HOOD CRUCIFIXION

GOD'S PLAN

BLOSSOM REIGNS

Acknowledgments

I want to thank everyone who supported me through this process of completing my first novel. Thank you to all that always encouraged me to keep going and never give up on achieving my goals.

Contents

TRIGGER/CONTENT WARNING

READ AT YOUR OWN RISK!

Chapter One

VITANI BANKS

"*Cum for God...*"

"Vitani! Wake up before you're late for work," my grandfather, Lee, yelled while banging on my door. He woke me up from what had to be the weirdest wet dream I'd had in my life. It was official, your girl had to get some, and soon, because I was tripping.

"Okay, grandad, I'm up."

I slowly got up out of my bed, heading towards my bathroom to take a shower. I loved sharing a place with my grandfather. He was cool as hell. Unlike my mom, Tamela, who thought her twenty-year-old daughter was still a child. Always saying things like, 'you ain't grown until you move out of my house'. Well, that's just what I did. I moved right around the corner with my grandfather as soon as I turned eighteen and got my first job to help him pay bills, because his social security check wasn't worth shit.

"Mommy, I hungry."

Dang! My three-year-old daughter didn't even give me time to brush my teeth before her greedy behind woke up. Before I could walk back into the room, my grandad burst through the door and scooped my daughter Ice up.

"I got my little chunk."

That's exactly what she was, too, a chunky baby. She started walking at nine months and talked more than me. Everyone keeps saying, 'she's moving out the way for another one'. The hell she is. I got that DEPO shot so fast the blood hadn't even been cleaned from the birthing table.

I hopped in the shower and did a quick wash, regretting that I even offered to go in for overtime today. As much as that job irked my nerves, I still had to feed my child. I refused to take money from the state or put her bum ass sperm donor on child support. He only came around to make my life hell. I finished getting dressed in my business attire and grabbed my purse and keys. I drive an older model Toyota Camry like it's a Lexus. I don't care what people say because it gets me from point A to B. I kissed my daughter and grandfather on the cheek and walked out the door as my phone rang.

"What, Rae? I know it ain't nobody but you calling before eight in the morning," I mused.

"Girl, fuck you. I'm just tryna make sure you up and at 'em. What time are you getting off?" My best friend Rae asked.

"You know damn well you have to approve the overtime schedule change requests, and I'm sure you saw my hours since you're calling me before my shift on my day off."

"Ooh, someone's grouchy. For your information, I do not have to approve them anymore, Erica does that. But I did look up your sched-ule to see if you would have time to go out with me tonight."

Ugh, this girl stayed going to somebody club. That was cool before I had Ice, but not anymore. Work and home are my life now. "I can't. I don't have a babysitter. Plus, I'll be tired."

"Get outta here with that tired excuse. You be acting like a grandma now that you have my niece. Ma said she'll watch Ice," Rae snapped, hiding her small chuckle, but I heard it anyway.

When Rae said "Ma," I knew she referred to my mom because her mom lived in Maryland. No matter how much crap my mom talks, she's a sucker for Ice, and I hate when she keeps her 'cause she spoils the hell out of her more than my grandfather.

My best friend Rae and I met in middle school and have been cool ever since. We live in Lakeland, Florida, also known as Orlampa because it is right between Tampa and Orlando. Rae and I both went to a vocational school for our Diplomas, but we also got our certification as Administrative Assistants.

"Where are you going?"

"You have to be kidding. The company party is tonight! I knew you would forget. That's why I went and changed your end time to 2 p.m. so we can swing by Ross or something and get you a cute dress. Alterations over off of Jewel might have some nice heels for you," Rae babbled.

"I really love you and dislike you at the same time. Bart would've blown a gasket had I not attended. Good thing this isn't my check for bills, or I'd be wearing my work clothes."

"Girl, please, I'd boost you an outfit before letting you go out like that," Rae laughed.

"Bye! Yo' scary ass ain't boosting nothing but an Instagram post." I hung up and rushed into the building to log onto my computer.

As a manager at IntelliCorp, one of the largest call centers in the country, I don't have to do that timeclock stuff. I've been on this job for eight months and am the top manager in the customer service department. While everyone else had a team of agents they were responsible for, my ass got to work directly under the Assistant Project Manager (APM) as more of an administrative manager. They made the position specifically for me when they saw my potential. Rae got hired at the same time in the HR department and worked her way up to the Recruiting Manager faster than I.

Knock Knock

I sighed as I heard a soft knock on my office door. I couldn't see who it was since I hadn't opened my blinds yet, but I did leave my door cracked, letting them know I was in here. The people at this job acted like they couldn't do anything without asking me first, trying to get in Bart's good graces. I rolled my eyes.

"Miss Banks, are you busy?" Bart asked as he walked into the office with a good-looking brother trailing behind him, except when Bart stopped, the man walked up to his side. That simple act showed me this man was not Bart's bitch like everyone else here.

"No, Bart, come on in." That got a laugh out of both men.

Bart was a tall Caucasian man. If I had to guess, I'd say he was about six-foot-three, and he is fine for a white guy. He was clean cut, but I could tell by his swag that he spent time around brothas. His dark, wavy hair was kept low, almost in what I would describe as a "white boy Caesar" that put you in the mind of Drake, and he had an athlete's build, slim and toned.

The brother standing next to him was the same height, but his build was more muscular and his skin was a smooth, even brown tone. Ole boy rocked square glasses like we were back in the sixties, but it was cute on him.

"I told you she was sassy. That's why she got promoted so quickly, no ass-kissing," Bart smiled before continuing his thought. I knew for a fact Bart's ass had a crush on me, but I didn't do that mixing business with pleasure bullshit. "I saw you were on the schedule today so I decided to introduce you to our company's new IT consultant. He is the real reason for the company party, but his incognito ass doesn't like all the hoopla, so we just made it a management party. Vitani Banks meet Teqwyn Lewis. Teqwyn, meet Vitani Banks," Bart concluded with introductions.

"Nice to meet you, Mr. Lewis," I stood and shook his hand.

"Likewise, Miss Banks, but you may call me Teq," he said as he released my hand.

"And you may call me Vitani," I said as I sat back down behind my desk. "See you fellas, later on. Oh Bart, can you open my blinds on the way out? I don't want to write any agents up today who think there's not a manager watching."

Bart nodded his head and opened the blinds before leaving out with Teq. He must know him personally for them to be clowning like that in front of me.

I rushed out of my house with Ice in my arms, jumping in Rae's car. She took off, going slow as hell, and I looked at her like she had lost her mind. We had thirty minutes to drop Ice at my mom and make it to the company party.

"Why are you driving so damn slow to get on the next street?" I asked, getting more and more frustrated. This bitch actually slowed down more. Going from 5mph to 2mph.

"Hoe, my niece not strapped in and if a muthafucka hit me with her in the car, I'mma beat they ass till 12 get here. You know I don't play about my baby," she paused, turning her anger towards me. "Why yo' ass ain't bring her car seat? What if your mom has to go somewhere?"

I couldn't stop laughing at her long enough to even answer before she stopped in front of my mom's house. I hopped out and ran to take Ice inside. Thankfully, my grandmother opened the door and took her from me. I did *not* want to hear my mom's mouth about what I was wearing. I power walked back to the car and Rae took off, this time driving fast as hell.

"FYI, my mom has her own car seat and clothes for your niece. Her ass is spoiled rotten. Where her car seat you bought her?" I asked, looking in the backseat.

"I had to move some boxes the other day, so I took it out and forgot to put it back in," Rae spoke softly.

I studied her while she drove. She'd decided on a fitted gown that showcased all her curves. My girl was full-figured and confident like Lizzo. Anyone that knew Rae knew she NEVER spoke softly. She was always with the shits. For two long ass years, my girl had a whole disloyal fiancé named Devun. Nobody liked him. His ass is somewhere from the islands, and he always bragged about his family dabbling in roots. Hopefully, he ain't put nothing on my girl but good dick.

We pulled up to the entrance and let the valet park the car. The company loved to show out when the big bosses came to town. This would be my first big meeting and Rae's second.

"I'll meet you inside. I gotta make a call real quick," Rae paused by the security desk.

"I don't mind waiting with you." Really, I just didn't want to walk in there alone.

Rae picked up on that and chuckled as she shooed me away. When I rounded the corner, the elevator was about to close.

"Hold the doors, please!"

I sped up just in time to catch the doors for myself. I was mad at the nigga just standing in the elevator staring at me like he was fucking stupid. No lie, though, this dude was fine. He was dark chocolate in a custom suit that hugged his body enough to show that he had a muscular frame. His lips were thick and juicy. The low-trimmed full beard made them look even more delectable, and his low-cut hair had so many waves.

If he wasn't such a jerk, I would be very much attracted to him. Let me stop lying. He was sexy, and I was attracted to him. Even while I stood there seething, I stared at him in the mirrors of the elevator doors. He was taller than me with heels on, but not by much. That meant he had to be like six-one because I was five-eight without heels. When he looked up and caught me staring, I scrunched my face.

"It be your own people thinking they're too good to hold a damn elevator door," I snapped just as the doors opened up on the third floor. I rushed out towards the restroom to calm myself down.

Godrique "God" James

"I'm so glad you could make it," Anita Porter, the CFO of Intel-liCorp, purred.

"I had time today," was all I said before she looped her arm in mine.

She knew damn well I didn't like her like that. I tolerated her for her father's sake, but truth be told, I came here tonight to give her a chance to show me what dat mouth do. She'd sent a picture to my phone a few hours earlier, and I decided to come see what she was about. The funny thing was, I couldn't stop thinking about the girl on the elevator. The fact that she wore a two-piece skirt set that showed about four inches of skin on her stomach to a company event let me know she was a rebel. The small belly ring was what really drew me in. Her tall, slim-thick, more on the slim side, ass could get the business on her worst day. She had ink on every part of her skin that was visible, and it turned me on.

"Come, let me introduce you to the man of the hour," Anita pulled me from my thoughts.

We walked over to a group of men who, all except one, gave me a look of sympathy when they saw Anita on my arm. I chuckled.

"Hey guys, meet God. God, this is Bart, John, Peter, Simon, and Teqwyn."

"Yea, we've met before," I said, not being able to hold in my laughter any longer.

The guys all joined in as Anita stood there, not picking up on the joke. I'd met these men before, but we rarely socialized here. Teqwyn was actually my cousin, but few people knew, and we liked to keep it that way.

We all shook hands just as the woman from the elevator was walking by with another beautiful woman. Bart turned and grabbed her hand in a way that made my eyebrows raise. *Are they fucking?* Anger coursed through my body. I flexed my jaw to keep from snapping. The elevator woman gave Bart a friendly smile as she pulled her voluptuous friend with her. *Her smile is so infectious.*

"I'd like you all to meet two of our youngest Managers, Rae Martin of HR and Vitani Banks of Customer Service," Bart said, finally releasing the woman's hand for us to shake.

Everyone shook the women's hands, but when it was my turn, Anita grabbed my hand.

"Vitani, this is my boyfriend, God," she said, speaking for me and a whole lie at the same time.

Vitani didn't seem bothered by not shaking my hand, and her head tilted slightly at my name. Anita sucked her teeth before speaking again.

"Just because you live in the hood doesn't mean you have to act like it. Have some manners when being introduced to a businessman."

"May I ask your real name, sir?" Vitani bit out.

I knew she was trying to hold it together after that little snide comment Anita made. I turned and walked away without saying a word. If I opened my mouth, I knew some off-the-wall stuff would come out, and she had been embarrassed enough. Anita followed close behind until I stopped near the hors d'oeuvres. "What was that?"

Anita frowned, "Nothing. I just don't like these disrespectful ass hoodrats they're hiring here."

I clenched my jaw before walking away from her and went to the bar before I got out of character. *Who talks shit to and about the people who make them money?* Without these "hoodrats," she and her father would be broke. I motioned for the bartender.

"Hennessey on the rocks, make it a double."

"Make that two," a silky voice said from beside me.

Damn, it must be my lucky night. Vitani's sexy ass sat next to me and was looking at me with her seductive eyes. Her brown skin contrasting with the ink was a sight to see. Her long locs only complimented her beauty.

"Godrique."

Her brow raised in question before falling. "Nice to meet you, Godrique."

She extended her hand, and I took it. The softness of her hand got me thinking about how soft her ass probably was. I usually liked big tittied women, but tonight, I would take on my father's philosophy "more than a hand full is too much."

"Likewise, Vitani. Are you enjoying your night?" I asked attempting to make light conversation.

"I would enjoy it more if I could get some dick." Vitani smiled.

I choked on my damn drink. When I finished coughing, I searched her eyes to find the humor. There was none. *What the fuck did I do to deserve this?* I was gonna be donating to the nearest shelter for more of this good karma.

I stood and said, "Lead the way."

We made it into an office on the same floor, and I grabbed the back of her neck, turning her to face me. "You sure this is what you want?"

"Yes," she whispered.

I still held the back of her neck as I walked her around the massive oak desk so we could be facing the door. I always faced any door in any room.

I hated surprises. I undid my pants and pulled a condom from my pocket before letting them fall to my ankles. Pulling her skirt up, I checked her readiness. *Damn, she wet. And she ain't got no panties on! I'm in heaven right now.* I slid a finger in her pussy and sweat started to form on my forehead from how tight it gripped. I tried adding another finger, but it was too tight. No way she could take this dick. If she could, it would probably be painful for both of us.

Removing my finger from her wetness, I used her juices as a lubricant and circled her clit until her breathing picked up. Whatever perfume she had on was clouding my senses as I sank back into her wetness with my finger. It was a little more ready. I did this a few more times before placing the condom on. The funny thing was that she hadn't moaned at all, but she was wet and squirming as her hand clutched the desk tightly.

I got in position behind her and started working my way into her center. This shit was gripping me so tight it felt like it was cutting off my circulation, even through the condom. It felt so good, though, like something forbidden. She needed to be locked away for safe keeping. I squeezed her hips as I pushed further into her wetness that gripped me and pulled me in deeper.

"Shit," she moaned.

There it is. I knew this dick had power. I gripped her waist with one hand and pushed her top half down onto the desk with my other to control the pace. That didn't work. She started throwing her ass back and creamed on me after two strokes. I pulled out to the tip and used my hand that held her down to slam her back down. She could throw it back, but I would make sure she knew who was fucking who.

"Damn."

I moved my hand from her waist to her clit. I lifted her a little to unzip her top from the front to play with her nipples. Vitani's nipples were hard as hell, and I knew they would be sensitive. She moaned loud as hell soon as I touched her nipple. She went into a shaking frenzy, causing her to start grinding harder. Not letting up on her clit I picked up the pace and pinched her nipple. I wanted her to lose it and make sure this pussy remembered me. I looked down to see her ass bouncing back. I didn't think I could get harder than I was, but seeing her cream each time I pulled back had me widening my stance. I slammed into her faster and harder. I couldn't stop watching my dick being swallowed because I was sure she wouldn't be able to take my full length. Before we left this room, she would scream my name. Her little ass would call on *God* tonight.

"Ugh. Oh. My. Fucking. God! Ahhh, God, yes!" Vitani screamed as she rode the wave of her orgasm. I stopped moving to watch her bounce her ass back on me as she came. I gave her time to catch her breath once she was finished cumming. Pulling out, I turned her to face me. This girl had tears in her eyes.

"You good?" I asked as I lifted her on the desk, finally seeing her perfect titties.

"Yes, I um. It's been a while." She gave a weak smile.

I stared into her eyes as I slid back into her opening. Her eyes rolled, and she bit down on her bottom lip. I started moving, trying to get my nut before someone came looking for us. Vitani wrapped her arms around my neck and started fucking me back. I removed her arms and pushed her down, so her back was flat on the desk. Seeing her titties bounce with my thrusts was bringing me closer. She started fucking me from the bottom again and moaning loud. I wish I didn't have this condom on, but at the same time, I was glad. After one minute, I probably would've bussed in this moist snuggie she called a pussy. I pulled her back up to my chest, then gripped her neck and squeezed that shit.

"Cum for God," I demanded in her ear.

Her eyes popped open, then lolled as she tensed up and grunted. Then I heard a squishing noise. I wrapped my arms around her to keep her from falling back and hitting her head on the desk.

The door opened, and I looked up and saw the voluptuous woman from earlier. She walked in with a phone to her ear.

"My bad, oh. Vitani! Are you okay?" Rae asked, concerned, but she didn't come further into the room as she muted her call.

"Ye-yes, I'm fine. Can you give us a minute?" Vitani spoke up.

"Yea hoe, then we can discuss my new desk coming out of your check," Rae mused.

When the door closed again, I backed away from Vitani as I removed the condom. I pulled out the empty condom wrapper, placed the used condom in it, and placed it in my pants pocket once I pulled them up. I ain't even mad about not cumming because watching her cum was lit. I watched as she fixed her skirt and zipped her top back up. Luckily, I had on black because my pants were wet from her juices. We both walked out without saying anything, and as she headed towards the restroom with her friend, Anita rounded the corner.

"Where were you? I'm ready to go," she said, rubbing her hands on my chest.

"Bye. I'm leaving, but not with you. Enjoy your night, Anita."

I walked off, thinking about Vitani. I don't get surprised a lot, but she was full of them. I had to see her again, and soon. I shot Teq a quick text on my way out for him to give me a call.

Chapter Two

TEQWYN "TEQ" LEWIS

Looking around the area designated for the company party, I noticed Rae and Vitani walking back in. Rae laughed at something Vitani said, and I couldn't stop the smile that crossed my face. Rae had to be around five-feet-five-inches of thickness, and her mocha skin was flawless. I initially didn't want to attend this event, but now I was glad that I did.

"I saw the way you looked at Vitani's friend. You might as well hang that up. So many guys here have tried to take her out, but she has a man," Bart interrupted my thoughts.

"Oh, yea? How do you know all of this?"

"Man, this place is like a never-ending game of telephone. There's not much I don't know," Bart paused. "I know Vitani is single and has been since she's been here. Nobody can get with her, either. But I'mma try my hand real soon. She's wifey material."

"Wifey? Do you even know her for real? Beyond work. Or you just see a fat ass and think she will make a good wife?" As soon as I spoke the words, I thought about Rae's juicy ass.

"Naw, man, she's really smart. Beyond looks, she is a sweetheart, and I know we'll be perfect for each other."

"I see. So you're in love, and you haven't even got the cookies yet. That fairytale stuff ain't real, Bart. You gotta get to know a woman first, outside of work, before making those kinds of assumptions. You don't even know if she likes white guys. From our brief encounter earlier, I think she only sees you as a friend."

"That's because I haven't told her how I really feel. I know she likes me. I sign her checks."

I slowly looked at Bart as he stared at Vitani as she made her way in our direction with Rae. Before I could respond, my phone vibrated in my pocket.

God: *Hmu when you leave. Tonight though.*

Me: *Bet.*

I wondered what had him leaving so soon? Anita was still here, so it wasn't to be with her. Hmm. My cousin God was a different breed of crazy. He looked chill on the surface, but he really was thinking of a thousand ways to kill people. I honestly didn't know how he and Bart became cool. They're polar opposites. But anyone cool with God was cool with me, so I fucks with Bart.

"Teqwyn, right?" Rae asked.

"Teq is fine."

"Cool. So, you're a gamer?"

"Yes, what made you ask?" *I'm curious now.*

"You have controller cuff links. I think that's very cool and different. You play online?"

I smiled hard. This woman pays attention to detail. "I do. Apex Legends and Grand Theft Auto. You?"

"I don't really play Apex. I do play Grand Theft Auto, but I'm mainly on Call of Duty. We should exchange Gamertags. I usually play on the weekends or late night."

"Bet. Hand me your phone."

Rae gave me her phone, and I entered my number for her to save it under whatever she wanted. From what Bart said, she had a man, so I didn't want to step on the guy's toes. If he slipped up, she would be fair game, though. She called my phone, so I would have her number.

"Hit me up when you're on. We can run a few." Rae smiled. She turned to Vitani and said, "I'm getting tired. Are you ready to leave?"

Bart's face flushed like he wanted to say something. Vitani nodded her head and shook my and Bart's hand. Rae did the same before they walked away.

"Aiight Bart, I'mma head out. I'll get up with you sometime this week."

"Cool, see ya."

I made my way to where John, Peter, and Simon were standing. They were in the cut, watching women. I wondered if they talked to God before he left. That's not like him to not let us know he's leaving when we're all in the same vicinity.

"Aye, did God say anything to y'all before he left?"

"Just chill, jit probably found him a lil' baby to pipe down. He sent us a text. He's alright," John spoke. He smiled, showing off his mouth full of golds.

At first glance, you'd think all of us were prim and proper businessmen, but when John and Peter opened their mouths, all you saw was 10k. Peter only had bottoms, but John had top and bottom. They're pullouts, but they wore them no matter what when they were out in public. Them two gave zero fucks. *None of us did.*

"You always got something slick to say. I got a text to call him when I leave."

That got their attention. All eyes went to Anita, who was now talking to Bart. I'm sure we all had the same thing in mind. If she's here, then he didn't have company.

"Y'all want to be around when I call? Just in case," I asked.

"That nigga don't need us. He told you to call, not us. Maybe he needs a post deleted from social media," Peter laughed.

"Y'all don't ever take anything seriously."

Simon chuckled, "We'll walk you to your car. All you had to do is ask."

"Fuck all y'all."

I turned and walked towards the exit, but they were right behind me. No matter how much junk they talked, they knew that wasn't like God at all. He would have said something to one of us. We made it to my car, and I hit the unlock switch so we could all get inside.

My phone connected to my car automatically as I dialed Godrique, and he answered on the second ring.

"Who are you around?"

We all laughed.

"I knew you would drag them into this," God paused. He cleared his throat before asking, "Where Bart at?"

"He was entertaining the guests, so we didn't involve him," I answered.

"Okay. Teq, I need you to completely wipe the elevator and third-floor hall cameras. I also need a new desk delivered to Rae Martin's office before Monday morning."

My heart stopped. "Wait, did you just say Rae? You did something with Rae?"

"Listen to this nigga's 'you did something with Rae' head ass," Simon clowned.

"Keep talking. I'mma wipe your entire client list," I snapped.

Simon's mouth immediately snapped shut. He knew I didn't fuck off.

"To answer your question Teq, no, I didn't do anything with Rae. Something did happen in her office, though. I need those cameras wiped ASAP. You know I don't like people in my business," he disconnected the line.

I hopped out of the car and grabbed my laptop from the trunk to access the camera feed. When I pulled up the video, we all stared dumbstruck as

God followed Vitani into the office. I fast-forwarded ten minutes, and Rae opened the door, closed it, and stood outside her office.

"Damn, shawty get off like that?" Peter questioned.

"Not from what Bart was telling me earlier. She doesn't be giving anyone the time of day, not even Bart. He has it bad for her, too," I answered Peter.

"I guess she made time for God. Bart bitch ass about to be pissed," John spoke as he opened the car door to exit. "Stay up, bro. We'll link before Simon leaves again. Let's do the club next weekend."

"Bet."

The rest of the guys said their goodbyes, and we all went our separate ways. I had to get home to shower and send the friend request to Rae. Hopefully, I wouldn't have to wait long to play with her.

I received a text from God asking to meet at his warehouse in the industrial warehouse district of Lakeland. When I pulled up, I noticed the other guys' cars. This was business, and all of us had a hand in each other's business dealings. I got out and was greeted by Chez, God's second-in-command. Chez was a big burly brother that loved to stay in the loop.

"Chez, how've you been? Staying out of trouble?" I asked, not even stopping for the two security guards to search me.

"Teq, I'm good. I don't get caught. Everyone has been waiting on you. You must be hella busy your way, man," Chez smirked.

"I guess you could say that." I paused outside of God's office. "You in on this meeting?"

"When have I not been in on a meeting? I see you got jokes today."

"Just checking. Never know."

We walked into the office to find God and the other "disciples" engrossed in a game of 2k between God and Simon. Simon scored the winning shot. God threw the controller across the room, then laughed.

"You're not right in the head." I said, but I couldn't help but laugh, too.

God continued laughing as he took his seat behind his desk. He suddenly stopped and got serious, then leaned forward.

"Simon got one of the guys who hit that lick on me a year ago. The only thing the nigga said before taking his last breath was that he didn't do it alone. These people can't walk around with the clout of breathing after stealing from me. No man can get away with robbing me."

"Apparently, they can," Simon laughed.

"You can't be serious for five minutes. Anyway, long story short, I need everyone involved touched. As far as business goes, I'm good on my end. The connect at the CIA just got clearance from the director to continue our contract for another five years. The weapons will sell themselves. Anything new on your end, Bart?"

"Nothing new. I am thinking of promoting Vitani, well having Anita promote her to Assistant Project Manager of a different department. She works her ass off, and I think that she won't give me a chance because of my position of authority over her," Bart concluded.

All eyes went to God.

"Do you think that is a smart idea? Once she is in that position, you can't fire her of your own free will. You might want to think on it for a few days, then let us know your final decision," God stated firmly.

"I ain't never heard of somebody giving promotions for pussy that is free," John laughed from his position in the corner. "If you ain't get the pussy by now, your goofy ass ain't getting it."

Bart cut his eyes at John with clenched fists.

"Moving along. Everything is set up on my end for your next shipment. Some of Teq's items will arrive with yours, so you two will need to coordinate on that." John paused. "Simon, I may need you to pick up Pete's load next week."

"Nigga, don't call me no muthafuckin Pete. Keep playing with yo' life," Peter snapped.

"I can do that since I wanna stay local to see what's up with the people that stole God's stuff. The one we know for sure was involved is in prison here, so I can slip in and take his ass out," Simon smiled. His psycho ass was probably visualizing his next kill in his mind.

"I got some things to handle at the shop. So far, I only have two big PC towers that are coming in. I'll hit y'all with the details when it's closer to the date." I paused. "God, that package has been delivered. I hope it was worth five bands."

"Five bands?! Ain't no bitch worth that much. Bitch would be suckin' this dick every day for the rest of the year," Peter gawked.

"I guess it's a good thing your cheap ass ain't spending your money—"

"Wait, what am I missing? Who did you spend money on?" Bart asked God.

"Rae," God smirked.

Bart's jaw dropped. I took that as my que to dip out because I did not want to be in on the bullshit.

"I'm out." I turned and exited the warehouse.

I made my way to my shop in twenty minutes, then went straight to cracking an iPhone that needed to be picked up by noon. I was the hood Tech guy everyone came to see when they needed anything done with electronics. Nobody could outdo me in the hacking world, either.

The door to my shop opened and Devun walked in with a different female than I had seen him with last week. This nigga wouldn't stop until I beat his ass. The only reason I spared him was that I didn't want drama in my shop.

"Aye, how much longer on that?" Devun asked.

"However long it takes me. I told you too many times about bringing different women into my place of business. I don't like a lot of new people in my shop, especially ones that ain't spending money."

"You got it, big dog. Carla, go wait for me in the car," Devun chuckled.

I finished up with the phone and handed it to Devun. He handed me three hundred dollars and turned to leave.

"Your business is not worth the heat that comes along with it."

Devun turned around and said, "Chill, man, I won't do it again."

Chapter Three

GOD

I couldn't get Vitani out of my head, and it had been a whole week since our little escapade. Her fine ass had a nigga regretting not finishing what we started. The pussy was good, but them eyes were what had me captivated in my thoughts. Her eyes are cat-shaped and seductive without any effort.

I looked down at the envelope in front of me with my full name on it. This damn girl was different from any other woman I had ever dealt with. A smile formed on my face when I opened the envelope.

Godrique,

I didn't know how else to contact you, so I gave this letter to Teqwyn with hopes of it finding you. Thank you for blessing Rae with a new desk. She deserves it. Thank you for blessing me with a temporary escape from all the things I have going on. Here's a gift for you.

Love,

Vitani

Three pictures fell onto my desk, and my eyes bulged. *Who still sends physical pictures?* I chuckled. If I wasn't thinking about her before, I was thinking about her now. She sent me a picture of her bent over with a nice arch. She held her breast while licking a nipple and with both of her legs behind her head. I unconsciously licked my lips. This girl was about to make me go find her. I put the pictures and letter back in the envelope, leaned back in my chair, and adjusted my now hard erection.

Knock knock.

"Come in."

"Hey, boss man, Simon and I are doing that thing tonight, so I'mma head out early. Do you need anything?" Chez asked.

"No, be careful. Text me when it's done."

Chez nodded, then walked out, closing the door behind him. Tonight, Simon and Chez are hitting up the prison for the nigga that stole from me. I had a new shipment of weapons coming next week, and I had to get everything ready for that. I was very selective regarding clients because I have a reputation and name to protect. IntelliCorp was a company my brothers and I started from the ground up.

I met all my brothers during different phases of my life, but we all clicked like it was nothing. Well, all except John and Bart. John couldn't stand Bart since day one and had been telling me for years not to trust him. Bart has never crossed me, so I don't treat him differently from the other brothers. We never fell out. It's always been love between us.

Checking my phone, I shot a quick text to my mom to let her know I would be stopping by for a plate. *I wonder if Vitani can cook. It doesn't really matter. There's no way a woman can keep me entertained enough to have to eat their cooking over my mom's.* My mom texted me back, saying dinner should be ready in two hours. I spent the next hour going through my business emails and getting ready for my shipment. Next week, there would be a meeting at IntelliCorp for Vitani's promotion, and I was a little anxious to see her. The letter she sent me let me know she was different, so I didn't mind her getting the promotion.

I finished up and headed to my mom's house to grub. I chuckled when I pulled into the driveway and saw Teq's car. This nigga stayed at my mom's house, eating all the food before I could get any. I walked in without knocking and went straight to the kitchen sink to wash my hands.

"Did I sleep with you last night?"

"Mommy, you be tripping. You weren't even in here when I walked in."

"And? You know I don't play that. How was your day, son?"

I started fixing my plate. "Good evening, mommy. It was productive. Where Teq?"

"He's around here somewhere. How long are you staying?"

"I'm not, just stopping by to get a plate. You need anything?"

"No, I'm good. There's a plate for Simon in the fridge. Be safe out there, son," she said before walking off.

I wasn't surprised Simon had called for a plate. All my boys loved my mom's cooking, and she loved them like they're her own. My mom Nichelle could throw down like no other. My father remarried, but we still had a good relationship. I finished making my fried chicken, yellow rice, and cabbage plate. I grabbed Simon's plate and then headed out, but I ran into Teq on the porch.

"What you about to get into, son?"

"I done told you about that son shit, bro. I don't care where you're from. You coming to the club tomorrow night?" I snapped.

"Miss me with that crybaby mess I can't change the way I talk. No, I won't be at the club. I got some things to handle at my shop. Plus, Sharese will be in town, and we gonna kick it."

"Tell Shari I said hey. I'll holla. Peace," I chunked the deuces as I headed to my car.

My phone vibrated, and I saw it was a message from Simon. I hopped in my car and sped to my duck-off spot on the city's far north side. It took me thirty minutes to get there. I jumped out of the car and into the house towards the room made explicitly for moments like this.

"I know your ass ain't leave my food in the car?"

"Kiss my ass, bro. I ain't thinking about no damn food right now," I yelled.

Stepping up to the man with the sack over his head, I snatched it off and took a step back involuntarily. I'd seen him before. I couldn't quite put my finger on where but I for sure had seen him somewhere.

"Why would you rob me?" I demanded.

"Nigga fuck you. You really walk around like you're God almighty. You're not! Your punk ass can get touched just like any other nigga in the streets!" The guy spit at me, and it landed on my shoes.

I kicked him in the face with the same shoe he spit on and watched as the blood gushed from his mouth. Reaching for the gun in my holster, and pulled it out. I hit him twice in the face making him throw up the contents of his stomach, while gasping for air.

"Now, I hope we can get on the same page soon, or you will regret waking up this morning."

"So you just gone have all the fun?" Simon laughed.

I flipped him off.

"All I know is it was two other niggas, and a bitch drove us there." I hit him in the mouth, and he started coughing, spitting out a tooth.

"Nigga if you mess up his mouth, he won't be able to tell us anything" Simon came and pushed me back.

"Stop playing all the time, Si, damn. Aye, you got five seconds to tell me something valuable before I put a hot one in your ass," I turned to the dude, saying.

"I didn't plan anything. All I did was what I was told by the lil young nigga that put us on the lick—"

Two shots rang out, and blood splattered over my clothes.

"What the fuck was that?!" I yelled at Chez, trying like hell not to snap his neck.

"He wasn't saying shit," he shrugged.

I was pissed the off, so I just walked out. Simon followed close behind. I'm sure to get his food. Greedy ass nigga. I got in my car and leaned my head back into the cream headrest. I thought of all the things I wanted to ask that idiot before Chez's dumb ass shot him.

"I'll get the next one alone, and we can do this the old way, just you and me."

I looked toward Simon and just nodded. He got out and walked back inside to ensure Chez did what the fuck he was supposed to do.

My phone vibrated.

"What?"

"Your baby wants some ice cream. Can you bring us some?"

"Yea, LiLi, I need to clean up. Have my stuff ready." I hung up.

LiLi was a lil chick I used to mess with heavy until I found out she wasn't it. Now, her trifling ass claimed to be pregnant with my baby. Well, she was pregnant, but I didn't know if it was mine. One thing I can say was she would have my back when I needed her. That's why I was headed to her place with the ice cream she requested so I could get me some pussy and rest.

I stood in the VIP section of Club ACE, watching the regular clubgoers below. LiLi had convinced me to let her come with me, which I didn't mind because she'd been in the house since I found out she potentially had my seed. She wore a red dress with some leopard-print high heels wrapped around her legs. I couldn't even lie. It was sexy. LiLi stood about five-four, light-skinned, and thick with some big double D's on her chest. My brothers were all in this section with a bunch of groupie bitches in their faces. I was about to turn to go sit, but something caught my eye. It looked like Vitani, but this girl had long curly hair down her back instead of dreadlocks.

My breath caught in my throat. That was Vitani. I could see the belly ring gleaming in the black jumpsuit with slits in an S shape that started at her shoulder and ended at her adjacent ankle. It was dark in the club, but I could spot her fine ass from a mile away. Rae was in front of her pulling her. Rae had on an all-white ensemble that was short, too short. Good thing Teq wasn't here. He'd probably go nuts.

"Tonight must be my lucky night."

I frowned. Ignoring Bart, I sat down on the leather couch and poured a shot of the first bottle I saw. I tossed back the Patrón just before Vitani and Rae stepped into our section. Bart must've sent the bouncers to get them. He was up in her face in no time, reintroducing her to the guys. He finally made his way towards me just as LiLi sat down beside me. I almost forgot her ass was there. I saw Vitani tense up, and I stood for the "introduction".

"Vitani, you remember God, right? This is his girl LiLi."

Vitani smiled and shook LiLi's hand, then extended her hand for me to shake. I took it and gently tugged her close.

"Thank you for the pictures," I whispered in her ear, then allowed my hand to slide down her back and graze her ass. She gasped but tried not to look frazzled. I could see the lust in her eyes until she looked at LiLi, then her eyes went slant.

"Hello, Rae."

"Hey God! We came here to have fun, so we're gonna head back downstairs."

"Y'all can stay up here with us. We don't bite," Bart chimed.

I watched as he stood behind Vitani and started dancing to the music. Bart may be white, but he danced better than me. So, I wasn't surprised when Vitani started winding her hips to the music with him. What did surprise me was that she was looking straight at me as she basically fucked Bart with clothes on.

Peter walked over and sat on the other side of me, then leaned over, and said, "That's how you're going out?"

I could feign innocence, but we both knew what I wanted. "If that's what she wants, then good for her and him."

"Good for who?" LiLi butted in.

"You, with your nosey ass." I looked up to see Rae dancing with Simon while Vitani still danced with Bart. Just seeing his hands on her did something to me, and I knew I couldn't take much more of this shit.

VITANI

I smiled up at Bart as we danced in the huge VIP section. I was actually surprised to see Bart at a club like this, let alone with the guys from the company party. I dang sure almost shit bricks when I saw God. He had on a dark suit with a silk dress shirt underneath with the buttons open, showing some tattoos on his chest. The pointy-toed dress shoes brought the look together, and it was sexy. The fact that he was here with a completely different woman was funny. I could only imagine the laugh he and his friends had about what we did at the office. I was impulsive and could've gotten fired, but I didn't care. I felt disrespected by Anita and wanted immediate revenge. Now, I was here looking like boo-boo the damn fool because I smashed a hoe.

"Has anyone ever told you that your body is so soft?"

I fought not to roll my eyes at Bart's words. I glanced at God, who was now whispering with Peter while staring at me. Since his hoe ass wanted to stare, I'd give him a show. I turned my back to him and dropped down to twerk in a squat position, but my face was coincidentally turned to face with Bart's hardened erection. I turned back to face God, then slowly wind my hips against Bart's hardened member.

Bart leaned into me and shouted, "I'm about to wake up. You gonna make me breakfast?"

It took me a second to register what he was asking.

"Vitani, come go with me. I gotta pee!"

Bart better be glad Rae came because I was about to curse him out. How dare he think me dancing with him means I would fuck him. We went into the upstairs restrooms for the VIP guests, and Rae burst out laughing.

"Simon and I heard what he said to you. The music is lower up here. I could see it all over your face that you were about to blow your cover."

"Forget a cover. He was about two seconds away from catching these hands. Does he think I'mma hoe? Oh gosh, do you think they all know what happened?"

"I don't know. Maybe. But why would Bart try to fuck behind his homeboy?"

"Rae, really? Don't act like dudes don't do stuff like that all the time." I touched up my lipstick in the large mirror.

"I don't know, sis. I don't think God would do that."

I rolled my eyes at her. How would she know what God would or wouldn't do? We walked out of the restroom, and I was immediately grabbed by my neck. I was pushed against the wall. I didn't fight against the familiar feel of the warm body behind me.

"I've been thinking of you."

I leaned into his warmth, feeling like I was being wrapped in a heated blanket. His hard dick pressed against my back caused my eyes to flutter.

He slid his free hand to twirl around my belly button. I smiled. *He really likes my belly rings for some reason.*

"Fuck you. You told Bart we smashed, didn't you?"

He stiffened. "No. Why, do you want to fuck him?"

"No."

"Who do you want to fuck, Vitani?"

His voice shook me to my soul and memories of the night at the company party flooded my head and I was ready to cream down my leg from just his voice and his touch. *Cum for God...* staring in his eyes, I remembered that I'd heard that before that night. In my dreams. Was this man the man of my dreams? I needed to stay away from him or I could be in some real trouble. Then again, I really liked the kinda trouble he put in me... I mean, me in.

A throat cleared behind us. I turned to see Rae trying to hide a smile. "Y'all nasty asses do know that this ain't my office."

God backed up and let go of my neck. I wanted him so bad my entire body felt like it was vibrating. I had never wanted anyone or anything as much as I wanted him to fuck my brains out. If just for one night, but he has a girlfriend. Hell, his ass apparently had two girlfriends.

"Have fun with your girlfriend," I tossed as I walked away.

"I'm single."

"Ooh bitch, that man got you wide open. What if that girl had walked up? We're too cute to be fighting Miss Piggy."

I laughed over the music as we neared the section. "I swear I was thinking she looks like a thicker version of T.I.'s wife."

Rae and I were both laughing as we walked back into the section. Bart was lounging on the couch, and Miss Piggy was drinking a water bottle next to him. Just as I was about to turn to Rae to say I was ready to go home, I felt a warm hand on my lower back. The contact was brief, but it sent my mind back in a spiral. *He better stop touching me before I fuck him in this club. Consequences be damned.*

I watched as he went to sit next to Miss Piggy. She smiled up at him like the Cheshire cat on Alice in Wonderland, then looked at me as if to say, 'what bitch?'. Let me stop. I could've been imagining that last part. Rae's phone vibrated, and she looked at me, letting me know we had to go. Devun's punk ass was probably home and asking where she was at. The clubs in Tampa closed at 3 am, and it was only a little past midnight. I was glad we had to leave early, though, because I probably would've ended up smashing God in the restroom before the end of the night.

I walked over to Peter, Simon, and John. "It was nice seeing you all again without being ridiculed about where I come from."

"It's not about where you come from. It's about where you're going. We all came from the hood, too. Let that shit fuel you, sis," John said, flashing his golds.

I smiled back, not missing that he had referred to me as sis. The others said their goodbyes to Rae and me. I walked over to Bart and hugged him, saying, "See you at work."

Thank goodness he didn't try anything. Rae walked over to say bye to God, and Miss Piggy stood up, looking at me, and said, "You got a problem?"

I closed my eyes, trying to calm myself from beating this bitch's ass. Rae spoke before I could.

"I can't stand a bitch that checks a female instead of checking her man."

"Well, ain't that the pot calling the kettle black. I know who you are. My girl Shanda be fucking on your nigga."

God stood up and grabbed Miss Piggy from the back, covering her mouth with his hand like a muzzle, just as Simon grabbed me, and Peter grabbed Rae. Rae didn't seem fazed by the comment, but I was livid. I don't care about a job when a bitch disrespected my sister.

"God won't always be around to save your ugly ass from me. Count your fucking blessings. I'm the bitch your mama warned you about. Oh, and your nigga, if I wanted him, I could damn well have him. Ask about me, bitch. Remember the name Vitani!"

I snatched away from Simon, grabbed Rae's hand, and walked away. These bitches were losing their mind over a nigga. I was gonna fuck him until I was tired and send his ass back to them.

Chapter Four

VITANI

Riiiiing Riiiiiing Riiiiiing.

Knock Knock.

"Hello?" I asked groggily into my phone.

"Why are you still sleep this late in the afternoon?"

"Because I am a grown woman and do what I want. How did you get my number?" I sighed as I got out of bed to go answer the door.

Knock Knock.

Who the heck was banging on my door like they don't have any sense?

"You gave me your number in the letter you wrote. How many niggas you gave your number to?" God questioned.

I rolled my eyes as I opened my front door to see a deputy and a woman standing in front of me. I was still mad at him about his hoe popping off last night.

"Are you Vitani Banks?" the short Caucasian woman asked, showing a Child Protective Services badge to identify herself.

"Everything okay?" God questioned through the phone.

"Let me call you back," I hung up and gave the two people at my door my full attention. "Yes, I am Vitani. What can I help you with?"

I knew my mom had Ice, and she was good. So, what did these people want? I started panicking on the inside. Ice was my whole world, and I couldn't imagine living life without my baby. Who would do something like this?

"Miss Banks, I received an anonymous report that you have neglected your child. Is the child present now?" the woman who identified herself as Susan asked.

"What? I would never hurt my child!" Tears filled my eyes, and I felt like I was hyperventilating. "My daughter isn't here at the moment. She's with her Nana. I was out late last night." Susan's eyebrow raised then she wrote something on her yellow notepad.

"May we look inside your home?"

"It's kind of a mess right now, but if you give me a second, I can straighten up," I said as I turned and closed the door. I hurriedly picked up the clothes I had scattered around from getting dressed for the club the night before. This was so unreal. I scurried back to the door and let Susan and the deputy in.

"How many other people live inside of your home?"

"Just my grandfather."

"Is he on the lease?"

That's an odd question, "No."

Susan scribbled on her notepad again before walking around the apartment. She kept writing in that notepad. You'd think she was drawing a damn floorplan.

"I need to see your daughter within the next twenty-four hours, or we will obtain a court order to have her removed from your care."

I broke down. I had tried to hold back the tears, but this shit was not cool. *How can they take my baby that I gave birth to away from me based on the word of someone who wasn't even bold enough to identify themselves?*

Knock Knock.

I was so distraught I couldn't even move to open the door. The deputy went to open it, and I kept my head down, not wanting anyone to see me so broken. I felt a hand on my shoulder and looked up to see Simon kneeling beside me. *Things just keep getting weird.*

"Get up. Everything will be okay," he said before standing to his full height. He and Godrique were the same height. "My name is Simon Grey. I am Vitani's brother. What seems to be the problem here?"

"I don't remember there being a brother listed on her background information. I would need permission from Miss Banks to discuss her personal information," Susan responded.

"You didn't need her permission to open her front door to allow me into HER home. What is your name, and who do you work for?" Simon asked calmly.

"My name is Susan West, and I am an investigator with Child Protection Services."

Simon nodded his head, took his phone out of his basketball shorts, and started texting on his phone. He then turned back to me and said, "Go get cleaned up, sis. I'm gonna fix me a sandwich. I had to leave my lunch date for this bullshit."

"Excuse me, sir, we were in the midd—" Susan's phone interrupted her. "West speaking. Yes. Yes. But. Yes, ma'am, I understand." Susan looked pissed, but the deputy that was with her was already heading towards the door.

"Enjoy your day, Miss West," Simon waved her off.

Once the two were gone, I just stared at Simon from my place on the floor. *How did he do that? Who were these people I had gotten myself involved with? If he could call off a whole government agency, what else could he do?* I stood and wiped my face.

"You said you're hungry? I can cook you something. It's the least I can do as a 'thank you' for helping me out. My mother will be bringing my daughter home in another hour or so, hope you don't have a problem with toddlers."

"You can cook? I want some soul food. Whatever you choose to make is good with me. As far as kids...I love them."

I smiled before walking toward my room to get cleaned up. God and his disciples were a mysterious group of men. *I wonder if Simon has kids of his own.* After getting cleaned up, I went into the kitchen and cooked some pork chops smothered in gravy, rice, and green beans. Simon smashed the food like his silly ass hadn't eaten in weeks. My mom dropped Ice off, and Simon started rolling all over the floor, playing like a big ass kid.

Knock Knock

Damn, I can't catch a break. I opened the door to see Ice's dad, Jack, standing there looking good as usual. He looked good but still didn't do anything when it came to his daughter. He thought he could come around whenever he felt like it.

"Who the hell drives a Maserati living out here?" Jack asked before his eyes went past me and landed on Simon, standing holding Ice. "Who is this nigga you got around, my child?"

"Jack, you need to call before you come to my house. What do you want?" I ignored his question.

"I came to see my daughter. Come here, Ice baby," he walked into the living room to where Simon was standing. They are around the same height, but Jack is a little more buff than Simon. Ice held onto Simon tighter.

"Aight Vitani, I'mma head out. That food was good. Let me know the next time you cook so I can stop by. Hopefully, I don't get another phone call tonight from you needing me." Simon winked as he put Ice down. She ran straight to me, and Simon's brow raised. "You need me to stay until your company leaves?"

"No, we should be okay. Thank you so much for coming through. It means a lot. You're the best."

"Don't thank me, thank God," Simon said before walking out.

Soon as the door closed, Jack was in my face, "Who the fuck is that nigga you have around my daughter? You 'round here fucking for money?!"

"I don't know who you are anymore, and neither does your daughter! She's three years old and doesn't know who you are," I snapped. I then picked Ice up to get her ready for a bath. I hated arguing in front of her, "You can let yourself out. We have a long day tomorrow."

Jack huffed, and I turned to walk towards my room when I felt a sharp pain in my back that knocked the wind out of me. I turned swiftly to protect Ice from hitting the ground first and broke her fall. I noticed Jack standing there with a sinister look on his face once I looked up.

"Ice baby, go in Paw Paw's room and watch Doc Mcstuffins, okay?" I pleaded with my daughter.

"Mommy, okay?" Ice questioned.

"Yes, baby, mommy just tripped. Mommy is okay," I kissed her cheek. She ran into my grandfather's room and closed the door. As soon as I heard the TV come on, I tried to stand but felt a foot in my chest. Tears streamed down my face as I bit back the pain.

"Please leave, Jack. Please, you could have hurt our daughter."

"That's your daughter. You running around here being a hoe for every Tom, Dick, and Harry with a nice car but won't give me no pussy. That stops today!" He reached down and yanked me up by my hair, and I bit my tongue to keep from screaming. I felt as if I was having an out-of-body experience. He threw me up against the wall and grabbed my neck. I went limp and then used the palm of my hand to smash up into his chin, but when I went to claw into his eyes, he kneed me in my pelvic bone. I gasped for air and willed myself not to faint from the excruciating pain.

"You must've forgotten I went to those dumb-ass self-defense classes with you," Jack laughed in my ear as he snatched my gym shorts down and my panties. I couldn't let this happen. I had to get him out of my home. He held my throat with one hand and roughly dipped a finger in my core.

"Umm, you act like you don't like it but look how hot you are for me," Jack moaned.

I had to think fast. I kissed his lips gently and started grinding into his finger. He thought I liked it, but I would do anything to get him away from my daughter and me. I pictured God and imagined how his kiss would feel and how his fingers felt deep inside of me. Jack kissed me back and increased his finger strokes. I came apart on his hand. I felt like shit for getting pleasure from him. He pulled his joggers down with his spare hand and fumbled, trying to hold my weight and penetrate my core while he continued kissing me. I bit down on his lip and simultaneously smacked my hands on the sides of his face over his ears. When he reeled back, I returned the favor and kicked him in his erection.

I wasted no time dashing into my room, grabbed my 9mm M&P, and then pointed it at his face. "Get the fuck out of my house and stay the hell away from my daughter and me, or I guarantee I will put this nine on your simple ass mind!"

I know I had to look crazy as hell. Gym shorts half down, juices leaking from my wet pussy, and Jack's blood dripping from my mouth. *I don't care about any of that. I swear my daughter is all that matters to me.*

Jack scooted back, holding his lip with one hand and dick with the other.

"You evil bitch! This ain't over. Your hoe ass can't even take a joke. I got you. I promise you that, bitch. I got you!" He kept scooting until he got to the couch and used it as support to stand, then walked out the door without even closing it.

I ran to the door to shut and lock it, regretting not making him leave while Simon was here. I never expected this from Jack. He was always weird when it came to me. He had seemed jealous when Ice was born as if he hated that I had to split my attention, but I never thought it would come to this in a million years.

Chapter Five

VITANI

I couldn't believe everything that went down yesterday. The fact that someone called CPS on me was just plain crazy. I told Rae about it after I put Ice to bed, and she came over to let me cry on her shoulder, and I had left out the part about what Jack did. Knowing Rae, her silly ass would be driving around at 2am looking for him. That crap had me stressed. Simon sent them away, but that bitch Susan didn't seem too happy about that. *How do they let a nigga in a t-shirt and basketball shorts send them away?* She was pissed. I was now on my way to work. I worked 12-8pm, and I loved it because I could have appointments in the morning and still get off early enough to go to bed on time.

I pulled into a parking spot at my job and dialed God's number. I forgot to call him back after all the drama.

"Speak."

"Umm. I didn't know that 'hello' wasn't customary when answering the phone nowadays. Dully noted. Did I catch you at a bad time?"

"My bad I didn't look at the phone before answering. I'm not busy. I will be in about five minutes. What's up?"

"I was just calling to say thank you. Can I take you out to dinner to show my gratitude?"

"How about you cook me dinner? I heard you can throw down in the kitchen."

I chuckled. "Fine, but it has to be at your house. I have roommates."

"That works. What time do you get off Friday?"

"I can get off at 6pm."

"I'll text you my address. Come straight to my house when you get off. Enjoy your day, Vitani."

"You do the same, Godrique."

His voice is so sexy. I don't know how I would be able to hold out from seducing him in his house. It was hard enough trying not to do anything at the club. *I love chocolate.* It was my weakness. What Jack did fucked my head up, though. I don't even want a man's hands on me at the moment. That should stop me from going too far with God. I went into the building and walked to my office to log into my computer. Not more than five minutes later, Anita opened my door without knocking.

"Vitani, my office in twenty minutes, don't be late."

She walked back out, and I counted backward from ten. That was rude, and she likes to talk about me being from the hood. At least I had some manners. Since I got hired, Anita had been down my throat, worse than the regular people on the call center floor. Even as a regular agent, I dressed to impress and kept my head down to stay out of the drama. The people here hated that I never entertained their bullshit, but I had a baby to feed, forget all that other nonsense. I came to work dressed in business attire every day, even during overtime. It took Anita two years to make it to her position with a college degree, and I am moving up the chain fast with just a trade. There were so many rumors circling around about me fucking and sucking on Bart to get the position. That's the real reason I would never give Bart a chance. I still didn't even know how I got involved with Godrique in the first place.

My phone vibrated, and I answered, "What have you gotten me into?"

Jenesis chuckled, "I just need a little more information before I come into the picture to take over. I don't want you getting hurt, boo. My boss has the hots for these guys and didn't want our fingers in the pot just yet."

"I don't know, Jen. These niggas ain't nothing to be playing with. Tell your boss I want out. CPS came to my home yesterday."

"What?! Why didn't you call me? You know I love Ice. That is handled. You don't even have to worry."

"I know it's handled. Simon Grey came over and took care of it," I sighed.

The line went quiet before Jenesis spoke again, "If anything like that ever happens again, call me first. You seem to be in good if they are coming to your rescue. Have anything yet?"

I was skeptical about Jen's boss, not her. We grew up together in the same church, but she moved to Kansas when she was fifteen, and I was thirteen. We kept in touch, and she moved back after she got out of the Army last year. That's when she came to me with a job offer. I took it because it could help me launch my career. Now, I was second-guessing my decision because these men seemed dangerous. But at the same time, they were sweethearts that I didn't want to screw over.

"I gotta go, Jen. I have a meeting with Anita. I will call you later to tell you about my weekend and what I learned."

"No need, I am stopping by your house later. I'll probably be in town for a few weeks," Jen said before disconnecting the call.

I made my way to Anita's office and was stunned to see Simon and Bart sitting at the round table in the far-left corner. Her office is massive. It would take five of mine to equate to hers. The guys stood until I took a seat between them, directly in front of Anita. *Am I about to get fired? Do they know about what happened with God?* Oh no, if it isn't one thing, it's another.

"Good morning, Miss Banks. As you may know, we have a new opening for an Assistant Project Manager in the Collections Department. Bart recommended you for the job. Although you are unqualified, word came down from the CEO that you should receive the job," Anita spoke with distaste.

I looked at Simon, wondering why he was there. He smiled and winked.

"I-I don't know what to say."

I was shocked, to say the least. That skank better be glad we weren't alone. I should slap her hoe ass for that slick comment.

"Would you like the position or not?" Anita asked.

"Yes, I would love the new position. What does that mean in regard to my schedule?"

"You will be a salary employee starting tomorrow, but your training doesn't start until next week. You already know most of the job requirements because you work so closely with Bart," Anita paused with a smirk. "You will be able to make your own hours and have the option to work remotely from your home as long as you come to the office twenty-four hours a week. You have been given the rest of the week off and a $20,000 bonus to thank you for your hard work and dedication to IntelliCorp. You need to stop by HR to complete the paperwork before you leave for the day."

"Do I have to take the week off? I want to do something nice for my agents."

"You want to do something for the people that complain to me about you?" Anita slipped. "I mean, um, you have to take the week off as it came straight from the CEO. I'm sure the agents will understand."

"You can plan something for your agents and come in for that day, but you will not be able to 'work' while you're here," Simon spoke for the first time.

"Thank you. You work here?" I asked curiously.

"Yes," he smiled before adjusting his tie. He wore a business shirt with a vest but no suit jacket. It looked nice on him, considering he had on basketball shorts the day prior in my home. "That food was good that you cooked. I'mma talk about it every time I see you."

I frowned. "I'm glad you enjoyed it. You're welcome over any time after what you did for me."

"Am I missing something? Do you two know each other outside of work? If you're dating, Miss Banks will not be able to get the promotion. There is a strict no fraternization policy," Bart chimed. His entire face turned red.

Simon looked at Bart with murder in his eyes like he wanted to say something but decided against it. I was in the middle of a hell storm, and I wanted nothing to do with it. "Vitani, go on down to HR to complete your paperwork. Bart, let's talk in your office."

I didn't waste any time getting out of that office. I felt like I was suffocating as I made my way to Rae's office. My body was still sore from the night prior, and I had to keep faking like I was okay, so nobody questioned me.

"What is wrong with you?" she asked from behind her desk.

I cocked my head. *Did she know?* I played it off, "I just got promoted to Assistant Project Manager."

"Oh shit! Bitch, you're making money money now! How are we spending them 20k?"

Whew, she doesn't know. I laughed, "I can't stand you! I might not even get the position because of Bart being on some bullshit." I gave her a quick rundown on what happened in Anita's office. She started laughing.

"Hoe, you play too much. You got the job, and we are celebrating this weekend! Simon is funny as shit. Why did he say that in front of them people?"

"He stupid. Says whatever comes to his mind. Where's my packet?"

Rae pulled out a packet and a highlighter. "I filled out everything for you. Just sign the highlighted areas. You're welcome."

I smiled hard, "Thank you!"

She knew I hated filling out paperwork.

God

I stepped out of my car on Second Street in Lakeland. My boy Turk ran the spot over here, and it was smooth sailing. No shootings, gang violence, or nothing. I loved that my people could come together and not be putting each other under the ground or in jail. Turk never sold drugs to people in the hood other than weed. We went way back to Pine Hills days in the O.

I walked in his spot and was immediately greeted by one of his runners.

"What's good, God?" He dapped me up.

"Chilling, I just got a new drop. Y'all good?" I fucked with my hood heavy. Everyone that knew me knew I didn't play about my people. Young and old.

"We might need a few 9's but nothing major. You know we don't get no smoke over here. Turk don't play that beef stuff. Thank you for looking out for my grandmother when I got pinched. That shit is love, fam," the youngin that went by Black said as he tried to hand me a stack of money.

"Don't disrespect me like that. Ma Tina is like family to me. Save your money."

Black nodded his head and put his money away. I had been trying to recruit him to my team for a little minute now. He had the three H's needed for this street life: Heart, Hustle, and Honesty. That goes a long way with a nigga like me. He was young, gotta be around eighteen or nineteen, but he was about his money.

"You tryna recruit Black again? You trifling as hell, dawg."

"One day he gonna leave yo' ass and come get some real money," I chuckled as we hugged.

"Keep dreaming. It's too boring on your side of the tracks. How you been?"

"Maintaining, definitely can't complain. Black said y'all good on weapons, so I guess I can be on my way."

"Yea, we're good. Let me put a bug in your ear real quick, though." Turk motioned for me to have a seat on the black leather sofa. I sat down, with him sitting a few feet away. "Some new lil' niggas been trying to move in on my spots. They hit two so far. You know I don't do that childish beef, but these niggas threatened my daughter's life, fam."

I sat up and pulled out my phone, sending a quick message to my security team. I don't play about my family, especially my goddaughter Alianna. Turk had gotten his high school sweetheart pregnant, and she died giving birth, so now he was a single father. We were all too young to be thinking about having kids, but he made it look easy.

"I got Alianna. You just focus on your money, bro. On the real, you know there will always be a spot for you on my team."

"You know I'mma live and die by this street shit. All I needed to hear was that you would look out for my baby girl. One love, jit," Turk said before standing.

"You're only four years older than me, with your slow ass. One love."

I always picked on him because he failed once and his birthday was late, so he was a junior in high school when I was a freshman. I stood and dapped him up before heading out to go home and get some rest. Tomorrow night would be my date with Vitani, and I was looking forward to seeing her again. I still hadn't gotten around to telling Bart about what happened. I needed to do that ASAP, but I didn't want to make their work relationship awkward.

I swerved through traffic in my black-on-black charger, thinking about what Simon had told me about the meeting when Vitani got promoted. He said Bart acted a complete ass. He better be glad I wasn't there. I would've had to knock his ass out. I don't play that power tripping. John texted in the group message that excluded Bart, saying he saw that coming. He ain't gone let us live this Bart junk down. I pulled up to my house, showered, and climbed into bed. It was only seven at night, I knew Vitani was up, so I texted her.

Me: *Hey, Beautiful.*

Future BM: *Hey Godrique. Are you canceling?*

Me: *Hell no! I was gone ask if you wanted to come over tonight instead.*

Future BM: *Really? No, I have a child. Adult responsibilities.*

Me: *Bring your child with you. A nigga hungry, I'll babysit while you cook.*

Future BM: *(laughing emoji) GTFOH! I don't even know you like that to be having my baby around you. Good night, see you tomorrow.*

Me: *I'll let you have that. Come to my house at 1 pm instead of 6. Don't be late. Enjoy your night Vitani.*

I needed to get my shit together. I ain't never been this anxious to see a woman I already fucked. The crazy part about it all was I had only ever been around my brothers kids, and they're older. I didn't even remember the toddler phase. That's why I usually didn't mess with chicks that had kids. I didn't know how to play stepdaddy.

Chapter Six

GOD

I chuckled as I watched Vitani on my door camera as she snapped pictures of my house and tags on my cars. I waited for her to knock on my door before I opened it with a straight face. She looked me up and down, and her eyes paused on my grey sweatpants. I wore these on purpose just to mess with her. I had on some Jordan slides and a plain white t-shirt.

"You need my social security number, too?"

"What do you mean?"

"I saw your sneaky ass taking pictures. Who are you sending them to, Rae?"

"If you know, why are you asking? I gotta be safe," she laughed.

"Let me ask you this. If I knocked you out and put you in my trunk right now, what good would those pictures do?"

I watched as she licked her lips and stepped forward, "Try it and find out."

The next thing I knew, this girl dropped her purse and started running, jumping on my white Mustang GT. I was lost for a second before I looked down and saw my babies standing on both sides of me. I doubled over in laughter.

"Get your goofy ass off my car. These dogs don't want you," I said in between trying to catch my breath, still laughing.

"No! Put them things away!"

"Hell naw, this their house. The fuck you think this is? Come here."

"No, I'm going home." She really started crying.

I walked over to the car with my dogs Midnight and Joy by my side. Vitani's crazy-ass climbed on the roof of my car screaming.

"HELP! HELP!"

This shit was funnier than any comedy show I had ever witnessed.

"Vitani, baby, just come here a minute," I said softly, motioning for her to take my hand. She hesitated for a minute, then took my hand as I picked her up, cradling her in my arms.

"I'mma put you down. Don't run. They just want to smell you. Are you okay with that?" I asked. She nodded her head yes. I put her down, and Midnight and Joy sniffed her jeans before running off in the yard to play.

"Who the hell were you calling out to? My neighbors live a good mile down the road."

She backed out of my grasp and wiped her face before saying, "I don't know. I wasn't thinking."

She walked back onto my wrap-around porch and picked up her purse before going into my house. Her ass looked good in the tight jeans she had on, and she felt good in my arms. She wore a pink spaghetti strap top with some pink Chuck Taylors on her feet. It was simple and cute. I followed her as she walked through my foyer and down the hall.

"Where is your bathroom? I also need a rag to wash my face."

"Down the hall to the left, there should be clean rags in the drawer."

I went to my kitchen, which was decked out in stainless steel appliances, to take out what I wanted her to cook and place them on the island. I wanted some fried ribs smothered in gravy, mashed potatoes, baked mac and cheese, and collard greens. I hadn't had any ribs in a long time because all my mom cooked is pork ribs, but all I eat is beef ribs.

"I'm guessing you want those fried since you have flour out." Vitani walked into the kitchen looking refreshed.

"Yes, how long will it take? I have a few calls to make."

"However long it takes. Just stay out of my way. I'll call you when I'm done. If them dogs come in this kitchen, I'm really leaving."

"Girl, shut that shit up. I don't play when it comes to my food. Ain't no animals been in my kitchen."

She smiled and then gave me her back. I walked to my office and made some calls. My workers handled all the groundwork for my business, so I really didn't have to worry about that. Chez pretty much ran the day-to-day operation. By the time I finished calling my clients, the house was smelling like a church that sold church dinners after a three-hour Sunday service. I made my way into the kitchen in time to see her pulling some cornbread from the oven.

"Where the hell you get cornbread from?" I asked, surprised.

"I made it. You had all of the ingredients I needed," Vitani smiled.

"Oh, so you cook-cook? Why nobody ain't wife you up yet?" I leaned against the marble counter and watched as she started putting all the food in separate glass bowls I didn't even know I had.

"I am only twenty years old. I still have some growing up to do before I think about becoming a wife."

"But you didn't have to grow before you became a mother?"

I watched as Vitani paused and then cocked her head to the side before placing the bowl she had in her hand on the counter. She turned to face me with a scowl, then walked towards me.

"No. My daughter is a blessing, and I have grown so much just from being her mother."

I grabbed her arm and pulled her close. "My point exactly." A look of confusion appeared in her eyes before I continued, "You grew AFTER you became a mother. Why grow before becoming a wife instead of growing as my wife?"

I released her arm. It took her a few seconds to regroup and finish putting the food on the table. She didn't respond, though, we sat down and ate in silence.

I watched her eat, and her skinny ass wasn't holding anything back. She ate just as much as me, and that cornbread was so good. I stood and cleaned off the table, then did the dishes since she had cooked. When I finished, I found her lying across my cream-colored couch.

"You want to watch a movie or something?"

"No, I just want to talk. You're right, you know. I guess I just never looked at things that way. You can never really be prepared for things like marriage and kids. You just gotta do it," she paused as I sat down beside her putting her legs over mine. She had removed her shoes to get comfortable. She rolled onto her back and looked up at me. "Do you have kids?"

"Naw, and before your nosy ass asks, yes, I want kids one day. Do you want more?"

"If I'm being honest, hell no. However, I would have more if my husband wanted some of his own. Tell me about yourself, Godrique. What do you do for a living?"

I told her about my childhood in Tampa and then Orlando. I told her about my arms dealing business. She didn't need to know all the details. I even told her about Turk and my goddaughter.

"What about you? Do you plan on using your private investigator license?" I asked.

"What did you just say?"

"You heard me loud and clear," I said. I was not about to repeat myself.

"I um. I don't know. I want to, but I am content where I am right now. The money is steady."

"Scared money don't make no money. Remember that, beautiful."

"So, how do you think Bart would feel if he knew we had sex?" she asked, changing the subject quickly.

"I honestly don't give a fuck. What we do ain't nobody's business but ours. How do you feel about him knowing about us?"

"Hmm. That depends on where this thing is going with us. Do you just want to fuck me? If so, we can go ahead and finish what we started and call it quits."

"Straight like that, huh? You wanna fuck me, or you wanna fuck with me?" I asked her as I looked into her seductive eyes.

"That's up to you. You're the one with two girlfriends. Cut them bitches off, because I don't share dick."

"I'll think about it." She punched me in my arm. "What is your hobby?"

"Reading. If I could get paid to read, I would. What is your hobby?"

"Getting money. Naw, I shoot hoops with the boys every now and then and play video games."

"You're just gonna leave them poor dogs outside all night?"

"Oh, now you care about the dogs. I'll let them in when I let you out. They have doghouses with food and water. They're okay."

I leaned down and kissed her lips gently. I had been thinking about how soft they would be all day. I wasn't prepared for her to grab the back of my head and give me full access to her delicious mouth. My tongue sailed into her mouth in search of hers as I began a slow assault.

"Mmm," she moaned into the kiss.

I pulled back, releasing her mouth as I stared into her enticing cat-shaped eyes. I bit her nipple through her skimpy shirt and watched as it hardened.

"Finish what you started." She tried to sit up, but I held her tight around her waist. She released her grip on the back of my head, and I leaned in to suck on her neck. I wanted to leave a hickey on purpose. If there were anyone else, they would know that she belongs to me now.

Beep Beeep

My camera alerted me that someone was on my property, but it had to be someone I knew because my dogs weren't barking. I pecked her lips again before I strolled over and opened the door to see Teq, John, Simon, Bart, and Peter standing there with beer and snacks. Their dumb asses pushed past me, but paused when they saw Vitani on my couch.

"Oh snap, I forgot to cancel with y'all tonight," I groaned.

"Oh, so you're just loving the crew?" Bart seethed as he grilled Vitani from where he stood near the door.

"Excuse me?" Vitani snapped back as she sat up straight.

"Aye, I'm not on that drama mess tonight, Bart, so you can go back out the way you came with the bullshit."

"I just want to know if you were ever gonna make your way around to me. You get around pretty fast," Bart continued as if I hadn't said anything.

"I don't think you'll be a good fit. For one, I don't do pink meat. For two, I don't do bitches. For three, God has this hook that hits my spot just right, and I don't think you could top Mr. Almighty himself. I've been blessed." She winked at him.

I was about to dig in Bart's ass, but Vitani's words had me cracking up. The other guys were laughing, too. Her goofy ass really be with the shits. I walked back over to my couch and sat back down beside her. She leaned over and kissed my cheek before standing.

"I have to get back to my daughter. I'll call you when I make it home."

"Let them leave. You can stay." I stood back up. She paused as if she was thinking about it.

"Spend time with your brothers. I'm sure we'll have plenty of time to get to know each other better. I might just reconsider becoming a wife." She smiled at our inside joke.

"Bye Sis," John, Teq, and Peter said in unison, being petty.

"Tell Ice to call me tomorrow. I leave Sunday, and I told her I would take her to the park before I go," Simon spoke.

Vitani nodded at Simon and waved bye to the others. I didn't miss the death glare Bart gave her as we passed by. She didn't even spare him a second glance. He would be okay. It ain't like I stole his girl. I walked Vitani to her car and gave her another kiss on the lips. This time she wrapped her arms around my neck and sucked on both of my lips as she twirled her tongue on them, teasing me. I immediately pictured how it would feel to have her do that to my dick. It bricked up instantly, and all I wanted to do was take her back inside.

"You sure you don't want me to 'finish what I started' on the couch?"

She chuckled as she got in her car.

"Next time. Good night Godrique."

I walked back into the house with a hard-on and an attitude, to find the guys sitting at my dining room table eating the food Vitani cooked for me. Their dumb ass had turned on the flat screen and put it on the channel that was linked to my outside cameras. They had smirks on their faces, all except Bart, who was standing in the cut with his arms folded.

"Damn, shawty really can throw down in the kitchen," Peter said in between bites.

"Hell yea, I see why she loving the crew," John added.

"Yo, you really in love. We see you out there all smoochy-smoochy, giving hickies and shit," Teq laughed.

"She ain't loving nobody but me. Y'all ruined my night. I know y'all seen that car outside that wasn't mine. And Si, I know yo' ass knew that was Vitani's car."

"Hell yea, I knew that was her car. I knew her ass was cooking, too. I could smell it from outside. You have a lifetime to fuck on that girl. Give her a break."

"You and Vitani fucked?" Bart asked.

"Didn't she just tell your simple ass that?" John snapped.

"Yes, Bart. I had sex with Vitani the night of the company party," I answered truthfully.

"Where? Why would you let me promote her if you two were fucking?"

John laughed. Peter smirked. Teq adjusted his glasses. Si kept eating.

"I said, 'we had sex'. It only happened once. If you wanted to promote her to smash her, then, by all means, go for it. That's none of my business," I said, Ignoring the 'where' part.

"So if I go fuck her right now, you'd be okay with it?"

"Absolutely, that's not my girl," I lied. Part of me would be pissed if that actually happened. I knew Vitani was not that kind of woman. If she was gonna fuck him, it would've happened by now.

"Fine, I'll catch you guys another time." Bart left out, slamming the door behind him.

"He's gonna be a problem," John said, shaking his head.

Chapter Seven

BART

I sat outside Anita's house, contemplating whether I wanted to go inside. After leaving God's house, I called her because I wanted to get even. He knew I wanted to be with Vitani, everyone with eyes could see that I was in love with her. Even knowing that she screwed God, I still want to be with her. She's so different from any woman I've ever met. I didn't mean to be rude to her earlier but I was hurt. It was obvious that her and Simon weren't fucking, but she had given God something after knowing him for one night when I had been trying for a year. I gave her the financial stability she needed to take care of my stepdaughter.

I got out and locked my door then walked up to the blue-painted mansion Anita lived in. I paid for this house too, if we're being technical. Anita's father wouldn't have a job if it wasn't for me. IntelliCorp was my business, I just shared it with my so-called brothers. They didn't know that I was using it to launder money. My father owned an oil company overseas so I came from money, unlike the other men I associated with. I was better than all of them, and that's why I would get my woman, by any means necessary.

I walked in and went upstairs to her master bedroom to find her laying on the bed in red lingerie set. It looked good on her and she was a nice-looking woman, but was no Vitani.

"Put some clothes on. We need a plan."

"I already have a plan in motion. Once I get God to leave that little hoodlum alone, everything will go back to normal. She's just the flavor of the month."

I shook my head. "I don't know about that. He seems like he really likes her. He needs to get his own woman so he can leave mine alone. I just need to get her away from him long enough for her to come to her senses."

Anita stood and walked over to where I stood and dropped to her knees. She pulled my dick out and started stroking it. I grabbed the back of her head, guided her mouth to my shaft, and she started slurping like her life depended on it. It felt like a wet vacuum on low. Then she reached around, stuck a finger in my butt, and I let off my load hard at the back of her throat. *Damn, I've never had a woman do that to me before.* It was something I had loved since I was younger. I released my hold on her and stumbled over to the chaise by her window.

"You know I'm not cheating on Vitani, right?"

She chuckled. "How can you cheat on someone you're not in a relationship with?"

"We are in a relationship, she just doesn't know it yet."

I stood and fixed my pants, then walked out. I refused to stick my dick in any woman other than Vitani. She would never forgive me if she knew I fucked another woman, let alone Anita. After Anita helped me with this situation, I would kill her just because she hated my wife so much. God better get his shit together or I would have to kill him, too. I was willing to do anything to be with the love of my life and our baby girl.

I watched as Vitani got into her car. It had been a week since that incident at God's house and I was still pissed. I had gotten another co-worker to start training Vitani because I knew she didn't want to be around me. That was about to end today, because I missed being near her. I followed her to a little hood store on Wabash Avenue. When she went inside, I got out and took her front tire off in record timing, so fast a pit crew would be jealous. I put it in my trunk and drove off.

I circled around a few corners then drove up to the store just as Vitani walked out and discovered her tire was missing. I acted like I didn't see her and headed inside the store, she walked in behind me and went to the cashier.

"May I use your phone please? Someone stole my tire and my phone is dead. I need to call my sister to come take me to get a tire."

"Vitani?" I acted as if I'd just noticed her.

"Bart, what are you doing on this side of town?"

"I come here to get some boiled peanuts, they have the best. Is everything okay?"

"Not really, May I use your phone to call Rae?"

"How about I do you one better. I can have your car towed to your home and you can ride with me."

She looked skeptical but finally nodded her head. She didn't look so well. This past week she had been sick with a cold so she only came in for a few hours a day for training. I wish she would stop playing and let me take care of her. She followed me to my car and I opened the passenger door to my grey Jaguar for her to get inside, then leaned in to put her seatbelt on. After I got in and started driving, I almost forgot to cover my tracks.

"Where do you live?"

"Oh, sorry, I have sick brain. I'll put my address in your phone's GPS for you."

"Cool, you don't have a spare tire?"

"No, that was my spare. If I did have one, I could've put it on myself. My mom made sure I could change a tire and change my own oil," she smiled faintly.

"That's cool, I wish my mom was that hands-on. All she wants to do is spend my father's money. I was her meal ticket."

"Sorry to hear that. I come from a family with hard-working women. May I ask you something?" Vitani asked me.

"You can ask me anything."

"Why the sudden change in attitude towards me? We always had a good work relationship. I don't think that should change because of what I do outside of work."

"You're right. I was wrong for saying the things I did. I would like for things to go back to normal, too. Can we start as friends again and see how that goes?" I smiled.

"I would like that very much. I'm up here on the left. Thank you for giving me a ride. You don't have to—"

I wondered why she'd stopped talking, but I looked up to see God's car parked outside her apartment. *What was he doing here? Did he spend the night with her?* I gripped the wheel to try to calm myself down. I had to go about this the smart way. I didn't want to run her away again, but this guy God just didn't learn. I was not going to let him have Vitani, ever. I got out and walked around to open the door for her to get out.

"I'll walk you to your door. My mechanic will be dropping your car off with a fresh tire within the next hour."

"You really didn't have to do that, Bart."

"Yes, I do," I waited for her to open the door with her key, but it opened before she could place the key inside. I put my hand on the small of her back because the door opening startled her enough to take a step back. God opened the door, holding my stepdaughter. He looked at Vitani, then me, and I smiled at him.

"Be safe, Vitani. I'll see you at work tomorrow."

I walked back to my car, smiling. God would seem fine to people on the outside, but I knew him well enough to know that he was pissed. His jaw twitched, and he masked his face to show no emotion. Gotcha bitch!

RAE

"Bitch, Devun don't want your fat ass! He is only using your dumb ass to take care of our kids. He still comes to my house every day to keep me satisfied," Meka, Devun's baby mother, yelled at me through the phone.

I disconnected the call, rolling my eyes. I feel so stupid for staying with a man like Devun. There was just something in me that felt like I would be like all the other women in his life that left him high and dry. His mom left him with his grandmother to raise, and she died when he was ten. He had been on his own ever since, and I didn't want to leave him to fend for himself. I loved him too much. I was parked outside this electronics place to pick up my phone Devun had dropped off yesterday. For some reason, my phone was locked, saying there were too many incorrect password attempts. I knew I hadn't touched my phone, and Devun said he hadn't touch it either, so I don't know what happened.

As I walked in the shop, my heart crashed into my ribs. *What is he doing here?* This man was fine as shit, and I hated being around him. He was too perfect, and we connected on so many levels. If only I had met him before Devun. *Who am I kidding? He probably would only see me as a friend.* Not even on some low confidence shit, I always get seen as one of the guys. My sis Vitani does, too. That's how she ended up having a baby father that wasn't worth a damn.

But, back to the fine specimen of a man that stood with his back to me. *I know that body from any angle.*

"Have a seat. I'll be right with you."

"Okay."

I watched as he turned around, slowly, looking me up and down, taking in every inch of my body. I had just left work on my lunch break, so I had on a navy-blue dress that showed some cleavage, a red blazer, and some red pumps. *I know I look good, and from the look he's giving me, he does too.*

"What a pleasant surprise. What can I do for you today?" His deep voice had my body tingling.

Hell, what couldn't he do for me? "Hello, Teqwyn. I am here to pick up my phone that my boyfriend dropped off this morning." His brow furrowed as I walked closer to the counter, "My boyfriend Devun."

"Oh. Interesting."

"What's so interesting?" I was lost.

"It's interesting that you would be with someone like him. That's not my pig and certainly not my farm, so wait here for a minute while I go get your device."

He walked to the back, and I stood there wondering what his problem was. I hadn't seen him in about two weeks, which was in passing at work, but we often played games online. He knew I had a boyfriend, so why he acting funny now is what's 'interesting.' He returned with my phone and placed it on the counter.

"Did I do or say something to offend you?"

"Not at all. This one is on the house. See you around, ma."

I frowned. His New York accent comes out sometimes when we play together, but it was really thick just then. He had just dismissed me like I was nothing, and I can't even front like my feelings weren't hurt. I'll just let him calm down. Maybe something happened that I don't know about, and he's just in a mood.

"I would rather pay you. How much?"

"A dollar."

My frown deepened, "Stop playing and just tell me how much it costs."

"You good ma, it's on me. Just make sure you get online tonight so that I can spank that ass."

I laughed. "I can't make any promises. I don't just lay down and take ass whoopings, but you can get a fair one."

"Bet."

I walked out of the shop cheesing. That is the Teqwyn I knew and had grown to like. He made me laugh more than Devun. I had been lying to Devun, saying I was playing online with a woman because he would trip if he knew it was a man. When he said he would get my phone fixed, he referred to the person as his homeboy. *Are he and Teq cool?* I hope not. That would be just my luck to fall for his boy. I am not a cheater, but my mama always told me to keep a spare. *Who am I kidding? That man just likes playing games with me.*

I went back to my job and still had a half-hour to spare, so I went to Vitani's office. It was on the same floor as mine now that my girl had got that promotion. I'm so happy that everything was looking up for her. She had been through a lot. I knocked on the door, then let myself in and looked at my girl. She looked as if she was down bad. Last week she had a cold, but she didn't seem to be getting any better.

"Sis, are you okay? I think you should take the rest of the day off."

"I have to get my hours in, and then I'll log in remotely from home tomorrow. I don't feel good at all. The doctor said it was a sinus infection. I gotta pick up the antibiotics when I get off."

I walked over and touched her head. She was burning up. "Let me take you home before I have to clock back in."

"No, Anita been down my throat talking about 'you won't be getting any special treatment,' so I'mma thug it out a few more hours."

"Fuck Anita, I'mma go tell that bitch about herself. You ain't no damn slave." I turned to walk out.

"Please don't do that, Rae. I don't want any more trouble around here. You need this job just as much as I do. I'm fine."

She started coughing, or should I say barking, because it sounded terrible. I had never seen Vitani this sick before, and I didn't like it one bit. It was taking everything in me not to go drag Anita all up and through this office building. Since Vitani wanted to do things the hard way, I got something for her ass. I reached in my purse, pulled out two NyQuil liquid pills, and handed them to her.

"Here, take these to get you through the day."

I knew she was sick because she took the pills without even asking what they were. I hugged her and then walked out of her office. When I got back to my office, I sent a quick text. He responded immediately with the information I had requested.

"Hello?"

"This is Rae. I need a huge favor from you."

"What's that?"

"I need you to come to my job to get Vitani, she's not feeling good, and I can't convince her to leave. I know—"

"I'm already here. I'll take care of it," he cut me off.

"Thank you so much!"

ANITA

God smelled so good and looked even better. He could have on the simplest outfit, and it looked sexy on him. I stood behind my desk as I watched him answer his phone. He had on a plain t-shirt, jeans, and some sneakers, but all I want to do is jump his bones. He hopped out of the chair and headed towards the door in front of my desk.

"Where are you going? We need to talk."

"That will have to wait. By the way, Vitani Banks is going home for the rest of the week."

"She can't do that, and neither can you. You do not run things here."

"Call your father and ask him if he is ready to lose his biggest client," he snapped as he walked out, slamming my office door.

I sat down and racked my brain, trying to figure out what that dirty ghetto bird had that I didn't. *How are all these men crazy about her when I was obviously the better catch.* I had a college degree, I was light-skinned with good hair because of my mixed race, and my body was way better than hers. Bart had been smitten by that dirty foot for a while now. But having God taken away from me was overkill.

Bart and I had been secretly messing around since I graduated from college. Once Vitani came into the picture, he stopped screwing me. The other week was the first time he let me touch him in a long time. I knew I had to pull out the stops to get him to come back around, so I tried something different, and he loved it.

God wouldn't touch me for some reason even before Vitani came in the picture, but he had started coming around. Now he doesn't want anything to do with me at all. I got him up here today by telling him I had a message for him from my father. That was a lie, and I'm sure he knew that, but he still came. Then that skank had to play sick. I was going to make her life a living hell. If I couldn't have the man I loved, then she wouldn't either. My phone rang.

"What is taking you so long?"

"Calm down. These are some powerful people, but I'm working on it. Just be patient."

"Fuck patience! I need this handled immediately. If you can't take care of it, I will pay someone else to do it," I yelled. I was upset.

"Calm down, princess. I will have it done by the end of the month."

"Fine, the payment will be transferred when the job is complete."

Click. That cunt hung up on me. My cousin works for CPS, and I put a little birdie about an unfit mother in her ear. Now that she has met Vitani, she hates her too. She didn't even know that I was using her to be with the man I loved.

Chapter Eight

VITANI

I woke up feeling better than I ever had. It felt like I was floating on a cloud. This had to be a dream. I felt strong arms wrapped around me, so I snuggled closer to the hardness that was emanating so much warmth. The movement behind me caused me to stir. I rolled over, seeing Godrique sleeping peacefully, in only boxers. I had never had a dream that felt so real, so I decided to take advantage of the moment. I reached down into his boxers and stroked his length lightly. He stirred a little before his eyes popped open, and he grabbed my hand to stall my movements.

"Go back to sleep," he grumbled.

"I will go back to sleep, but only if you put me to sleep," I murmured. This dream me was brazen. I liked her.

He rolled over, forcing me to remove my hand from his boxers. I sucked my teeth.

"Take your sick ass back to sleep, girl."

I sat up and hit his arm. That got him to roll onto his back but sent me falling over. For some reason, this dream me was clumsy as hell. I climbed back on top of him and realized I only had on my bra and panties. I positioned myself on his erection and started slowly grinding on him in a circular motion, but really, I was about to make myself cum, because the pressure on my clit was just right. I guessed this was what wet dreams felt like. Godrique bit his bottom lip as he grabbed my hips and started controlling my movements. As soon as I was about to explode, he pushed me off of him.

Oh hell no, this dream Godrique was evil. I screamed. I was so pissed off because I wanted my nut. His hand went over my mouth and partially over my nose, so I could barely breathe.

"Stop screaming before you wake the baby up. The fuck is wrong with you?"

He released my mouth, and I gasped for air. What baby was he talking about? I didn't even care at this point, I just wanted him inside of me. He climbed on me, placing his knees on my sides, and raised my arms. Before I could figure out what was happening, my arms were stuck above my head. He turned around and did the same thing with my legs, then he stood and walked to a dresser drawer that was floating on a separate cloud. I tried not to panic because it was only a dream, but this might be a damn nightmare.

I heard plastic ripping. Then I saw him walk back over and cover my eyes with a blindfold and felt a ball in my mouth. Did he just gag me? Oh damn, I'm about to die in my sleep. I tried moving again, but that didn't work. There's no use. I'm done for.

"I told you to go to sleep, but you didn't listen. Instead, you challenged me. Let me show you what happens when you challenge God."

I felt his warm mouth near my ear, and it caused a chill to run down my spine. He started at my neck and took his time licking and sucking. I was sure he was leaving hickeys everywhere he touched. I could feel my juices soaking my panties. He moved down to my collar bone, and this muthafucker bit it. As much as I wanted to hate it, that shit had me shaking. He used his teeth and rubbed them against the bone. Oh my, I didn't even know that was my spot.

"Are you cumming already? Tsk. Tsk. Tsk. You might not last long at all. People always want things they're not ready for."

I rolled my eyes. I was glad he couldn't see them, or I probably would have had to pay for that. He made his way down to my breasts, removed my strapless bra then licked and sucked everywhere except my nipples. I started whining. This was torture of the worst kind. My body felt like it was on fire. His tongue was like a torch scorching everything in its path. He finally grazed a nipple, and I came so hard my body lifted off the cloud. He covered my nipple with his warm mouth, and I sunk back into the cloud. I needed to wake back up because I was sure I was having a heart attack.

My chest was heaving, and I couldn't catch my breath. God gave the other nipple some attention, and I couldn't take it anymore. Then I felt orgasm number four. I had cum again when he sucked the other nipple. I felt him licking lower, and he swiped his tongue over my clit in my panties unexpectedly, and boom, another orgasmic wave crashed into me.

He made his way down my legs, leaving no skin unscathed. Then he ripped my panties, and the anticipation alone had me shivering. He took his time licking and sucking on my nether lips, then sticking his tongue in my core as if he was exploring a new candy flavor. He licked from my core back up to my clit in one long stroke, then latched onto my clit. I jerked like I was being shocked back to life after going into cardiac arrest. I came, and I could feel my juices flowing out of me like a river.

God went back to my core and started licking every drop like it would give him eternal life. He was even moaning. I have known death. This had to be what it felt like to die because I couldn't move, I couldn't breathe, I couldn't see. My body was releasing my soul through my pussy. When he had his fill, he stopped. I felt him releasing my arms and legs from whatever held them hostage. Then he removed the blindfold and gag. I looked at his face glistening with my juices on his beard and wished I had the strength to kiss him.

"Oh, God! Please, baby. Don't stop. I...I want," I moaned as I bucked my hips.

Godrique must hear my thoughts in this dream because he leaned down and let me taste myself on his lips. I savored every drop. No wonder he was down there eating like a starving man. It was sweet.

He positioned himself in between my legs and asked, "Are you on birth control?"

Why would that matter in a dream? Okay, I'll go along with it. "Yes."

When had he removed his boxers? This dream Godrique was smooth as hell. He worked his way into my warmth, and I felt like I had been struck by lightning. Paint me white and call me Powder because this nigga is Powerline. I started squirming to try to get away and moaned from the intensity of his strokes. He was deep inside me, hitting walls I didn't know existed. I didn't want it to stop when I felt another orgasm coming.

"I should've left your ass tied up."

He grabbed my legs, put them together, and put them on his right shoulder. Now my legs were closed, causing even more friction with each stroke.

"Oh God, you're... you're."

"Yea, I know. But don't cum without me this time."

"Mmm, fuck, this feels sooooo good. Riiiight thereee. Yesss."

He put his hand over my mouth again, stopping my ability to speak and breathe. I was still making noise, but it wasn't as loud. I felt his nut rising through my inner walls, and that paired with not being able to breathe, had me cumming so hard my pussy muscles held him captive. He had no choice but to release everything he had inside of me. I came so hard that my eyes rolled back into my head as I moaned and groaned while grinding against him. I was lightheaded and sated, something I had never felt before taking hold of me. I wanted this man, not for a night or two but longer, maybe forever. I blinked sleepily as he pushed deeper inside me, and I felt

"Seven."

That's the last thing I heard before I blacked out in my dream.

I woke up to a persistent beeping noise and a terrible headache. *Where am I?* I gave my eyes time to adjust to the bright light and forced myself not to freak out when I realized I was lying in a hospital bed. The smell of hospitals always made me sick to the stomach, and this time was no different. I looked frantically around to find something to throw up inside of and saw a barf bag hanging beside my bed. I grabbed the bag and started dry heaving, and the pain made me groan as tears welled in my eyes. I heard movement and looked over to see God looking at me from the couch near the hospital room window with Ice on his chest. She was sleeping peacefully, and I knew he didn't want to move to wake her.

After the wave of nausea passed, I stood and unhooked myself from the monitors and went into the restroom to discard the barf bag and get cleaned up. Good thing I wasn't attached to an IV. The whole lower part of my body was sore and felt like I had been hit by a truck. There was an extra hospital gown and a toothbrush with toothpaste, so I took care of my hygiene, exited the restroom, and laid back down in the bed just before the doctor and nurse entered.

"Mrs. Banks, I am glad to see you are moving around this morning. You gave your husband quite the scare," the short chubby white man said. "Do you mind telling me your full name, date of birth, and what day it is?"

"Vitani Seline Banks, June seventeenth, today is March twenty-eighth. You must be mistaken. I am not married." I frowned.

"Oh, I am sorry, I just um assumed, but I need your full date of birth," he rambled as he looked from me to God, who had now sat up on the couch because Ice was waking up.

I gave him the year I was born as the nurse that looked like Velma from Scooby-Doo took my vitals and temperature. The doctor seemed to be pleased, but I was still trying to figure out how I ended up here.

"I can see the questions in your eyes. You were rushed here last night because you had stopped breathing for a few seconds and alarmed the gentlemen here. Your heart rate was elevated when you arrived, and you had a slight fever. However, you kept screaming, 'God is evil,' so we called for a psych consult. Had you woken in that same state, we would be forced to Baker Act you. You seem perfectly fine now, so we should be able to discharge you later on today and send you home with stronger antibiotics for your sinus infection," he smiled. "We are still waiting for some blood work to come back before releasing you."

The dream rushed back into my memory. That damn dream where Godrique had fucked me to sleep, literally. The doctor and nurse left, and Ice came and jumped on the bed with me, hugging and kissing my cheeks. I hugged her close and tickled her tummy. God just stood beside the bed, watching us. I was nervous around him now based on what happened in that dream. I probably would never talk about it. It was too raunchy. There was a knock at the door, and it was a clown in the doorway. He looked like Krusty the Klown off the Simpsons walking in with some balloons in his hand.

"Clown! Clown! Clown!" Ice yelled excitedly.

"What is a clown doing in my room?" I leaned over and whispered to God.

"I heard you liked clown niggas, so I asked him to make an appearance to help you recover," he smirked.

I gave him the side-eye, then said, "Ha, ha, ha, you're so funny."

He started laughing as the clown made balloon animals for Ice, then he handed me a balloon poodle saying, "I heard dogs are your favorite."

I couldn't help laughing at the lengths this fool would go through, to make me smile. Ice joined in on the laughter, not even knowing what she was laughing at.

"Thank you," I smiled up at him.

He leaned down and kissed my forehead, and Ice put her forehead near mine so he could kiss hers. We all laughed again. This felt so right. Ice had been attached to God since she met him the week prior. I thought God would be upset about Bart giving me a ride home when I had a tire stolen that night, but he was chill. He spent the night on the couch, and I knew then he was different. He just said he wanted to make sure Ice and I were safe. I knew that him not being able to contact me had caused him to worry.

"What are you thanking me for?"

"For everything. You made me leave work. I guess you picked up Ice from my grandfather and brought me to the hospital. I can't thank you enough."

I smiled up at him as he picked Ice up from the bed as she showed him her balloon heart. It was like I wasn't even there anymore. He gave Ice his full attention. My memory was so foggy. I really didn't remember anything after taking those pills Rae gave me. *Them things must've been strong as hell.*

The clown made his exit. I closed my eyes to try to get a quick nap but quickly reopened them when I heard, "What is this? I know you're not fucking this bitch."

God placed Ice on the bed with me before I could get up to knock this dumb bitch out. Miss Piggy must have lost her rabbit-ass mind coming in my room talking like that around my child.

"LiLi, get out. Now," God spoke in a low tone as he walked towards her in long cool strides.

"Fuck that! How are you in here playing house with the next bitch while I'm pregnant with your seed?!" God grabbed her elbow and pulled her out into the hallway.

"Goddy! Goddy!" Ice called behind him.

"Shhh, baby. It's okay."

I rubbed my daughter's back. I'm sure she was just as confused as I was. Miss Piggy had on what looked like a cafeteria uniform. That had to be how she stumbled into my room. Pregnant or not, that bitch had an ass whooping coming her way. Her face ain't pregnant.

"I apologize about that. I forgot she works in the kitchen downstairs," God said as he came back into the room.

"I have a baby, and I don't need this drama. Tell your little girlfriend she better watch her back because I'm coming for her head. This is the second time I let her slide."

"What?"

"You heard what I said."

"I'm not telling her anything. You won't be touching LiLi while she's carrying my child."

His words were like a hard slap to the side of my face. A dowse of cold water to my entire body. *What was I thinking? We could be together forever and be a happy little family? Yea, right, I just received the wake-up call of the century.*

"Leave. Stay the hell away from my daughter and me," I snapped. "Ice baby, say bye to God. He has to go away for a long time."

"Bye Goddy, hugs," Ice leaped into his arms and hugged him tightly.

"I'll see you soon, Ice," God smiled as he looked into my eyes. I felt like he could see into my soul, but at the same time, like he was taking me for a joke. He put Ice down and leaned close to my ear, "You got me fucked up if you think you can keep me away from my daughter. After last night, you're my wife, and she's my stepchild. See you around, wifey."

He swaggered out of the room like he owned the hospital. *What have I gotten myself into?*

I think his dumb ass needs to be Baker Acted cause he lost his damn mind. He was acting just like the Godrique in my dream, and I didn't want anything to do with that monster. Jen needs to set up that meeting with her boss asap so I can stay the hell away from these people. Bart was the initial target, but after meeting God and mentioning his name in a friendly conversation, Jen asked me to get more intel on him and his crew. I still don't know much about what he does, though. Besides being a little off in the head, he seemed like a legit businessman.

What was he even talking about, 'after last night, you're my wife? Because he brought me to the hospital? That ain't no grounds to act crazy. He coulda let me die if he was gonna hold it over my head like I owe him something. We had sex one time about a month and a half ago, and he was acting like we had been together for years. Why do I attract crazy men?

"Excuse me, Miss Banks, we have your blood work, and it explains what may have brought you in," the chubby doctor walked back in with the nurse.

I sat up. "Is everything okay?"

"Yes, for the most part. The gentleman that was here before informed us that you had taken two NyQuil pills, but according to your blood work, it seems you may have had a bad reaction to Ambien. You will need to speak with your Primary Care Physician about lowering your dose."

"You must be mistaken. I have never taken that medication in my life. I don't even know what it is."

"There was a very high dose in your system..." the doctor's voice faded as he looked at the nurse. "Call for a social worker to come down. We need to do a rape kit as well."

"Social worker? Rape kit? Y'all not doing no damn rape kit on me. I wasn't around anyone that would rape me yesterday," I snapped.

"Ma'am, this is standard procedure for women who have been drugged, and you have passion marks all over your body."

"Forget your procedure. I said you're not doing a rape kit on me."

"Okay, you can refuse the rape kit, but you have to speak with a social worker before you leave. One will be in to speak with you shortly."

The doctor and nurse left out of the room just as my mom was walking in. I started crying, trying to figure out who the hell would drug me. *Was it God?* My mom walked over and picked Ice up, then wiped my tears away with her hand.

"Vitani, I don't know what's going on, but I'm sure it is nothing God can't fix."

I started crying harder because God's ass is probably the problem. I tried to get myself together because I hated crying in front of my baby. I'd never had this many off-the-wall things happen to me in such a short amount of time.

"I am gonna take Ice to get something to eat from the cafeteria. We'll be back. Remember what I said, baby, just pray and ask God for help." She smiled before walking out.

A few minutes later, Susan walked into my hospital room, and I knew this was only the beginning. This bitch had a goofy smirk on her face, and that's when I noticed she looked kinda familiar. I know she was the same woman that came to my house a few weeks back, but there was something else. She looks like someone else I know, but I can't quite put my finger on it.

"Miss Banks, can't say I'm surprised to see you here today. Do you make it a habit of overdosing around strange men with your daughter present?"

I gasped in shock at her cold assumptions, "I-I never took any drugs. My daughter was safe."

"How long have you known the man that brought you to the hospital? Why did he leave you here alone?"

"It's none of your business how long I have known God. I told him to leave. He didn't want to."

"Lovers quarrel so soon? Or you couldn't pay your dealer, so you had to find other ways to settle your debt? You have different men around your daughter frequently? Do you even care about your daughter?"

"Of course, I care about my daughter! I am not a prostitute." I pressed the nurse button. In less than a minute, the Velma-looking nurse walked in and asked what was wrong. "I would like this woman out of my room."

"I have no problem leaving for now, but I have probable cause to be concerned for your child's safety. Have a nice day, Miss Banks." Susan walked out.

I was at a loss for words. Everything seemed to be coming together and falling apart at the same time. Jen and her boss better get this handled before I lose my mind. I dialed Jen, and she answered on the third ring.

"Hey V, let me call you right back. I'm in the middle of something."

"No! I want a meeting with your boss next week. I can't do this anymore," I cried.

"Shhh, Shhh, what's wrong?" she asked, concerned.

"What isn't wrong would be easier to answer. I have to get away from these people. That crazy social worker is trying to take my baby, and someone drugged me. I am falling in love with a sociopath. I may just let Ice stay with my mom until this shit dies down."

"Calm down, friend. We will get through this. I am out of town until Wednesday, but we can meet then. I need you to log into your secure email as soon as possible and send me everything you have on IntelliCorp. Also, give me details of everything that happened to you. I will be doing what I can on my end. I love you, friend."

Jen ended the call.

Chapter Nine

GOD

I bobbed and weaved through traffic like a racecar driver, mad as fuck. First, LiLi shows up at the hospital on some bullshit. Now I get a call from one of my men that my god daughter was being tailed. After Turk filled me in on his little beef, I had two of my best men following her to ensure she was safe at all times. My men were all trained as independent contractors by Simon. Technically, they were his men on paper because of his company, but they worked under me.

I pulled up behind the dark sedan that was two cars behind my god-daughter in the line at the Beverage Castle on old Hwy 35 and climbed off my all-black Yamaha MT-10. I pulled down my ski mask that I had custom-made with the Greek alpha symbol on the front and omega symbol on the back. Walking up to the driver's side, I opened the door. This caught the driver off-guard as his eyes bulged. Them bitches were already big as hell. His bug-eyed ace hood on crack-looking ass had me fucked up. I pulled him from the seat, pulled my gun from my waist, and placed it on the back of his skull. My men were on the passenger side dragging his friend out by this time.

"Who sent you?" I yelled, smashing the butt of my Glock into his head.

"Nobody, man! I don't know what you're talking about," Bug-eyed whined.

Pew-Pew. I sent two shots to his dome piece and then walked to the other side, where his accomplice lay face down.

"Your boy gone. R.I.P., but you can live a little longer if you tell me who sent you."

"We don't know. Some nigga rolled up on us and asked if we wanted to make twenty bands, so we took the job."

"What was the mission?"

"Kidnap the lil bitch in that little pink car. She's wanted dead or alive."

Pew-Pew.

I ended his life with no remorse. He was young and money-hungry as usual and had fallen prey for some weak nigga.

"Damn boss, I thought you said you were gonna let him live," one of my men asked.

"I did let him live 'a little longer' than the other fool. Word is bond."

Both guys laughed.

I turned around when I heard a car pull up. The silencer had delayed any initial uproar, but the car that pulled up behind my bike was packed with females that started screaming at the sight of blood. I hopped back on my bike, drove through the Beverage Castle, and stopped beside my goddaughter's hot pink mini coop.

"Go to my house. I'm right behind you."

She nodded her head and did as she was told. We had been through this plenty of times before as a safety precaution, and we had a specific route to a few safe houses. Alianna knew what her dad did for a living, so the street life was in her blood. My men would handle the bodies, and the police would never find them. Once I made it to my home, I pulled my bike into my garage and met Alianna in my living room.

"Have you talked to your dad? Did you know they were following you?"

"Calm down. I can handle myself. I can't believe you had those big goofballs following me around, even at school! They got hired on as Janitors. You be doing way too much."

"Hold on, little girl. I just saved your life. Can I get a thank you first?" I chuckled because this was the demon Turk had created.

Alianna pulled her 9mm from her purse, saying, "I had it. You and dad never let me have any fun."

"I refuse to let you catch a body before the age of sixteen. It's bad enough you are driving with only a permit. Now you want to add murder to your list of transgressions? Hell no."

She put her gun away and plopped down on the couch as Joy came over for her to pet her head. My dogs loved my goddaughter, and she loved them. Her dad was allergic to dogs, so she couldn't have any of her own.

"Alianna, this is not a game. This is life and death—"

"Ali! What happened?" Turk burst through my front door yelling.

"Chill. She's good. I handled it. We can talk about it later, but she's staying with me for now. At least until you get this handled."

"I'm cool with that."

"I'm not! I'm staying home, y'all two need to boss up and let the streets feel that heat. Stop running like some punks," Alianna folded her arms over her chest.

I shook my head at her. Although I would never admit it to her, she ain't far off from the truth. The streets knew Turk ain't one for the beef, and they must've forgotten who I was. We gotta show these pussies we ain't nobody to fuck with.

"If you're not staying with me, go to Teq's shop when you get out of school from now on until your father or I tell you otherwise."

"Fine. That's not so bad. Teq is the fun uncle," she rolled her eyes and then walked towards my kitchen.

"What are we gonna do with her?" Turk asked.

"You created that demon. Now you wanna talk about WE. That's your problem."

We both laughed, knowing damn well I was lying. I pulled out my phone and tried to call Vitani to make sure she made it home safe. The line went straight to voicemail. I tried again and got the same result. She blocked my number, and I'mma fuck her up. That pussy had a nigga tripping. I couldn't even imagine her being with someone else, or I'd have to kill them both. I let Bart slide before, but she became mine after I got that gushy gushy a second time. I know her lil' feelings hurt, but she'll get over it. I sent Teq a quick text to let him know to come to my house when he left his shop. We couldn't discuss this over the phone. I gotta put my own problems on hold to get this handled because my goddaughter was my top priority at the moment.

"Yo, Turk, I think it's time for you to get out the game," I whispered.

"What you whispering for? Get away from me," Turk responded, pushing me back.

"I'm serious 'jit.' Your life is too precious to your daughter to be dying for a street that's going to move on with or without you."

"I'll do you a solid and think about it...right now, let's figure out how to dead this shit."

VITANI

It had been a month since the incident at the hospital, and I was still fire hot about that bullshit. LiLi better hope I don't see her ignorant ass, or it's on-sight. That bitch had me all the way fucked up. I had a meeting with Jen and her boss today after work. I'd had enough of the stalling. Jen was supposed to be my friend, but I think she had ulterior motives. She had pushed our meeting back three times now. I was getting nervous.

When I walked into my office, I sighed. There was so much paperwork on my desk. I sat down, and a red coffee cup caught my attention, but I couldn't remember if it was mine or not. I sniffed the cup and then opened it up, realizing it wasn't coffee at all. It was tea. Then the memory of a door dash driver delivering the tea to me popped into my mind. I couldn't remember who the hell bought it for me. I would take this with me to meet Jen. Maybe it could add some pieces to the puzzle of what happened that day. I didn't want to think God would do something so horrible to me, but I didn't know him at all. I put the cup in my bottom drawer with my purse and got to work. This was my first day back since I had to recover from that terrible sinus infection. Time passed by faster than expected, and I rushed out of my office.

I was on my way to Rae's office because we decided to go to the mall for lunch today. I walked in on the surprise of my life: Teq had Rae up against the wall in a lip lock. I cleared my throat, and they both jumped apart.

"So y'all didn't hear the door open?" I smirked.

Teq backed up and fixed his shirt as he turned to offer me a smile. "I heard it. I just didn't care." Rae smacked his arm.

My eyebrows arched, "How long has this been going on, hoe? You got some explaining to do."

"Girl, please, there's nothing to tell. What you walked in on was merely two friends sharing a kiss." Rae fixed her pink floral dress that had bunched up around her waist.

"I don't go around kissing my friends like that." I scrunched my lip.

Teq smiled and nodded before walking out and closing the door behind him. "Spill the beans, hoe!"

"Ain't shit to spill. Devun and I broke things off last night after catching him at his baby mother's house again," Rae paused. "Then Teq came in to update my computer software, and one thing led to another."

"Just don't hurt Teq by getting him involved. You know Devun ain't wrapped too tight. His ass might do something crazy."

"His scary ass ain't gone do shit. I'm the hitta in that relationship."

We both laughed. "You ready to go?" I asked. She nodded, and we headed out to the mall.

We decided to eat at the Chinese BBQ spot in the food court. Everyone used to say it was rat meat, but we didn't care. Hell, that's some good-ass rat meat. We ate our food, and when I stood, I saw a guy that had a crush on me in high school. He was buff as shit now, the complete opposite of what he was in high school. He started walking my way, and I smiled.

"Vitani, how you been, girl? How ma doing?"

"Chez, I'm good. Just taking it one day at a time. My mom is doing fine, still in the same spot. I heard your mom passed. Sorry for your loss."

I wouldn't tell him that my mom didn't really care for him. Only because she said, there was something off about him, like he would kill me one day if I got serious with him. My mom might get on my nerves, but I learned a long time ago to listen to her. If he wanted to be friends, I would be cool with that, though.

"Thank you for that. I might have to stop by to see ma. Hey Rae, you been good?"

"Hey Chez, I'm good, too."

He turned his attention back to me, "Are you still single?"

"I sure am, niggas in Polk County ain't 'bout shit but making babies and playing games."

Chez had lighter skin and hazel eyes because of him being mixed with Puerto Rican and Black. He went away for college, and I hadn't seen him since. Now he was beefy and looks better than he did in high school.

"Take my number and hit me up when you're free. I would love to take you out to catch up."

Instead, I gave him my number because I didn't feel like searching for my phone in my purse. I was smiling when we walked outside.

"I don't know why you're acting like you're single. God sees all and knows all, hoe."

"Fuck God," I snapped.

"You already did."

I rolled my eyes. Rae played too much. She received a call from Devun saying he needed her to pick him up because he got a flat tire. I said I would get an Uber back to work because I did not want to be in the car with him. Rae apologized, but she didn't need to. I knew she wasn't completely over that fool, no matter how much she wanted to be.

"Hey, get back here! I'm calling the police!"

I heard a mall security officer yell from behind me just as someone crashed into me. I looked at a young girl and thought how pretty she was. She has long natural hair held back by a dark blue headband, bright pretty round eyes, and dark skin. I noticed she wore a school uniform that said McKill Academy, her plaid skirt was a little on the short side.

"Excuse me, Miss, I'm sorry," she mumbled, trying to move past me.

I grabbed her arm. "There you are! I've been searching that entire mall for the last thirty minutes looking for you. Your lunch hour is almost over. Come on." I looked over to the security officer. "I'm sorry for the misunderstanding. My daughter can be a handful sometimes. May I ask why you were chasing her?"

I really wanted to make sure she hadn't stolen anything.

"It is illegal for kids to skip school. You look a little too young to be her mother," he eyed both of us skeptically.

"Black, don't crack. We must get going, or she'll be late."

I leaned in and whispered for her to lead the way to her ride. Surely, she wasn't old enough to drive. When we walked to a pink mini coop, I cocked my head to the side, saying, "How old are you?"

The young girl put her Foot Locker bag in the passenger seat before sitting in the driver's seat and opening her backpack. I was not prepared for this little girl to pull out a .22 and aim it at my chest. What is this world coming to?

"Listen, ma'am. I am not a weak little girl that you can force to go have sex with some nasty old men!"

I started laughing. She was a character. I stopped laughing when I noticed a familiar face on her dashboard. Ugh, I couldn't get away from his crazy ass.

"I assure you, I do not want to take you to an old man to lay up with. I was merely trying to help. I do have a question, though. Do you know God?"

"I go to church every now and then, but I ain't no saint. What are you? Jehovah's witness?"

"No, no, not that God," I chuckled. "Godrique."

"You're a cop?" The young girl asked, still holding the gun to my chest.

"If I was a cop, you would be in cuffs by now. I know him, that's all."

"Ohhh, you smashed my goddaddy, now you're stalking me?" She scrunched her face up.

"I. I. I mean, I, well, part of that is true. I'm not stalking you, and I damn sure ain't pressed about God. I just remember him mentioning having a goddaughter, and I see the picture on your dash and wondered if you were Alianna."

"In the flesh," she finally lowered the gun. "So what? You want me to put in a good word for you or something?"

"No! Well, if you could tell him to leave me alone, that would be great." I sucked my teeth, wondering why in the hell I was having this conversation with a fifteen-year-old.

She frowned. "My goddaddy, don't chase women, so you must be on some type of drugs or fatal attraction shi- stuff. I don't believe you."

I took out my phone and showed her my call log. Although his number was blocked, his calls would still appear in the recent calls list. She burst out laughing, which caused me to join her because her laugh was infectious.

"Dang lady, you must be who the guys talk about in that throat baby song."

"Hey! Watch your mouth. You should not be talking like this."

"I'm young, not dumb. I know all about the birds and the bees or whatever y'all old people call it. Do you need a ride somewhere?"

"I can call an Uber. You need to get back to school."

"I have a free period. Get in. I like you. Just know that I shoot just as good as I shop, in case you wanna try anything. What's your name?"

"Vitani. But don't tell God you met me. I don't want anything to do with him."

Chapter Ten

GOD

I sat in Vitani's office thinking about everything that had happened since I met her. I'd been slippin like a muthafucka. There have been no updates on the people that robbed me. Simon was out of the country, and he's the lead investigator on the incident. But now he's back, so there should be some new developments soon. Although that practically runs itself, Chez has been handling everything with my firearms business. I convinced Alianna's badass to stay with me until shit dies down with her dad. It must be serious if Turk didn't object. I looked at my watch to check the time, wondering what Vitani was doing. I knew her lunch break was over ten minutes ago. The lady Keisha over in HR gave me everything I needed to know, and all I had to do was flash her a smile and compliment her perfume. It was a nice scent, although it seemed to be something older women should wear.

The door opened, and Vitani rushed in, closing it behind her. She rolled her eyes when she noticed me sitting behind her desk. I smiled at her.

"What do you want, Godrique?" she snapped as she walked over, pulled her bottom drawer open, and placed her purse in before closing it.

I concentrated on keeping my facial expression lax because something had caught my eye in the drawer. I had so many questions I needed answers. I had to get Si to run a federal background check on Vitani to find out what she's into. Since she wanted to keep secrets.

"I just came to check on you. The last time I saw you was on your death bed. I miss my wife." I kept calling her that to piss her off.

Vitani groaned as she kicked the bottom of the chair, causing it to roll back a few inches. She leaned over in front of the computer to sign in and ensure she was on the clock, then locked the screen. She turned around, standing at her full height over me, and put her hand on her hip. I licked my lips at how beautiful she looked when she's mad. She had on a loose-fitting black skirt that stopped just above her knees and a white silk button-down top with some red open-toe high heels that showcased her calve muscles.

"First of all, I wasn't on my deathbed, and if I was, it was your fault! Second, you don't need to check on me. Third, I am not your wife!" She poked my chest, and I grabbed her finger, tugging gently, making her fall on my lap, right into my arms.

"What did I do to get you on your deathbed?" I questioned, licking her lips as she straddled my hips. Her eyes glazed over and I could see the fire in her eyes, but it wasn't anger.

"You drugged me, then fucked me."

I laughed. She couldn't be serious. Looking into her eyes I saw that she was. "I wouldn't call NyQuil 'drugging' you. Technically your homegirl gave that to you. I just picked up your antibiotics and gave them to you. You're a little dramatic."

She rolled her eyes again.

I hope those bitches get stuck in the back of her head.

I grabbed her hips and started moving them as I stared deep into her eyes. She tried to look away, but I released one hip and grabbed her face to make her look at me.

"I would never intentionally hurt you. I'm really feeling you, and the sooner you stop fighting this attraction between us, the sooner we can be married and start a family." I pecked her lips.

Vitani's eyes closed when our lips touched then she seemed to snap out of a daze and pushed away from me, standing back up. "You better go marry your baby's mother."

I grabbed her arm again and pulled her back down with her back to my chest. I wrapped a hand around her throat, and she moaned. I used my other hand to lift her skirt and found her dripping wet when I pushed her skimpy panties to the side. I caressed her tight bud as I whispered in her ear, "I only want you. I swear you're gonna be my wife one day."

Vitani's breathing became labored as she worked her hips to fuck my fingers. "Ummm, that feels so good, Godrique. Don't...Stop."

I removed my hands from her center and released her neck. I lifted her off my lap, stood up, then placed her down on her chair. Walking around her desk, I sat down in one of the guest chairs. Vitani stared at me in disbelief, but she would learn quickly I didn't play that shit.

"Why did you stop? I was about to cum," she frowned.

"You said 'stop,' so that's what I did."

"You're such an asshole! I also said stay the fuck away from me, but you didn't do that," she retorted.

"Calm down before someone thinks something is wrong with you. I did stay away from you. You never said how long. I don't force myself on women, not even my wife, so don't say stop unless that's what you want."

Vitani stood fixing her panties and skirt, then walked around the desk and dropped to her knees. "Stand up."

I contemplated my next move. I probably shouldn't indulge, but who am I to deny her what she wants. I stood up. "I must warn you. I am not easy to please."

She smirked as she unbuckled my belt and undid my button to ease my pants down. "Grab your phone and put on a timer for three minutes," she said before licking her lips.

I chuckled. She was confident. I wouldn't tell her the only woman to ever make me nut from head was LiLi, and that took months for her to master. I set the timer on my phone and turned around to face the door. She rotated with me with no complaints.

I watched as Vitani lightly gripped my length and stroked it, going from the base to the tip. I leaned against the desk, loving the sight of her hand wrapped around me. Her fingers looked small in comparison. She started using her thumb to swipe over the tip with each stroke up, and I felt that shit in my toes. She slowly wrapped her succulent lips around my tip and licked it with her moist tongue. She put her tongue under the head, and I glided inside. I moved in and out of her mouth like a sailboat in the wind.

"Ahhhh!"

My eyes drifted closed, and she seized her movements, causing me to look down.

"Watch me."

Oh, she wants to control. I'll let her believe she got some control for now. Vitani allowed me to ease back into her mouth as her hands began to rub up and down my thighs, causing a heightened sensation in my dick.

"Damn, girl."

She let me slip all the way to the back of her throat, and I grabbed the back of her head, pumping it into her mouth. She took all of it, and it made my dick harden even more.

"Uhnn, fuck."

I felt my nut rising, but I wasn't quite ready to cum yet. I tried to pull out of her mouth, but her jaw and throat muscles held me captive as she began to caress my balls gently.

"Ohh, damn. Vitani! Suck dat shit, just like that," I groaned as I bussed it all down her throat.

I held her head as I pumped my seed down her throat while her tongue made circular motions, causing me to jerk. She swallowed every drop I gave, and I felt like I couldn't stop cumming as I continued fucking her throat.

Beep! Beep! Beep! Beep! The timer beeped.

Finally, the waves passed, and I continued to lean on the desk in awe. Vitani might as well marry me now because I swear couldn't another nigga look at her without getting bodied. I watched as she stood and walked into the restroom that was inside her office. I followed her and watched her brush her teeth. When she was finished, she sat a spare toothbrush and a rag with a soap bar on the counter for me to freshen up.

I freshened up, and just before I was about to walk out, I heard a knock on her office door, which caused me to stay put. I didn't need anyone thinking she's fucking on the job.

"Hey Bart, what can I do for you?" Vitani asked as I ear hustled.

"I wanted to know if you would attend the Governor's ball with me in two weeks. As friends, of course."

"I um, I would have to check my schedule." *Why does she sound uncomfortable? Did Bart do something to her?*

"Sure. I mean, that's understandable," Bart paused. "Why is your lipstick smudged?"

"Is it? I just came from lunch with a friend."

"A friend that you kissed?" Bart questioned. I chose that moment to walk out of the restroom. Bart looked like he had seen a ghost. "I thought you two were no longer doing," he waved his arms, "whatever it was that y'all were doing."

I walked over to Vitani, wiped a smudge of lipstick from the side of her mouth, then leaned down to kiss her. Then I turned back around to Bart, saying, "I don't understand how that's your business. No, she will not be going to the ball with you to answer your question. Or anywhere."

"Really, Godrique? I can go wherever I want to go and with whomever I please," Vitani scowled.

"Try me." I kissed her lips again and walked towards the exit. "Bart, let me holla at you for a minute." He followed me into the hallway, and I stood in front of Vitani's door. "Why are you doing this?"

Bart feigned confusion. "Doing what?"

"Testing my fucking patience. I have never tried to fuck behind you or any of my brothers. So why are you so hellbent on fucking with Vitani?"

"She was supposed to be mine. You stole her from me!"

"Had you told me you wanted her, I would've left her alone," my eyes slanted. He was really on some bullshit. I could see why because Vitani was wife material, but he was a little too late. She was my wife now.

"Leave her alone now then," Bart stated simply.

"No. I allowed you to continue being her friend, but if you keep trying me I'mma dead that shit, too."

"You would ruin our brotherhood over a woman you barely know? A woman I am in love with?" Bart whined.

"Gladly. I am sorry you fell in love with my wife, but our brotherhood is the only reason you're still breathing." I walked away.

"Is that a threat?!" Bart yelled from behind me, causing people to stop and stare. I kept walking because I would have to break my foot off in his pale ass if I turned around.

VITANI

Godrique has lost his mind if he thinks he can control my life. I escaped one crazy person to end up in the grasp of another. But God was so different from Jack. He was selfless in the bedroom, loved being around Ice and me, and gave me my space when I needed it. I hated for a nigga to be all up my ass like I birthed him. It irked my nerves. I wish I could've heard him and Bart's conversation outside my door. All I heard was Bart saying something about a threat, but I hope God didn't threaten that man. I didn't want to come between their friendship, but I actually liked the way God made me feel. The way I was when I was with him, I felt like I could be myself. I didn't have to watch what I said or did, and my grandfather loved him. I was scared for my mom to meet him because he's older than me, and the way he carries himself makes him come off even older, although I knew it was just maturity.

I checked the time, and it was almost time to meet with Jen and her boss. I straightened up my desk, walked out of my office, and then rushed back in to grab the Ziploc bag with the red coffee cup. I hurried back out of the office and ran into Rae.

"Sorry, did you need anything?" I quizzed.

She put her hand on her hip and squinted at me. I looked everywhere but in her eyes. I knew her nosy ass had questions. I was sure the gossip mill had been talking about God being in my office or about Bart shouting down the hall. Hell messing with God was proving to be just as dramatic as any other work romance the way Bart was carrying on. I just want things to go back to how they were.

"I refuse to stoop to your level at these people business. I am cooking tonight. Let's have a girls' night."

I sighed. She was onto me. "Fine, what time? Why can't it wait until Friday? Who has girls' night in the middle of the week?"

"I do, be there at seven. You can bring my niece, too."

"No, my mom wants to take her to Legoland tomorrow, so she's keeping her tonight."

"Okay, well, see you later. Bring some wine, that pancake stuff you be drinking on."

I giggled. "It's cupcake, not no pancake. See you later." I chucked the deuces then walked away.

I arrived at a disclosed location that looked like a normal building in the Ruthvan Plaza near 33. The name on the front was LATX, and I was starting to think I was at the wrong place, but the door opened, and Jen motioned for me to come in. She was scanning the area as I walked past her. Once inside, she stopped me.

"Were you followed?"

I shook my head no. This was getting real. *Who the would follow me?* We walked to the elevator and went to the second floor. I don't understand why we couldn't use the stairs since it was a two-story building. We rounded a corner and entered a conference room with only one other person sitting at the oval-shaped table. I willed myself to walk up to the man that stood when I came close, he was a sight to see. A little too on the light side for my taste. But he was still good-looking, standing at around six-four with a muscular build in a navy-blue suit. His skin was the color of toasted butter, and his lips were nice and full.

"Vitani Banks," I extended my hand.

He took my hand in his and kissed it. "Lexington Sharpe, but you may call me Lex."

I smiled as I removed my hand from his and took a seat to his left while Jen sat across from me. His voice was smooth and commanding. I could see how he became the boss. His eyes were dark, and I could tell they hid some deep, dark secrets. He intrigued me, to say the least, but he wasn't Godrique. Godrique's eyes were a chocolate brown like his skin, and when I stared at them under the light, it was as if I was seeing the moon, the future, something otherworldly. I got lost in his gaze, and a chill raced down my spine just thinking about him and the way he looked at me.

"Let's get started. What can you tell us that isn't in the report you gave Jen?" Lex asked.

"Nothing really. All I know is that Bart has been laundering money through the company. I am still unsure of the source, but I know it is some form of drug money," I rubbed my hands together, suddenly getting nervous. My hands started sweating, and I felt a little nauseous.

"What about Godrique James?"

My brows furrowed, and my lids lowered, "What about him?"

"I understand you and he had some dealings, would that cloud your judgment?" Lex leaned forward.

"What are you insinuating?" I leaned forward as well.

"Vi, what Lex means is, are you in love with Mr. James? You falling in love with him can blow our whole case to shit."

"I am no—" my throat suddenly became dry. "May I have a glass of water?"

Jen stood and walked to a separate table that held a pitcher of water and poured me a glass. She walked back over and handed the cup to me. Gulping down the contents, I was hot and would probably break out in a sweat at any moment. I placed the glass back on the table and looked back up at Jen and then at Lex. He made me nervous for some reason.

"I don't understand what Godrique has to do with IntelliCorp. He's just an investor. From my understanding, he really doesn't have any ties to the company outside of that. He nor the other investors, I can only tie Bart to the money laundering."

"Is that so? Is that what you were told? Let me guess. You think Anita Porter's father owns the company?"

"That's enough, Lex. She did what she was supposed to do. Pay her." Jen frowned at Lex.

"What the hell is going on here? You sent me in a situation blind and had me spying on dangerous people?!" I yelled. "I have a child to protect."

"You not knowing anything is for your best interest. I can put you in protective custody if you'd like."

"Protective custody?" I gawked. "I know for a fact that won't do anything but have them kill me sooner rather than later." I was starting to panic.

"Calm down, Vi. Your cover wasn't blown. You are free to leave now. If you cut ties now, they won't suspect a thing. I am stepping in and taking over, if anything happens, put it all on me." Jen came around the table and sat next to me, grabbing my hand.

A tear escaped my eye, not because I was scared of what The Disciples would do to me, but because I was scared of what I had done to them. I liked all of them. It pained my heart to think of anything happening to them.

"I do need one last favor before signing off on the building for your PI Firm," Lex interrupted our sisterly moment.

"I don't want shit from you anymore. I don't need a building. I need a fucking bodyguard."

"That can be arranged, too. You will attend the Governor's ball with me as my escort. He would like to meet you to thank you personally for your contribution to stopping crime in his state. Oh, and before you decline that was not a request. Meet me here on the 22nd," Lex smiled.

"Thank you so much for your kindness. Dick," I stood and was about to rush out of the office until I remembered I did need a favor. "If you want me as your date, I need to know the contents of this cup and fingerprints if possible." I flashed a fake smile.

Lex stood up and took the cup from my hand, rubbing his fingers on mine. I snatched my hand away. His eyes told me he was hiding something, but I didn't know it was bullshit. I walked outside of the office and headed for the elevator feeling like garbage. Jen caught the elevator and smiled faintly at me.

"If it makes you feel any better, I didn't know anything about that last part."

"It doesn't." I frowned.

"What are you getting into tonight?" Jen asked.

"Hanging out with Rae. You?" The elevator door opened, and we stepped off, heading towards the exit.

"I didn't have plans. Can I join?"

"Sure, but no work stuff!"

"Cool, I'll meet you there," Jen said before hugging me.

I knew I was questioning Jen's loyalty before, but that was out the window now. She had a job to do just like me. I took the job knowing its risks, so I couldn't blame her for my situation. I decided to stop by my mom's house to see Ice. When I got there, my grandmother was sitting on the porch.

"Hey, granny." I gave her a hug.

"Hey baby, look at you. Your hips are spreading like rice in water. You pregnant again?"

I sighed. "No, granny, I'm not pregnant. I am on birth control." She smacked my butt, causing me to jump. "Granny, you be doing too much!"

"Naw, I ain't. You must been doing something to get pregnant. I saw your eyes wondering if I was right. That roach control stuff doesn't always work, you know. You better start making them menfolk wear protection."

I chortled. "It's not roach control, granny! I can't with you."

"It is roach control. Lord knows I love my grandbaby Ice, but her daddy is a damn roach. I don't know what possessed you to lie with that rascal," my granny continued.

"Ma! Come get your mother," I yelled in between, laughing with tears in my eyes.

My mom walked out on the porch holding Ice, who jumped out of her arms soon as she saw me. I picked her up and hugged her close, being sure not to kiss her. "Ma, granny out here tryna convince me that I'm pregnant. Tell her I'm on birth control."

My mom squinted at me, "I dreamt about fish that night you got out of the hospital. I see why you would be pregnant. That young man looks like his soldiers can march through hell and back." My mom fanned herself.

I groaned. "Both of y'all tripping. What man are you even talking about?" I hoped to hell she wasn't referring to Jack's punk ass.

"Goddy."

My head snapped up from Ice as she started cheering, "Goddy! Goddy! Goddy!" *What the fuck?*

"Mom, how do you know what Godrique looks like?"

"He was in the hospital cafeteria that day. I took Ice down there."

I seethed. *He probably went down there to talk to that bitch! I'mma fuck him up.*

"He was sitting alone, and Ice ran over and jumped in his lap. He introduced himself and asked me for your hand in marriage. He's so swe—"

"He what?!"

"Don't cut me off when I'm talking. Your ears work fine. That man is serious about you, and you want to try to be all independent. Let that man take care of you," my mom scolded.

"Ugh, ma. You and granny on one today. I don't even know him like that."

"I didn't know your grandaddy like that either when I was bussing it wide open for him," my granny started twerking.

I kissed Ice, handed her to my mom, and walked away. They were doing the most. *Godrique ain't shit!*

Chapter Eleven

TEQ

"**K**nocked one. To the left! Good shit. Oh shit, behind you! Behind you! Damn," I yelled excitedly into the mic. Rae and I had been playing Call of Duty for the past two hours and I was enjoying every bit of it.

"Nigga, get off the game with your rude ass!" I felt a pillow slam into my head as I turned to see Simon run away.

These niggas had no boundaries. Here I was in my den, chilling, minding my business and these idiots wanted to ruin my moment. I muted my mic.

"Add me in," Meesha yelled over my shoulder.

"Man no, I am playing with someone," I bellowed.

"I'll cut this off, call me another man see don't I split your shit," Meesha snapped.

I snorted. "Word." I turned around to see all eyes on me. "Y'all ain't got nothing better to do today but be in my space?"

Simon now had a plate in his hand full of some type of island food John bought from a local restaurant. He sat down next to God and started smashing his plate. I turned back to the game and immediately felt a piece of something warm hit the back of my neck. I'd had about enough of their shit for today.

"Get out yo!"

"Ooh he's mad now. Somebody go find me a fuck to give," Meesha laughed and the other guys joined in. The only person missing was Peter, but his little sister, Meesha, was here. She was like an older, more annoying version of Alianna. But she will peel a nigga's cap back so I be letting her slide. Peter and his sister had been boxing since they were younger so she could hold her own with just about anyone. Ironically, she's our attorney and you would never suspect her of packing such a powerful punch.

"Aye Meesh, you got one more time to try me, ma." I scowled.

"So, Rae got your nose wide open, bruh? Usually, you let Meesha hop on with you," John started.

I unmuted my mic, ignoring him, "Oh no, I just muted my mic to talk to my sister."

"Is that what you're calling me now?" Meesha yelled.

"Your sister is funny," Rae laughed.

"You have no idea, ma." I muted my mic back and gave everyone the bird. Rae muted her mic too I guess since everything got quiet.

"Your mic muted?" God questioned.

I double checked then nodded.

"Let me tell y'all about Bart ass today, his bitch ass tried me for the last time. Next time I am runnin' off in his shit and that's on everything I love," God stood up and started pacing.

"What happened?" John asked.

"This nigga come up in my wife's office on some ra-ra shit, not knowing I'm in the bathroom."

"What were you doing in the bathroom? Couldn't have been taking a shit because he would've smelled you and kept walking," Simon said, causing everyone to laugh.

"Who is your wife?" Meesha asked.

"Fuck you, Si! So, he questions my wife, Vitani. You haven't met her yet Meesha, but you will. He on some 'why your lipstick smudged?' I stepped out the bathroom like nigga the fuck you on?" God stopped pacing and started rubbing his beard. "He asked her to the Governor's Ball, too! I didn't act a fool in front of wifey but I told him to step outside and checked his ass."

I heard a noise in the mic again and it sounded like crying. *The hell?* I listened close then decided to remove the cord from the controller so that God could hear.

"Did you tell God?" Rae asked.

"Why would I tell him? We're not together! His ass is crazy too, you should've seen the way Bart looked when Godrique stepped out of my office restroom today. I swear his fear radiated through me," Vitani cried.

"Hoe, that wasn't no fear, it's called lust. What did Jack do?" An unfamiliar voice asked.

"He was mad I had a nigga in the house and won't give us another chance," she paused as she started to cry harder. "He-he kicked me in my back while I had Ice in my arm." Vitani continued. "He tried to rape me and I started fighting back, but he was getting the best of me so I let it happen."

"He raped you?!" Rae exclaimed.

"Not all the way. I was able to stop him." Pause. Sniffle.

"You did what you had to do Vi, that is what any mother would do." The unfamiliar voice spoke.

"I got him to let his guard down then kicked him. I ran to grab my gun and made him get out. This happened over a month ago and I am so afraid to be home alone. I been at my mom's house when my grandfather has to go somewhere." Vitani's voice shook.

"Fuck this!" God walked out the front door. We all jumped up and climbed in his Charger as he sped through the city.

"This nigga touched my wife. My daughter. He's dead. Muthafucka betta count his days," he mumbled.

"Let me drive, you don't even know where Rae lives," I suggested.

"Tell me where to go."

"Victoria Cove," I replied. He sped up and I was scared for my life. *How the hell can we help Vitani if we're wrapped around a pole somewhere?* This nigga ain't got no sense, but I would be the same way if something like that happened to Rae.

Rae

I sat there listening to my sis pour her heart out and get the weight she had been holding off of her shoulders. *What kind of friend am I that I didn't pick up on it?* When I went over that night, she cried on my shoulder but didn't mention any of what happened with Jack. *If I see him I'mma beat his ass like a runaway slave.* There was always something off about Jack and I told Vitani but she never listens. Devun may be a lot of things but he never put his hands on me. I wished she would tell God because I knew he would handle it. He texted me pictures of rings asking which one I thought Vitani would want and I asked her oblivious ass which one she liked best because I was gonna get myself a wedding ring. I didn't know what she put on that man, but he was stuck on her and I was so happy I would get to be a maid of honor soon.

Jen returned with a cool rag and put it on Vitani's neck as she lay on my lap silently allowing the tears to fall. I was usually not one for get back, but Jack had something coming for him.

Boom! Boom! Boom!

Who is at my damn door knocking like the police? "Who is it?"

"God."

Oh shit. Vitani sat up from my lap as Jen walked towards the door. "You want me to let them in?" Jen asked.

"Are you crazy? When God knocks on your door, let his ass in!" I chided.

Jen opened the door and all of The Disciples walked in with him and a young beautiful woman. That must be the sister Teq referenced earlier. "How do you know where I live and why are you here?" I quizzed.

"Vitani," God lowered his voice dropping to his knees in front of her. "Why would you keep this from me, baby?" His hands found hers as she began to cry again.

"I...I didn't know what to do. How do you even know..." Vitani's eyes landed on me.

"When exactly did this happen?" Simon asked from his place near the door.

"The day the social worker came—" she hesitated.

"The day I left you there with him?" Simon edged. Vitani nodded.

"Your baby father is dead," God snapped, standing to his feet.

Vitani raised up with him. "No, he's not! Remember what you told me when it came to your child's mother? Keep that same energy!"

God stepped closer to Vitani's face. "I don't give a fuck what you have to say, he's dead."

"That's Ice father whether you like it or not," Vitani retorted.

"I am her father, whether you like it or not!" God roared. Vitani started crying again.

"Stop yelling at her like you're a big bad wolf," Meesha chimed. I only knew her name because Teq had said it earlier.

God grasped Vitani's neck and forced her to look at him, "I only want what's best for you and Ice. I love you and my baby girl so I can't imagine what I would do if something happened to y'all." All eyes went to them with his declaration of love.

"That's what that demon pussy do to you," Teq mumbled.

"I give you my word I won't kill him," God conceded.

"You won't lay a finger on him?" Vitani clarified.

"I won't lay a finger on him."

Simon tried to sneak out the door but Vitani stopped him, "Si and the rest of y'all guys have to promise the same thing."

"We promise," they all said in unison.

God picked Vitani up and slung her over his shoulder as if she weighed nothing "You're moving in with me tonight."

"Put me down, stop." Vitani screamed.

God dropped her on her ass with a thud, "I told you about that stop shit."

"You asshole, I was just kidding!" Vitani jumped on his back and he carried her out of the house.

"Welp, shows over guys, time for y'all to head out." I fake yawned. Simon ignored me and walked in the kitchen. John sat on the couch and started flipping through channels. Teq stalked over to my gaming set up and started touching stuff. Jen poured another glass of wine.

"So, you're Teq's gamer girlfriend?" Meesha asked.

"I am. I'm a girl gamer that's his friend," I chuckled. "You must be his sister Meesha, he talks about you and how good you are on the trash box. My name is Rae, nice to finally meet you," I extended my hand. She shook it then folded her arms over her breast.

"Trash? Sound like a hater. I actually own a PC, Xbox, and PS. I'm good on all of them." Meesha winked.

"Oh, you got me beat. I only play PS. We have to exchange gamer tags!" I got excited talking about gaming. Simon walked out of the kitchen and sat at my small dinner table with a plate of food as Teq sauntered over to sit between me and Meesha on the couch. He put his arm around me and I snuggled into him. There was just something about Teq that gave me comfort, my body was so relaxed around him.

I sat up then looked up at Teq and scrunched my face, "Why you make that comment earlier about 'that's that demon pussy' or whatever you said."

He laughed. "Y'all don't know what Vitani's name translates to?"

We all observed on curiously, even Simon paused from eating to hear what Teq was about to say. "What does it mean?" I pressed. He paused for dramatic effect and shit.

"Vitani translates to demon of war," Teq stated simply.

"Oh shit, bruh didn't stand a chance from jump. Her little ass done infiltrated The Disciples and took down God. Not even God can resist temptation," John laughed at his own joke.

Everyone else were still laughing when Simon suddenly paused saying, "Aye blue hair, how old are you?"

I looked at Jen because she was the only one with blue hair styled in a straight bob, that paired with her dark complexion made her stand out. Her skin was flawless and she looked like a baby doll, but she was older than me and Vitani. I was the shortest of the three of us and Jen was the tallest. She was six-feet and if you did a quick glance she could be mistaken for Naomi Campbell in her younger years. Jen was thick, though, like big booty Judy type thick.

"Who wants to know?" Jen stood to her full height.

"A grown ass man that doesn't need to be saying inappropriate shit around minors walking around with colored hair and shit like a big ass child." Simon stood as well. He was only a little taller than her.

"I am a grown woman that completed two tours in Iraq."

Simon smirked. "You're childish, got it." Dismissing Jen, he turned to me saying, "that food was good. If bro ain't tryna wife you, can I put in my application?"

"Okay, baby Bart," John chuckled.

"Nobody would marry your rude ass unless they're desperate. You have some nerve insulting me and your punk ass don't even know my name.

Better be glad I'm not who I used to be or I'd make your bitch ass beg for forgiveness," Jen snapped.

"Hey you two, what the hell? Jen this is Simon, Simon this is Jen. Play nice." I looked between them two like they were children on a playground.

"The game is called Simon says, not Jen says. You'll be the one begging in the end," Simon quirked before walking out the door.

Teq went to stand, but I stood and walked onto my porch. Simon was deep in his phone but looked up for a second to see who had followed him.

"What's up? Jen's presence can be overwhelming sometimes, but you were rude as shit and should apologize," I spoke.

"There is something about her I don't trust. I'm never wrong. How do you know her?" He asked.

"I don't really know her like that, that's Vitani's homegirl. All I know is they went to church together and she moved away, then popped back up a year ago after she got out of the military."

Simon nodded his head up and down taking in the information. *Shit! I hope I didn't give too much information that would put either Jen and Vitani in danger.* My simple ass forgot just that fast about Vitani's other job. A dark car with tented windows pulled up and John and Meesha came outside and hugged me goodbye then climbed in the backseat of the car. Simon hugged me and was about to walk away when the door opened and Jen walked out.

"Aye, I apologize for some of the things I said in there." He flashed a dimpled smile at Jen.

"You're good," Jen held out her hand.

When Simon took her hand in his, he frowned, then walked away to the vehicle that was still waiting for him. They were a strange bunch. I'd never seen Simon act that way. Jen hugged me and said she needed to go handle some business. I walked back into my home and locked the door. I was tired and needed to take a shower. I told myself I would wash the dishes in the morning. Someone had already straightened up the living room. I went to my bathroom connected to my room and turned the shower on, then I found a teddy that had the matching boy shorts. I got in the shower and began lathering my body with my luffa. When I was finished rinsing off, I opened my shower door, but something caught my eye in the mirror.

"Ahhhhh!" I screamed from being startled then slipped on my tile floor and went tumbling forward. I felt strong arms around me and opened my eyes that I didn't even know I'd closed. My face was inches away from the floor as I admired the muscled arms that saved me.

"Yo, you good, ma?" Teq asked looking over my body to be sure I wasn't hurt.

"Get out!" I pushed him outside of the bathroom then slammed the door. *Oh my gosh he just seen me naked! I know I look good and all but that should come later.* I put on the teddy and boy shorts then surmised that this wasn't much better.

I opened the door to find him sitting on my bed. When he looked up his eyes dropped low and a slow smile spread across his face. I smiled, too.

"You scared the shit out of me. I don't know why I thought you left with everyone else."

"I was cleaning the kitchen, I was coming to tell you I was about to head out. I see you're trying to seduce me with the red lace and shit."

I giggled. "I sleep in nice things. You never know who has to come in your home."

"Shit, I should get going." He licked his lips seductively, "I will call you tomorrow."

"You can stay if you want," I offered. I hoped he would take me up on it because I haven't been laid in a few months. Devun has been running around and I have been too scared to sleep with him from fear of catching an STD. Teq stood and leaned down to whisper in my ear.

"I'm not your rebound." I dropped my head. He straightened to his full height and lifted my chin, "When I spend the night, I want to know that I am the only man you will be with from that moment on. Take your time, figure out your feelings, but know that real men do real shit. You're the prize."

He kissed me and palmed my ass lifting my two-fifty-pound body like it was one hundred. I wrapped my legs around his waist and palmed his face. His erection pressed hard into my stomach and I wished he would just give me a taste. I loved the fact that he had a tongue ring. I had never met a man that had one, but the way he commanded my mouth had me soaking my panties. His tongue wrapped around mine and I melted.

"Umm," I moaned.

He abruptly stopped and placed me back on my feet before leaving my room. I half hoped he was going to get a condom but when I heard the front door open and close, I knew he was gone. My phone vibrated on the bed and I sat down, slightly upset.

Teq: *Lock the door. Sleep tight ma.*

Me: *GN*

Chapter Twelve

GOD

I felt the sun shining on my face which forced my internal alarm clock to go off in my head. I kept my eyes closed but lay awake still wanting to rest my eyes a bit. Yesterday was a lot to take in and it made me realize how quick life could change. One minute I was minding my business and getting paid, then the next I was confessing my love to a woman I met two months and some change ago. I had a daughter now and I was working on another one with my wife, so I hoped she was ready for more kids. I was twenty-five years old and I'd been wanting my own family ever since my goddaughter was born. Yes, I was too young to be thinking about starting a family, but oh well. I had to manifest that shit into fruition. Now I got it. Vitani was half crazy and a little ditzy sometimes, but she was different from any woman I'd ever met.

"So, you're just gonna lay there and pretend to sleep?"

My eyes popped open at the sound of Vitani's voice. She was sitting Indian style on my bed staring a hole in my face. I continued to lay there.

"I was hoping you would go brush your teeth before talking to me with that stank ass breath."

She grabbed a pillow and hit me with it then straddled me, holding my hands over my head, blowing her hot breath directly in my nose. I flipped her over and returned the favor, she faked gagged and both of us started laughing. *This the type of shit I'm on right here.* I could never have a moment like this with LiLi or any other woman I'd been with. They would fix their hair and brush their teeth before I woke up. I held her down, gazing into her cat-like eyes. She smiled up at me, showing all her teeth. I leaned down and kissed her nose.

"Get your big ass off me!" she joked.

I didn't have my weight on her because I was on my knees, but I dropped on her for real after she said that. She dug in the side of my neck with her sharp pointy nails.

"Ahh," I yelled as I rolled off of her. She jumped back on top of me and put her nails to my neck as if they was a knife in a hostage situation.

"Please don't kill me, I have a family!" I begged. I dug my nails in the apex of her pelvis where her thigh met her pussy.

"Owwww! Why would you do that?!" Vitani cried. I knew that was her weak spot from us playing around before.

"Why you scratching me? Play pussy get fucked."

I smirked. She hit me with the pillow again, still straddling me with my dick poking her love spot. My phone began ringing and I reached over to the nightstand to grab it without checking the caller ID.

"Speak."

Vitani hit me on my arm, she hated when I answered the phone like that.

"Your baby wants you to cuddle with us," LiLi's voice pulled me out of the marital bliss I was in. I was sure Vitani heard the voice because she moved to get off of me. I held her still with one hand and placed the phone on speaker with the other.

"My baby is sitting on my lap right now."

I traced my fingers up and down Vitani's arms to calm her. I could see her heart pounding in her chest since she only had on a bra and panty set.

LiLi paused on the line before saying, "Don't tell me you got that bitch laid up in our bed! I just know my ears are playing tricks on me. I am pregnant with your first child!"

"Call my wife another bitch and you'll be contacting my assistant to give me messages. I don't know what gave you the impression that you were having my firstborn, but I already have a daughter," I bit out. "Now is there something you need to tell me concerning my child?"

"Wife? Never mind allat, I have an appointment tomorrow morning because I have been cramping and pre-eclampsia runs in my family," LiLi sobbed.

Vitani rolled her eyes.

"Just text me the time and I'll be there," I said before disconnecting the call. "Aye, you gotta chill with all that hostility. If you're gonna be my wife you will have to accept my child too, regardless of who the mother is."

"I don't want to be your wife and I don't have to accept shit. I'm going home today."

Vitani snatched away from me and went into the bathroom, slamming the door. *There she goes with that dramatic bullshit.*

My phone rang again but this time I checked the ID. It was a facetime call from Ice.

"Good morning, baby girl." I smiled at her cute little chubby cheeks.

"Goddy! Nana take me to Legoworld!!" she yelled excitedly. "Girl, who are you talking to this early in the morning?" I heard just before Miss Tam walked into view. "Oh, hey Goddy."

"Hey Miss Tam, how are you doing this morning?" I asked smiling. Vitani favored her mother a lot. The only thing was Miss Tam's skin color was the same as mine, dark. Vitani was a caramel complexion.

"As good as I can be at eight in the morning. You're the first person she called on this iPad this morning but I know she's just getting started. You worked things out with my daughter?" Miss Tam asked.

"I'm still working on her. But she's here now, so I'm making progress. I got her to move in with me, so you can bring Ice here after y'all leave Legoland," I grinned.

Miss Tam chuckled, "I know you're up to something. You won't put me in the middle of y'all mess, you can come pick her up from my house. Oh, and if you're not busy this weekend, I am having a BBQ. Bring as many people as you like."

"Thank you for the invitation, Miss Tam. I probably won't be able to make it since I had previous plans with my brothers." Miss Tam gave Ice back the iPad. "Baby girl, I will see you later today. I love you." I blew a kiss and she kissed the iPad.

"Luh you, Goddy."

Just as I ended the call Vitani came out of the bathroom dressed in a floral maxi skirt with a tank top and some long socks on. We had stopped by her place last night to get her some clothes. She decided to work from home today so she would be using my office. I watched as she walked around my room comfortably as if she'd lived here forever. She came to stand in front of me and placed her hand on her hip.

"Do you sell drugs?"

"No," I answered. That question caught me off-guard because it was a little too late to be concerned about that now.

"Do you have illegal business dealings?" she prodded.

"Yes," I answered truthfully. "I don't discriminate on who I do business with. I don't knock nobody's hustle because I don't know why they went the route they did. It could be me out there slanging drugs and going in and out of jail, but I was fortunate to not be put in a situation like that. I won't lie, I was selling weed in middle school and got jammed up, that's where I met John."

Vitani looked surprised, "John sells drugs?"

I shook my head no. "John wasn't locked up for selling drugs, I was. Everyone has a past and if you want to know about John or any of my brothers, you have to ask them yourself. They're very transparent."

Her eyes shined with a curious light but then they dimmed and she turned around, walking towards the door.

"I'm cooking breakfast. Do you have any special requests?"

"Are you on the menu?" I licked my lips.

"Not with that hot ass dragon breath you got, that shit will scorch my clit."

"Fuck you!" I jumped up and she ran down the hall. I went to shower and fix my hygiene, opting to put on a V-neck and some jeans. I texted Chez letting him know I would have to postpone our meeting. Then I texted the group message with the brothers asking if they wanted to go to a BBQ this weekend. I was even being considerate and invited Bart, although he would be out of town visiting his father.

Me: *Vitani's mother invited us to a cookout on Saturday, y'all tryna slide there instead of the club that night?*

John: *We can do both!*

Peter: *I can do both. I need to do some reconnaissance at the club tonight.*

Simon: *Who cooking?*

Teq: *I can do both*

Me {replying to Simon}: *Greedy ass, I guess her mom since she's the host.*

Simon: *I'm in. If Vitani cooks like that, I know her mom can throw down. Moms single?*

Me: GTFOHWTBS. I'll send y'all the details later. Teq don't wear a suit to the cookout.

Teq: *Word. God, don't wear a turtleneck to the cookout. [laughing emoji]*

Bart: *I'll think about it.*

I heard a knock at the front door that snapped me back to reality. The smell of bacon wafted my senses and my stomach growled. I stood to go answer the door, but I heard the door open and Vitani scream. I grabbed my Glock-18 from my nightstand drawer and ran to the door. I had to rethink these long ass hallways because it took way too long to get to the living area from the master bedroom. I rounded the corner seeing Vitani hugging Alianna as Turk and Black stood there looking just as shocked as me.

"Why aren't you in school, young lady?" Vitani asked her.

"I got suspended this morning because a bi— I mean a chick tried me over a guy I don't even like!" Alianna whined.

"So, what did you do to get suspended?" I asked, coming to stand behind Vitani.

"I punched her in her mouth. She was talking too much," Alianna shrugged.

Black smiled as he watched her from his place by the door as Turk and I shook our heads. *I don't know what we will do with this little girl and her attitude.*

Vitani looked her over to make sure she wasn't hurt then asked, "Are you okay?"

Alianna gawked. "No, I'm not okay! My dad took my car."

All of us laughed at her theatrics.

"Wait, did my goddaddy kidnap you on some 365 stuff?" Alianna asked Vitani. "Blink once for yes and twice for no."

Vitani blinked once.

I don't know what either one of them were talking about at this point, so I tuned them out as they walked into the kitchen and I walked over to Turk and Black. "What y'all two got going on?"

"We gotta make some moves, so you're on babysitting duty for the next three school days. Who is shorty and how do she know Ali?" Turk said.

"Cool. That's my wife I been telling you about. The hell if I know how they know each other, your guess is as good as mine." I shrugged.

Turk looked deep in thought before saying, "Wife? Does she know that?"

"Kiss my ass, bruh. Ali starting to rub off on you," I chuckled.

"She's fine. A little on the thin side, but she still got an ass," Black said nonchalantly.

"Aye lil' nigga, don't be checking my wife out. Niggas get killed for less," I faux warned.

Black chuckled, "I was just making an observation."

I shook my head as I walked towards the kitchen, "Y'all might as well come eat breakfast. I know Vitani cooked more than enough."

We entered the kitchen and I placed my gun on the island as I walked by it to get to the dining room table. I sat at the head of the table with Vitani on one side and Alianna on the other. Turk sat on the other side of Vitani and Black sat beside Alianna. The table was stacked with pancakes, bacon, sausage, grits, and some muffin egg looking thing.

I scrunched my face, "What is this?"

"Quiche. Basically, baked scrambled egg. It's good," Vitani answered.

I took a bite and my eyes instinctively closed. Damn my babe can cook her ass off. It was moist and creamy but fluffy and flavorful at the same time. I put three more on my plate and looked around at everyone else devouring their food.

"So how do you know my goddaughter?" I questioned.

"I met her a little while ago at the mall. I asked her for a ride because my car was acting up," Vitani said.

I looked to Alianna asking, "You just giving rides to strange women?"

"You fuck strange women," Vitani slipped then covered her mouth. Turk snickered. Black kept his head low as he stuffed his face.

"I'm sorry about that, but I actually saw your picture with her on the dashboard and remembered you saying you had a goddaughter so I asked for her name," Vitani concluded.

"Yepp, and she showed me all the calls between you two. I thought she was lying," Alianna chimed. "You thirsty, Goddy"

I chuckled, "Yea I am thirsty. I need a tall glass of water."

My eyes connected with Vitani's as she stuck a piece of bacon all the way in her mouth slowly then pulled it back out and bit the tip. I knew the temperature raised a few degrees and I needed some water for real now. I picked up my glass of orange juice and gulped it down. *I was still thirsty.*

Vitani smiled as she stood and walked to the fridge, making a show of swaying her hips. Her ass looked extra fat in that thin ass skirt and it showcased every crevice. I knew she had to have on a thong because there was no panty line. She dropped a piece of ice on the floor and made a show of bending over to pick it up. I checked to make sure I was the only one watching. Everyone else seemed to be consumed with eating their food. Vitani put the ice in the sink then brought a cup of ice and a pitcher of water. She placed the cup on the table in front of me then leaned over my shoulder, grazing her soft breast on me, filling the cup with water. I took a deep breath then turned and grabbed her by her locs swiftly pulling her ear to my lips.

"Keep playing, you will be bent over this table with this dick deep in your guts," I whispered. Everyone had paused because I was holding her hair and forcing her neck at an angle. I released her and resumed eating as she sat back in her seat and stared at me with bedroom eyes.

"Awkward," Alianna uttered.

Chapter Thirteen

LIQUESHA "LILI" DEVINE

I was mad as hell with God yesterday when he told me about that bitch being at his house. I had never even been to his house and I was pregnant with his baby. I know I be doing me most of the time but that doesn't give him the right to treat me like a gutter rat. I had my own place, car, and I made my own money. I sold lashes and hood fits on the daily and had made a name for myself aside from working part-time at the hospital. I knew the lil' chick he was messing with on the side ain't got no hustle like me. I was lying about that pre-eclampsia shit just to get him to come see me. If I could get him alone, I could make him cheat on his lil hoe so I could throw it up in her face. *She seems like the type that will leave a nigga if he cheats one time.*

I looked out the window and saw God's Charger pull into my driveway. I opened the door and stood there with my arms folded. He stepped out and sauntered over to me looking like a snack with a black t-shirt, blue jeans, and some black J's.

"Hey zaddy."

He looked at me with a blank expression, "Where your shit? Let's go."

"We have a little time to spare, come in so we can talk," I pleaded.

He turned around as if I hadn't said anything and got back in his car. I walked to the car and tried to get in, but the door was locked. He'd leaned his seat all the way back and closed his eyes.

"Open the door God!" I yelled.

He kept his eyes closed saying, "Wake me up when it's time to leave. If you bang on my window, you can go to the appointment alone."

I sucked my teeth, walked back to my house, and slammed the door. He has never treated me this way. I knew it was because of that thot he was fucking with. I dialed Chez.

"We have a problem."

"What's that?"

"God won't talk to me," I whined.

"Nobody told you to be a hoe. Should've stuck to the plan and not get knocked up," Chez raged.

"I know, but our plan won't work if I'm on the outs."

Chez chuckled, "I always have a contingency. You were never plan A"

I hung up in his face. I had to find a way to get rid of that skinny bitch he seemed to be so stuck on. My cousin on my dad's side, Chez, was God's right-hand man, that's how we met. I told Chez about that bitch and he got defensive like I did something wrong. He had the nerve to tell me to watch my back because she was known for fighting when they were in school. He must have forgot, I'd been dragging bitches my whole life and could go toe-to-toe with any hoe, especially about my nigga.

I walked out to God's car and we headed to my OB/GYN, looking over at God I couldn't help but wonder what that bitch had that I didn't. Why was he going so hard for her so fast? *I am having his child and his mother loves me, so why not me? I have been holding him down when he needed me most, and this is how he repays me?*

"You're giving me a headache with all this drama, LiLi. I swear shit was good with us before you got pregnant."

"What is that supposed to mean?"

"It means play your fucking position. You had your chance and blew it. So why are you trying to mess up my life?"

"You never gave me a chance! I never told Cedrick to come to my house that night. You saw his car outside and flipped out. You claim to be done with me but you still wanted to fuck me when it suited you. Make it make sense, God."

I sighed.

"You should've sent that nigga packing and not let him in your crib knowing you had a man. I really don't feel like doing this shit with you today. Just let the past stay in the past. what's done is done. I've moved on, so should you."

He pulled into a parking spot and I didn't miss the hint of pain I heard in his voice. That meant I still had a chance to win him back. He must still have feelings for me if he's still hurt by what I did. To tell the truth, I didn't fuck Cedrick or anyone while I was fucking God. He was over that night to pay me for the lick I did with him. There was virtually no one in the waiting area, so the medical assistant called us back in no time. The doctor was a black woman that I had searched, because I didn't want one of those doctors that cut people open for the money. I wanted to have my baby natural.

"Hello mom, how are you feeling today? I know you said there was some pain yesterday, can you explain a little more?" The doctor finished and started touching on my stomach. I had changed into a gown just before they checked my vital signs. God's dumb ass stood outside the room while I changed. He really irked my nerves sometimes.

"My pain level is about a seven right now and it is in my lower stomach area," I lied.

The doctor nodded, "Okay, let me do a quick ultrasound to ensure everything is okay."

I was excited for God to hear the baby's heartbeat again, the last time we both ended up crying and fucking all night. Hopefully that could happen again so I could get that other bitch out the picture. A phone started vibrating and I looked around for my phone before realizing it was God's phone.

"Hey wifey," he answered.

"I know you didn't just answer the phone for that bitch at my appointment. This is my time!" I yelled and tried to sit up but the doctor wouldn't let me. She better be glad I liked her or I would've slapped her ass, too.

God pissed me off more when he ignored me and turned to the doctor saying, "I am gonna step outside for a minute."

Once he was outside of the room the doctor proceeded to do the ultrasound and I became alarmed when her facial expression changed. "What is it?"

"I'm sorry to inform you but it looks like you miscarried, Miss Devine."

"I what? This can't be real. When? How? I have been still having cravings," I cried in disbelief.

"It seems like the fetus has been dead for a month now, there has been no developments since the last visit. We will have to send you to the hospital immediately for an emergency D&C to remove the fetus. I am so sorry for your loss."

"How have I still been gaining weight? I don't understand."

"It is called phantom pregnancy. Your body still thought you were pregnant, so it continued to require extra hormones and put on weight. Again, I am so sorry."

God chose that moment to reenter the room and I was panicking at the thought of him discovering I was no longer pregnant. I would lose the leverage I have to get that bitch out of our lives. It was all her fault I lost our child and she would pay!

"Get out! Go be with that bitch that is so important. I hate you," I cried and tried to throw everything I could reach at him.

He ducked and dodged as confusion etched across his face. "What is wrong with you?" He turned to the doctor, "Is everything okay?"

"Don't you dare play the concerned father now. Me and MY child are okay and we will continue to be okay without you! I don't want him knowing shit about us Doc and if you tell him anything I will sue your ass for everything you have!"

God stared at me for a minute then turned and left the room. The pain in his eyes hurt me more than it hurt him. I knew he loved our baby, which was why I would use this to get his ass back. He was my man and no bitch would change that!

VITANI

This nigga's really off his rocker, I wanted to scream! I pulled up to my apartment to find a "For Rent" sign on the door and the locks changed. I marched to the rental office because I knew damn well they didn't evict me and I'd just paid my rent last week. Them simple bitches in the office said my husband said that I was moving in with him and had all my things moved out yesterday, then they handed me a check saying it was my deposit back. Something told me to stop by my house yesterday while he was at the doctor's office with that bitch, but I had Ice and she didn't want to leave God's house because she was having a ball with the dogs. She kept calling them big ass pitbulls puppies. *The hell they were.* I drove around the corner to my mother's house, furious. He can't keep trying to control my life like he's my daddy. I dialed my grandfather as I pulled up to my mom's house.

"Hello?"

"Grandad, where are you?"

"Good afternoon to you, too. I'm at my house, where are you?" he laughed. *I didn't see shit funny.*

"I'm serious Grandad. Why didn't you tell me what God did with our apartment?" I sighed.

"I was supposed to tell you? I figured you and him had already discussed it. What is going on? I thought you were happy with him," Grandad asked concerned.

"I am, well kinda. That doesn't matter though, Grandad. Where is your house? I need to come make sure you're okay."

"Little girl I'm the one that taught you how to shoot. I'm fine, just up the road from where your husband lives. Are you sure you're okay? I need to put my foot in his ass?"

"I'm okay Grandad, I'm just glad you're safe and happy."

"I have never been this happy in my life. Being far away from your big mouth ass grandmother gives me so much joy. I love you, baby girl," he chuckled.

I smiled, "Love you, too."

Chapter Fourteen

VITANI

"Ugh," I slammed my car door, still upset with Godrique.

My cousin Zelaya was on the porch and looked up from her phone when she heard the door. Zelaya, also known as Zee, was hood through and through. She was what you call a project queen. She had four kids and all of them had different daddies, but she works two jobs and made shit happen with or without a nigga. I still kept her ass at a distance, because I couldn't trust her as far as I could throw her.

"Hey cuz," Zee stood to hug me as I stepped onto my mom's porch. I could hear the cookout music blaring in the background.

"Nothing much, just frustrated."

"Yo' ass stay stressed about something, I hope it ain't no nigga," Zee frowned.

Bitch wouldn't you like to know. Any nigga I showed interest in, she made it her business to fuck with them first. I loved my family but I stayed away from most of them because they be on some other shit half the time. My mom stayed on my neck about reaching out to my cousins, but I don't be with the family drama, and I couldn't dead them like I could a person in the street.

"Naw cuz, I don't stress over a nigga or a bitch."

I walked into the house and went to the restroom. I felt sick as hell. I think them antibiotics fucked my stomach up. I splashed cold water on my face and hoped it would hold off the sickness for a few hours until this cookout was over. My mom would kill me if I left before it got started. I dried my face and headed to the kitchen. I grabbed some dill pickles out of the jar in the fridge and poured me a cup of milk on the rocks. I walked outside to find my mom and granny dancing with Ice on the "dancefloor" my mom put in her backyard a few years ago when she had her home remodeled. It was a 13x13 wooden deck in the middle of the yard. Her backyard was fenced in and it was about an acre. So, the multiple tents set up didn't cover the whole yard, but it gave enough shade from the Florida sun.

"Mommy!" Ice yelled running over to me. I put my last pickle in my mouth and used my free arm to scoop her up and rest her on my hip. She bit the other end of the pickle that was hanging out of my mouth. I took it out my mouth, then laughed at her greedy ass. That's why she stayed calling and trying to be around Simon, his stupid ass be sending food delivery services to her spoiled ass and all. I broke off the part of the pickle that was in my mouth and gave Ice the rest. She let her legs fall from my waist, signaling for me to put her down. I felt used as she ran back over to dance with my mom and Granny.

I walked over and gave them hugs as my Granny turned her nose up at me. "Girl, you must be pregnant."

"Granny, we been through this," I sighed. I was not feeling good enough to be dealing with her today.

"That is a pregnant person combination," Granny nodded to my cup and the pickle.

"I didn't have any cravings with Ice nor did I get sick. I think those antibiotics messed up my healthy gut bacteria." I reasoned.

Granny didn't respond, she just started back swaying to the music. I had on some daisy dukes that were ripped at the bottom near my ass, some black sandals, and a black tank top that was ripped down the front middle so it showed my belly ring. Ice had on a yellow Jordan outfit with the matching sneakers. Mom and Granny both had on jean shorts with t-shirts that matched their shoes. I spotted Jen and Rae standing by the drinks. Rae had on a sleeveless pastel pink silk button up dress that barely covered her ass and Jen wore some nude biker shorts with a black Nike shirt and some black Nike shoes with a nude Nike check on them. They were cute and neither of them had on makeup, either. It was too hot for that today.

I walked over to my girls and as I approached them, I felt a wave of nausea pass through my body like a shockwave. I found the nearest chair and put my head between my legs.

"The fuck is wrong with you?" Rae questioned as she touched my forehead.

I sat up. "I don't feel good. I think I'm getting a bug or something."

"Did you eat this morning?" Jen asked.

"No, that could be it. I just ate two pickles before I walked over here," I frowned.

"Bitch, come on. Let's get you some bread or something. I have an e-band to help with nausea, you know my hypoglycemic ass keep some on hand."

Rae reached in her purse and pulled out a pink band to slide on my wrist. I instantly felt a little better, but I still wanted some bread. I stood and walked back into the house behind my girls. We entered the kitchen and I grabbed two slices of bread.

"How you get sick on the day of ma's cookout? Is God coming?" Rae asked leaning against the marble counter.

"I honestly don't know. God wasn't invited so I doubt if he'll show up. You know he took that bitch LiLi to her impromptu appointment yesterday. Well, while he was out apparently, he had time and had all my shit moved out of my apartment," I whined.

"You can't be mad about that hoe, she was in the picture before you. He savage for that last part, though!" Rae laughed.

"Who is LiLi?" Jen's eyebrow arched.

"Some thot from around the way. She's not important," Rae summed. "I'm sorry again about not muting my mic the other day. It's all my fault you aren't in your apartment anymore."

"It's not your fault, sis. I smashed the nigga before knowing he wasn't wrapped too tight," I laughed.

"Hey beautiful." I heard drift from the side door, it was Chez. He walked over and shook Jen's hand and hugged Rae and me. "I'm Chez," he said to Jen.

"That's Jen, my friend from out of town. How have you been, Chez?" I asked as I turned to head back outside. I felt better after eating that bread and finishing my cup of milk.

"I'm good. Tryna see what's up with you, Slim," he called me by my old nickname.

Rae and Jen snickered.

"We can kick it for a while, we need to catch up." I walked to a corner tent near the back of the yard and sat with my back to the crowd that was getting bigger by the minute. My uncle Ant was doing his thang on the grill and I was starting to feel a little hungry. Chez sat facing the crowd, *I guess he is like Godrique in that regard.* I got comfortable and put my legs on his knees as he massaged my calves. He used to do that all the time when we were younger.

"So, what's been up with you? How was college?" I asked.

"College was fun. I have a shorty but he lives in Daytona with his mother. I got my degree and began working for my current boss. He's pretty chill."

"You like what you do?"

"Yea, I want to run the company one day..." his voice faded as he stopped massaging my legs. I had allowed my eyes to drift closed so when he stopped, I opened them to see what was up with him.

"You good, Chez?" I moved my legs and leaned forward and touched his face to make him look into my eyes, "Are you okay?"

"Tell me how that's any of your business, wifey," the deep voice said from behind me.

My head jerked so fast I felt a wave a nausea pass over me again as I went to stand. I wavered a little and Chez grabbed my elbow to steady me. I watched as Godrique's head tilted slightly. Chez immediately moved his hands. *I'm so sick of this shit!* God and all of The Disciples were present except Bart. All of them towered over me, but I wasn't scared of them. They weren't about to scare my friend away with their foolishness. God reached out and grabbed me by my neck and kissed my lips gently, I rocked side-to-side as I swooned with lust. Just that fast I forgot what I was about to say. His lips released the hold they had on mine and I wrapped my arms around his waist.

"Boss man, it ain't even like that. I didn't know you two were together," Chez stammered. That caused me to snap out of my temporary insanity. God still had his muscled hand around my neck as I released him.

"Don't be trying to intimidate my friend with your bullshit! You haven't been here two seconds and you're already trying to ruin my mom's BBQ." He kissed my lips again and let go of my neck to grab my ass as his tongue seduced mine.

"Oh, my damn. Lord, I don't know what I've done to be graced in the presence of such fine young men, but oooh, I thank you!" I heard Granny say as I stopped kissing God to look past him. My granny was walking our way with her eyes on Simon.

When Granny got in front of Simon she turned around and dropped it low in front of him then started twerking on him saying, "Fuck me daddy, fuck me." Simon's arms were flailing in the air as he looked around for help.

"Granny!" My mom and I said in unison.

"Y'all better get her because if she gets me up I'mma let her put me back down. And if she cooks like Vitani, y'all gone be calling me granddaddy," Simon smirked as everyone watched in shock.

"Granny! Stop it!" I yelled. I was so shamed of her actions.

"Don't Granny me, girl. How you think your mama and uncle got here?" Granny stopped twerking and turned to Simon asking, "You want something to eat, baby?"

"A woman after my heart," Simon said following her to the food table.

"What do you have on?" Teq asked Rae as she walked over speaking to the guys.

"Something I paid for. You like it?"

"Hell no, ma, you need to go put some clothes on," Teq frowned. Rae smiled and walked away with him following close behind her.

I turned around to find Chez deep in thought. I was about to ask him what he was thinking about but God would probably hit the man with his ignorant ass. But I was curious about something, "Chez, who is your boss?"

"I am," God spoke in my ear. A chill ran down my spine and I visibly shivered, "You cold?"

"No, I'm good."

"Aight boss, I'll get up with you later." Chez shook my hand and dapped up God.

Turk, John, Peter, Black, Meesha, and Alianna walked up. *Why are all of them here?* God wrapped his arms around my waist as he stood behind me. I was really hiding his massive erection. My pussy was dripping after that kiss and I was contemplating sneaking off into my old room. I haven't had dick in a long time and it was starting to make me think crazy. It's weird because I'd gone without it before with no problem, but now I felt like I was craving his touch.

"Hey sis!" The guys and Meesha said. "Hey godmom," Alianna added.

I smiled at them, "Hey y'all, who invited y'all?"

"God, well I was invited by Miss Tam," Turk said.

My brow raised, "How do you know my mom?"

Just as I asked my mom walked over and hugged Turk and Alianna. "Glad y'all could make it." She smiled genuinely. "Vitani this is Turk from the block, he used to buy all my dinners."

I squinted. *Oh shit,* the beard threw me off but it was him. *Damn, small world.* My mom used to babysit Alianna and everything. I can't believe I didn't remember them.

"Wait, this is little Tani? Had I known that I would've kept God far away from her," Turk joked. *At least I think he was joking.* God hadn't said anything since Chez left, I knew his narcissistic ass was still mad, but he'd get over it. We were not together.

"I gotta pee," I said as I went to pull away from God. He moved with me and I just shook my head. *This nigga clingy.* I decided to go into the ensuite that was connected to my old bedroom. He waited in the room while I peed. After washing my hands, I walked out to find him looking in my high school yearbook.

"Oh, so that's how y'all know each other. You fucked him?"

"No, the only other person I ever fucked was Ice dad."

"It better stay that way," he said as he stood and closed the book.

I rolled my eyes. He walked over and locked the door, I wanted to run from the predatory look he was giving me. "What are you doing?" I backed up into the dresser.

"Shut up," he turned me around so my back was now to his front. I fell mute as he unbuttoned my shorts and pulled them and my panties down. He pushed his thick length into my tight slit and I shuddered from the feel of him being so deep. He started stroking me slow and deep and I was trying to take it like a champ but that shit was hurting.

"Oww," I half moaned, half whimpered.

"It hurts?" He stopped moving waiting for an answer. *Fuck the pain, him stopping had me ready to pout.*

"It's fine. Just keep going, please."

He eased into a steady rhythm as the feel of him inside me took over my senses. He lightly stroked his finger over my spine as he nibbled my earlobe.

"Fuck wifey, take this dick like you own it."

I forgot all about the pain and started throwing my ass back to meet his strokes.

"Just like that, wifey," he grunted.

Knock! Knock!

I couldn't stop if I wanted to, I felt the orgasmic waves burst to the surface of my core and I let out a moan. God covered my mouth with his big ass hand and I moaned louder as he stroked me deeper and harder. We both started cumming together and he grabbed the sides of the dresser to steady himself. *Oh shit, someone was at the door.* I decided it was best not to say anything. Hopefully they'd go away.

We both went into the bathroom and he washed off in the sink as I took a quick shower. We brushed our teeth and walked out of the room hand-in-hand with big ass smiles on our face. Thank goodness my mom kept spare toiletries in the bathrooms.

"That's why your ass pregnant now," Granny said from behind me. I nearly jumped out of my skin as I turned around seeing Granny smiling.

"You're pregnant?" God asked.

"I'm on birth control, plus we only had sex that one time with protection, and you didn't cum."

He looked even more confused. "We have to talk about this later."

I nodded, but there was nothing to discuss. "What were you doing anyway, Granny?"

"Ice fell asleep and I went to lay her down in your old room but the door was mysteriously locked. So, I put her in my bed." Granny walked past us and lead the way back outside.

I felt like everyone was watching us when we stepped back outside. My cousin Zee approached us and I prepared myself for the bullshit.

"Zee this is God, God this is my cousin Zee."

"I know who God is," she said with a smile that didn't meet her eyes.

"Hey Zee, do I know you?" Godrique's rude ass asked.

"Um no, not personally, we run in some of the same circles." Zee said as God's face visibly scrunched. I bit back a laugh. He was so mean sometimes.

"Alright Zee, we're gonna head over to get some food." I pulled God away before he embarrassed me again. I started fixing both of our plates as John walked over to ask about one of my other cousin's friends. I gave him the scoop that she was a good girl, so he went over to shoot his shot.

Just when I thought everything was going great, I heard someone gasp saying, "Jack, I don't think you should be here."

God's head snapped up at the name. I stepped in front of him, knowing what was going through his mind. He placed our plates on the table then picked me up and moved me to the side as all The Disciples, plus Turk, Black, and Meesha, materialized out of nowhere.

Giving up on trying to stop God, I ran over to Jack and pushed him yelling, "You need to leave!"

Jack looked at me with disgust and I knew this wouldn't end well. He pulled out a gun and pointed it at my head. My eyes bulged as all The Disciples had their guns out and pointed at him. He looked unfazed and that was not like Jack's scary ass.

"Jack, please don't do this here. Your daughter is in the house sleeping," I pleaded as God walked up calmly pushing me behind him.

"That's your daughter pussy hoe. You fucked at least two of these niggas in here," he laughed. "Do they know they're sharing with each other?" Jack spat.

"Let's take this out front and handle it like grown men," God spoke with authority.

"Fuck nigga, you don't run shit. I'm calling the shots here. This bitch been fucking and sucking niggas and your duck ass up here playing Captain save a hoe." Jack raised the gun to point it at God's head.

"Jack, leave my house with your foolishness. My daughter may be many things but a hoe is not one of them," my mom interjected.

Jack laughed cynically.

I saw Meesha come up behind him stealthy as she removed her earrings and handed them to Teq. God nodded his head to her and she walked up on Jack as if he was nothing but a nuisance. He turned as she got in his personal space, but when he looked in her direction, God did a quick kick to Jack's nuts. When he bent over, he kicked his wrist disarming him in a matter of seconds. My mouth fell open as Meesha cracked her neck and went into a southpaw stance, before decking Jack in the nose when he stood up. He didn't know what hit him, Meesha threw two more quick jabs to his body then went straight for his face. Jack didn't stand a chance.

"Stop her! You promised me!" I cried.

"I kept my word," God said as he watched Meesha beat the shit out of Jack.

"Meesha, stop!" I yelled but she kept throwing haymakers. Jack was a bloody mess by now and all I could do was watch and cry. "Simon! Teq! Stop her! What if Ice wakes up?"

That got them to say something. Jack was crying like a bitch. I ran over to him yelling, "Someone call an ambulance!" Nobody moved. Jack must've blacked out because there was no more crying from him. I must've left my phone in my room because it wasn't on me. God picked me up as Peter and Turk carried Jack out of the backyard.

"Where are they taking him?!"

"Keep carrying on this way and I'mma be led to believe you still have feelings for this nigga," God snapped still holding me around the waist.

"Fuck you!" I spat. If my family wasn't around, he probably would've beat my ass, too.

Chapter Fifteen

GOD

Rubbing my hand down my face, I tried to calm myself, but it wasn't working. Vitani is starting to make me question her loyalty. First Chez was all in her face and she all smiles and now she was crying over a nigga that attempted to rape her. *The fuck is wrong with this silly ass girl? Better yet, what the fuck is wrong with me?* I was standing in the middle of her mother's living room ready to kill for her and she was trying to be a saving grace for a nigga that don't give a fuck about her or my daughter.

"God, you have to understand where I'm coming from. I don't want to look at my daughter knowing I let someone kill her father. If we plan to be together, I don't want you having to look Ice in her eyes knowing you took her father away from her."

I didn't say anything, just stood there staring at her thinking about what she was saying. I would love to say that changed my mind, but it only fueled my anger. I couldn't dead dude anytime soon anyway since all the people at this BBQ saw our little altercation. That would put me and my fam in the bullshit investigation of his murder. Peter dropped Jack's dumb ass off at the twenty-four-hour ER on the southside and went to do damage control at the station. Turk had to head out of town with Black to handle business since Alianna was staying with me. They were supposed to leave Thursday but they decided to wait a few more days. I knew my god daughter would be sad if I messed this up, because Vitani was a woman worth compromising for.

"I feel you. I will keep my word, but just don't bring that nigga up around me." I licked my lips, then pulled her into a hug, "I'm sorry baby."

I kissed her lips softly. She wrapped her arms around my neck and deepened the kiss, sucking on my bottom lip and nibbling lightly. My dick jumped to life. I pulled back and gave her a small smile, she didn't know how beautiful she was, even with dried tears on her face.

"Go wash your face so we can go get something to eat."

She nodded and walked down the hall. I watched her until she disappeared, but then I heard chuckling and turned to see Simon standing there as Jen and Rae rushed to find Vitani in the back of the house.

"You're going soft lil' bitch," Si said as he sat down on the brick-colored suede couch. Miss Tam had her living room decorated brick red and grey, two colors I would never think to put together but they came together good.

"Stop cursing before Granny hear you," I sat down in the love seat adjacent from where he sat and threw a grey plush pillow at his head. "I know I must be in love bro, because if it was LiLi out there beggin' me to spare another nigga, she'd be dead with him."

Si smirked, "I can't even front, my G. You been slippin' lately. You been so busy stalking lil' sis you haven't been thinking about the people that hit your house. They know where you lay your head, but more importantly they know where Ice and Vitani lay their heads now."

I dropped my head because he was right. I had to find them and dead this shit so I could rest peacefully. My brothers and I ain't into no illegal shit, except Turk, so there was no reason for them to break into my home and hit my safe. I only kept a grand and a Glock in it for show. "You're right, I will have to personally work on it with you. This should've been handled a long time ago, I just don't be trying to go back to my old ways," I sighed.

The girls walked back into the living room and Vitani was wearing a yellow short sundress with her locs up in a high ponytail. She walked over and stood in front of me with her hands on her hips. I pulled her closer and pressed my face into her stomach while grabbing her fat ass.

"Umm, you smell good, wifey."

"Stop playing, I'm hungry," she tried pushing my head away and I nipped her. "Oww, let me go, goofy!"

"Not until you apologize for trying to push me away."

She laughed, "I can't stand you."

"I'm waiting," I nipped her again.

"Ouch," she turned to the others. "Y'all just gonna stand there and let him abuse me?" They all ignored our display of public affection and kept talking amongst each other. "Okay, I'm sorry. Stop it and come feed your wife."

That made me smile as I stood to kiss her cheek. We all walked back outside and the sun was starting to set. Vitani fixed us some plates and we sat and watched her uncle and mom play a game of spades against Simon and Rae. Teq, Meesha, and John had left to get ready for the club.

"Stop cheating, Uncle Ant!" Simon called out.

"Prove it youngin', call the book," Ant snickered.

Simon leaned back and eyed the books Miss Tam had lined up and contemplated whether he wanted to try to call the wrong book to lose two of his own. They were five to six and this could make or break him and Rae. He turned to look at Rae.

"Aht, don't even think about talking across the board," Miss Tam chimed.

"Just run me my last two," Simon threw out the big joker and the two of spades.

"Take one book, but that two of spades is mine," Miss Tam laughed throwing out the two of diamond and three of club.

"How?" Simon wined.

"You went out of term so your joker didn't lead to pull my two. Your partner has two clubs so that would've led, and let's just say we don't know how it would've played out," Miss Tam stood and did the Charlie Brown.

Vitani and I were cracking up laughing as Simon fumed. Rae looked at Simon like she wanted to slap him, then reached across the table and mushed his face. Miss Tam and Uncle Ant started doing the Kid 'n Play dance, clowning Simon.

I leaned over to Vitani and asked, "You ready to go cuddle?" She gave me the side eye with a small smirk, nodding her head yes. I stood and dapped up Simon and Uncle Ant, then hugged Miss Tam and Granny. I motioned for Alianna.

"Let my grandbaby stay here tonight, since she's already sleep," Miss Tam said.

"Okay mom, I'll be back to get her tomorrow evening."

"Miss Tam, can I stay here tonight? I have a friend that lives around the corner that I want to go see tomorrow," Alianna asked.

"What friend? It better not be a boy."

"Leave that child alone. You can stay Ali, you know you're welcome here anytime."

Vitani and I walked towards her car hand-in-hand as my phone started ringing. I knew the tone belonged to LiLi so I ignored it. I stopped in front of Vitani's driver's side door and opened it for her to get inside.

"I was supposed to go to the club with the guys tonight, but I can stay in with you if you want."

"No, you can go. I'll be fine."

"I'm not leaving you home alone. I'll follow you to the house."

I leaned down to kiss her lips then closed the door and walked to my car. My phone rang again as I followed Vitani to my house. This time I answered.

"Speak."

"I was just calling to check on you. Yesterday you seemed a little stressed out."

"LiLi, you don't need to call to check on me. I seemed stressed out? Naw, you're the one that was on some other shit. I am on my way home with my wife, so don't call me unless it's an emergency."

"Why are you treating me this way? We were friends before anything else, God. I was stressed out when you left me in that room alone."

"When were we friends?" I chuckled. "What's my favorite color? Have you met my goddaughter? The only thing we have ever did is fuck and that didn't even happen often. I don't give a damn how stressed you are, don't ever try to pull no shit like that again. You won't always be pregnant with my child."

"Wow, you really don't care about me. Glad to know where I stand."

She hung up and I chuckled again because she was emotional with this pregnancy. It had her dreaming up a relationship that she and I both know never existed.

"Vitani, this is my mother, Nichelle. Ma, this is my future wife," I introduced them.

Vitani went to hug my mom, but she put her hand out for her to shake. I was gonna have to ask my mom about that backwards ass bullshit. She ain't do that with LiLi, and the only reason she met her was because she's pregnant with my seed. I ended up not going to the club last night and just spending time with Vitani, getting to know her better. I could listen to her soothing voice all day and night.

"Hey, I didn't know you were bringing someone to Sunday dinner. I invited LiLi over so you two could talk things out." My mom smiled.

I cocked my head to the side and contemplated leaving, but I don't want Vitani thinking I'm trying to hide something. I looked down at my wife and I could tell she was getting upset because she was staring into space, not blinking or anything.

"Ma, why wouldn't you run that by me first?"

"I'm sorry, I didn't know you were the one that birthed me and I owe you some type of explanation. You need to show your mother some respect, son."

"I am, it's just not right," I grabbed Vitani's hand and turned to head out the door. "We will come back later when she leaves."

"Son, you haven't came by to see your mother in over a month. I could understand if you were just working, but you made time for LiLi I mean Vita here and can't make time for the woman who birthed you?"

I paused before turning back to face my mother. I was trying to not disrespect her, but at the same time, she was being very disrespectful. "Her name is Vitani and I can come back another time because today is not your day."

"Uhp, son, stop being dramatic. I will call her and tell her I'll take her a plate later. Go have a seat at the table and let your mama fix you a plate. You know can't nobody cook like your mama and I'm sure you've been starving."

I smiled because she was halfway coming back to her senses. "Vitani, are you okay with staying?"

"Yes, as long as you keep your baby mama away from me, I'm not gonna pass up a free meal," she smiled back and I led her to the dining room table. "Where is the restroom? I'd like to wash my hands."

"Down the hall to the left." I watched her then stood to go wash my hands in the kitchen sink.

"Son, you know I don't mean any harm but there's something about that girl I just don't like," my mom came to stand beside me saying, not even trying to whisper.

"Well, when you can give me a valid reason, let me know. Until then, it's irrelevant. I love her and her daughter and I plan on marrying her one day."

"You don't even know that girl. And she has a baby? Where is the baby? Why wouldn't she bring her baby?"

"Chill ma, she didn't even know we were coming over here today. We woke up late and were gonna go to a restaurant but I decided to stop by here instead so you could meet her. We're gonna pick Ice up later before we go home."

"Go home? You moved that girl and her child into your home? Son, I know I taught you better than that. She must got gold between her legs to make you lose your mind." My mom clutched her invisible pearls.

"I'm back. Miss Nichelle you can have a seat I'll fix our plates," Vitani walked over to us. I wondered how much of the conversation she heard.

"Oh no, I will fix the plates, I don't like all type of people in my kitchen."

My head snapped at my mom's words and I had to bite my tongue to keep from cursing. Vitani grabbed my hand and pulled me around the corner to the restroom and closed the door. "Wifey, I promise my mom is not mean. I don't know where all of this is coming from."

"Godrique, I can handle a lot but I don't tolerate disrespect from anybody. I have been in a bit of a mood myself lately and extra snappy. I want to stay because that food smells good as hell and I'm starving," her stomach growled.

I chuckled. "Your greedy ass always thinking with your stomach. If you want to leave, we can, if not, we can stay. It's up to you."

"Kiss me," Vitani moaned as my lips automatically found hers and locked us in a sensual embrace. She pulled back with her eyes still closed saying, "I'll stay."

We went back into the dining area and sat down, all eating in silence. That was short-lived as my mom began with the bullshit again. "So, Vitani. How old are you and how old is your daughter?"

"I'm twenty and my daughter is three."

"So, you started young. Is your baby daddy around or you're just trying to pawn her off on my son?"

I knew damn well she didn't just ask her that. "Ma where are you getting at with these questions? It's really none of your business since I'm the one that has to raise Ice and not you. Hell, if her mother ever tries to leave me I'mma take my daughter with me." Vitani started laughing thinking I was joking. I didn't crack a smile and my mother looked at me with bunched eyebrows.

"Son, you might need to go to church with me tonight. You know these lil' hussies be doing them roots on men."

It was my turn to laugh, the only roots Vitani put on me was that demon pussy and that hellfire mouth. Vitani finished off her food except the yams and stood to grab my plate but I took hers and started eating the yams.

"I'm sorry wifey, I should've fixed your plate. I know you don't eat yams."

"That's right, son, we don't waste food around here. I don't know why people be such picky eaters around men," my mom scowled. I wasn't sure where all this sneak dissing was coming from.

"I can attest to that, Miss Nichelle, your son doesn't waste a single drop. He can't get enough and I give him as much as he wants," Vitani smirked at me and I choked on a damn yam.

ANITA

"Please tell me you have something for me, Su," I pulled my cousin to the side as our parents chitchatted in the family room. Both of our fathers are white brothers who married black women. My cousin Susan chose a noble profession in social work although our parents had old money and we didn't need to work, I chose to work for my father. "It has gotten to the point where he won't even answer my calls anymore."

"I just went by two days ago and discovered she had moved out, which she neglected to inform me or the office. I am in contact with a judge now to have her daughter taken from her custody, it might take more than an address change though. I am sure the grandmother will get her, so she won't be in the state. But that slut will have to jump through hoops to get her parental rights back," Susan smirked and I smiled.

"I want you to arrest her so everyone can know that I have been right about her along. Keep me informed and don't fuck this up."

"I won't. I hope you get the man. He is a sight for sore eyes I'll tell you that. The Simon fella is too, but I don't do their kind," Susan frowned in disgust.

See this is why I can't be around her too long, they despise my choice in men and would much rather I be with Bart, but I don't see forever with him. *I need a God.*

"I will chat with you later, cousin. We should get back before they send the help searching for us."

As I listened to my family discuss casual irrelevant topics, I thought about the look that will be on Vitani's face when all of her dreams come crashing down. I smiled at the thought alone.

CHEZ

"Devun, my guy, you ready to hit the shop?" I asked, walking into the crib he shared with his baby mama Meka.

"J-dawg got hit up by your boy and his crew yesterday, so he can't run down just yet. We gotta hold off a few more weeks, but that nigga God and them other pussies he be with are all on my list."

"What? J got fucked up? They let him live?" I was surprised I hadn't received a call about this.

"Hell yea, the brawd Vitani that God is fuckin with is Jack's baby mother. She ain't gonna go for him getting killed, but some bitch put heavy paws on the kid. I feel a lil' sorry for him on the real."

I rubbed my hand down my face. "I know Jack is Vitani's deadbeat." Devun's head shot up and I had to clear up my slip-up. "I mean, you know we all went to the Hill together. I hope the nigga recover fast, because I need this fake ass wannabe gangsta nigga God out the picture."

"Word. My girl broke up with me and I think that bitch Vitani had something to do with it. I told her I'd kill her before I let another nigga take what's mine."

I shook my head because this dude was dumb. He was laid up in his baby mom's house worried about what his ex was doing. "Vitani ain't have shit to do with it, leave her out of it."

Devun stood and folded his arms over his chest. "Yea, you're probably right. You like her, too? Bitch must have liquid gold between her legs."

"I'll let you know when I find out. Stay up, my G. I'll hit yo' line when it's a go."

I walked out of the house and felt someone watching me but I didn't see anyone around. I needed to stop being paranoid before I gave myself away. Normally I wouldn't pull up on Vun, but I knew Turk and Black were out of town because my cousin had started some beef with him on my behalf. Everything was starting to fall into place. I had God's house robbed and only took one thing that would be his downfall and my come up. I'd take Jack and Vun out after they finished up what I needed them for. A light bulb went off in my head and I turned around and walked back in the house to find Vun still sitting on the couch.

"Aye, where can I find Jack? I want to see for myself that he's okay."

"He's at his crib in the trails."

I dapped him up then headed to my home to get what I needed to put my final plan in motion. The next time I saw God, he'd be in a jail cell, signing his company over to me. They'd be calling me God when it was all said and done.

Chapter Sixteen

VITANI

"**B**itch, these men are dangerous. I was doing some digging, plus you know I be talking to Teqwyn. God may as well be a leader of a cult. Hoe GET OUT while you can!" Rae warned.

"Cult? I already told the Feds I'm no longer working with them, if they want God, they'll have to do it on their own. Were you able to find anything on Anita?"

"That...ooh, let me calm down...she has been communicating with someone that has a burner phone sporadically, the messages are cryptic, but it seems like she's paying someone to set someone up."

"How did you get this info if they were on a burner."

"Damn V, God doing a number on you, you're acting slow as hell. I hacked the dusty bitch phone, she's not smart enough to use a burner, but the person she hired is," Rae summed.

"Oh, are you still going to the Governor's Ball? I need you there with me. By the way, can you try to find out what Jen has been up to for the past year. Something seems off about her, but I can't put my finger on it."

"Yes, I am still going to the ball. Jen been off grid, I already looked into her a week or so ago when Simon said he had a funny feeling about her."

"Simon? Oh shit, if he has a funny feeling about her, she needs to stay away from them. I don't know for certain, but I think Simon is the killer, hitta, Mad Max of the crew."

"He is. From what I could find on him that wasn't locked away behind a damn impenetrable firewall, he is a contractor for the government. That's why he was able to make Susan leave the day she came to your crib. Jen should tread lightly because that fool crazy with his greedy ass," Rae chuckled.

The front door opened and in walked God, holding Ice, with my grandfather and Alianna close behind. He looked at me and licked his lips then winked, causing my heart to flutter like a butterfly's wings on a warm day.

"I gotta go sis, I will hit you up later." Disconnecting the call, I stood up from my perch on the couch asking, "Did you all have fun?" Ice jumped up and down in God's arms with excitement but didn't try to get down like she normally did to hug me. A ping of jealousy tugged at my heart.

"We get ice cream, Mommy! Ice cream, ice cream, my cream!" Ice pumped her fist.

"Your cream? Did you share?" I laughed at my daughter thinking all the ice cream in the world was hers, knowing Godrique, he probably encouraged it. I walked over to her and held my arms out. This thang reared back and turned around circling her arms around God's neck saying, "My Goddy," with her lips poked out. *It be your own damn kid!* I rolled my eyes heavenward.

"She did share after her greedy little butt tasted everyone's ice cream. I thought I was spoiled but baaaabae, Ice takes the cake!" Alianna laughed as she sat on the couch.

"My lil' chunk will only go as far as you let her. What have you been doing all day? Why are you still in sleeping clothes?" Grandad asked.

I snatched Ice out God's arms and we laughed when she hugged me tight and let me love on her.

"I haven't been feeling good lately and today is my day off, so I am lollygagging around."

"All that ends now, go get dressed."

"No."

"Don't start your mess, Vitani. Put on something sexy but not too sexy."

I didn't argue as I took Ice and Alianna in the room with me. I took a quick shower, put my locs in a high pony, and then put a light beat on my face. Alianna picked out a mauve dress that crisscrossed in the front stomach area and the back, but it still showcased my whole back and dipped low enough to show my tramp stamp. The shoes she picked were strappy and fuchsia as was the coach bag she had me wear.

"Mommy perty," Ice smiled.

"So, I'm usually ugly?" I frowned.

Ice nodded her head up and down causing Alianna and I to laugh. *Damn, my daughter better know how to fight when she gets older because she already has no filter.* I strutted into the den to find God talking to my Grandad, but both of them stopped when they saw me. God's eyes slowly raked down my body, then glided back up to my face, as he rubbed his beard biting his bottom lip.

"Turn around, let me see the back."

"You can have a better view of that later. Let's go before I change my mind. Grandad, Ali said she is about to give Ice a bath and put her to bed, so you can chill and watch your westerns."

"Sounds good to me."

We headed out to wherever he was taking me and I stared at him as he drove his all-white mustang GT, cruising down I4. "You got a problem?" he asked without taking his eyes off the road. I smiled.

"Yes, but it can wait until we get to where we're going."

"We might not make it to where we're going. Speak."

"Why do you like me? What did you think when you first saw me?"

"I thought 'damn this woman has a nice ass and pretty feet'. From the first moment you opened your mouth calling yourself tryna check me about my name, I knew you would be mine. I didn't think it would be so soon, but I would have pursued you either way. You are like a breath of fresh air, you're my peace and my headache. My world is yours now."

Tears lined my eyes. "What about your mom. She doesn't like me."

He reached over lacing his strong hand in mine saying, "What about her? It ain't your job to make her happy, nor is it mine. She'll be alright." He kissed my hand.

"You are not what I expected. Hell, I thought you were a damn drug dealer the way people talk about you."

He smiled. "Naw, I hang heavy with one so, of course they believe that birds of a feather bullshit."

We pulled up to Valet at The Capitol in Orlando, a well-known high-class restaurant. God walked around, opened my door, and escorted me inside the elegant establishment. As we were being shown to our seat, he grabbed my ass and squeezed it, getting a giggle out of me. He just wanted all the men that were staring at me to know what type of relationship we had. *Men are so territorial.* Before the hostess could walk away, a waiter came to get our drink order. He ordered a bottle of Petite Sirah and I hoped it tasted as good as it sounded.

"So, Mrs. James, what do want out of life?"

I was caught off-guard by that broad deep question. It made me think about all the things I had aspired to do in life and the steps I had or hadn't taken towards those aspirations.

"I'mma let you slide with that Mrs. James shit for now. I personally have not thought about what I want in a long time. I want more than anything to ensure my daughter doesn't want for anything in life. I want to be a wife one day and be loved unconditionally. I thought I wanted to be a private investigator, but I love my current job, minus the drama. That's why I've been working hard to move up in the company so I can implement some positive changes to help IntelliCorp flourish."

Godrique's smile covered his face and I admired his white straight teeth, then his smile vanished as he caught my gaze in an intense stare down. "I have to ask you something, because it has been eating me alive since last weekend. You said we only had sex once when Granny suggested you could be pregnant, but we have had sex three times so far."

My breath lodged in my throat as I took a gulp of the wine he ordered. I gagged and hurriedly spit it back out in the glass.

"Ewww! What the fuck kinda wine is that, you trying to kill me?" I gulped the water down instead, attempting to get rid of the bitter taste on my tongue. The waiter came and took our order, he ordered steak and I ordered king crab legs. I also requested more water and a side of pickle chips. Godrique still smiled as he tried to conceal his humor that had caused other patrons to look our way. "You said we had sex twice after the first time. When?"

"The night I took you to the hospital."

My head tilted as the dream crashed into my memory. "Walk me through that day after you picked me up from work, because it's still hazy to me."

"I stopped by the apartment and picked Ice up from Pops because he had a doctor's appointment. I stopped by the pharmacy to pick up your antibiotics, then took you and Ice to my crib. You were knocked the fuck out so I undressed you and showered you, which was hard because you kept waking up trying to grab my dick. After I got you settled, me and Ice watched Doc McStuffins until she fell asleep. I didn't want to give her a bath because I didn't know how you would feel about that, but Pops said she had a bath that morning so she should be good when I hit him up to update him on you," he paused when the waiter brought my pickles. "I took my shower and got in bed then your freaky ass basically tried to rape me again. I tried to hold out but you seemed hellbent on fucking, so I gave you what you were begging for."

I rolled my eyes as I smacked on a pickle. "I begged? You should've known I was high as hell!"

"Off NyQuil? That shit doesn't last that long in your system. Shit weak as hell now. Do you remember us having sex?" A tinge of worry laced his words.

"Apparently, I had a high dose of Ambien in my system. The doctor thinks someone drugged me. But I do remember the torture you inflicted on my body, I thought I was dreaming."

"Damn, your homegirl roofied you?"

I threw my napkin at him, "No! There was NyQuil in my system, too. I think it was this tea I had delivered to my office that day. I thought it was from you or Rae, so I drank it."

"Yea, you need to hang up that private investigating career dream because who the fuck drinks something without asking questions? The fuck you been, under a rock?"

I frowned. "Sorry we can't all have all the sense in the world."

"I'm not asking you to have all the sense, just the common ones."

The food arrived and I welcomed the interruption, he was so brutally honest and it hurt my lil' feelings. I knew I had to stop being so trusting, but if I wasn't so trusting I wouldn't have given him a chance.

He took a few bites of his food before saying, "I'm sorry if I came off rude."

"You were rude, but you were also right." The king crab was so sweet and buttery and I leaned over to feed him a piece. He opened his mouth and as I moved quickly to put it in, his tongue snaked around my finger and sapped up every drop of butter with the crab. I moaned, wishing I could trade places with the crab meat.

Still holding my gaze, he said, "That is delicious," licking his lips.

"Uh. Um. I—I was wondering, why do you have so much security on your home?"

"I was robbed a little over a year ago, so I have to take extra precautions, especially now that my family is living with me." I blushed. "I feel like the person that robbed me is someone close to me. They only took my gun."

"That is odd, you have any leads?"

"Naw, but Teq and Simon are on it."

"Speaking of the guys around you, what do they do? I know you didn't want to tell me before, but I am curious."

His brow furrowed, "Curiosity killed the cat."

"So did God," I winked. That got a laugh out of him.

"Teqwyn is my cousin and he has his own electronics shop, I'm sure Rae told you about that," I nodded. "He also is a genius that can hack into any system in under a minute, but he rarely does that. Simon is a contractor for the government, I can't really discuss what he does or you might come up missing. John is a broker for his trucking company and Peter is a detective."

"So, all of y'all are legal businessmen?"

He squinted. "Yes. Turk was the only one selling drugs, but he is getting out the game since it's getting crazy out in these streets."

"What about Bart?"

"What about him?"

"What does he do?"

"He owns IntelliCorp."

My jaw dropped to the floor. *I know damn well this muthafucka didn't say what I think he just said.* "Run that by me again."

"Technically, we all own equal parts of IntelliCorp, but he runs the show."

"I thought Anita's father owned the company and Bart is just a manager."

He smiled, "That's what you were supposed to think. Now that you'll be my wife soon, I think you should know the whole truth."

WOW. This new information completely blew my mind. "Did you get me my promotion because we fucked?"

"Hell no, I had nothing to do with that. It was all Bart."

I smiled because that was nice of Bart. It eased my mind knowing God and the men around him would have nothing to worry about with the Feds.

"Would you like dessert?" Godrique asked.

I shook my head from side-to-side because I was stuffed. Godrique was on one knee in front of me in a split second with a red velvet box containing a ring with a nice size rock on it. Tears streamed down my cheeks and he hadn't even spoke a word yet.

The restaurant grew quiet as he said, "Vitani, you have made me the happiest man in the world since the first night I met you. From the cat and mouse games you play to the wild sex and stellar head game." I felt my cheeks flush at that last part. *He gets on my damn nerves.* "You take care of business and home with ease and I swear I just want to live happily ever after with you and our daughter. Will you do me the honor of becoming my wife?"

"Godrique, I—I wish I could say yes, but I need time to think."

He slipped the ring on me finger that fit perfectly. Finally looking at the ring I gasped because I had sent this to Rae. *I'mma kill her!* "You have two days to give me your answer. Either way, we're getting married, wifey." He kissed my lips.

What kinda shit is that? How he gone tell me I have time to basically only have the option to say yes anyway. *I knew he was a lil' off but this was some real life YOU shit.* It kinda turned me on the way he always took control of a situation. I guess I would be getting married soon.

Chapter Seventeen

GOD

Sitting behind my desk in my office at the warehouse, I smiled again thinking about my date with Vitani. *How the hell does a person grow up in the hood and ditzy as fuck?* She continued to amaze me every day I spent with her and my daughter. Everything was coming together and yesterday she had agreed to be my wife. That shit made a nigga misty-eyed just thinking about it. Even though her rebellious ass waited an extra day past the two-day timeframe I gave her.

Knock. Knock.

"Come in." Teq, Simon, Peter, and Meesha strolled in. Teq held a manilla folder that got my attention. "What's up?"

Tech placed the folder in front of me and when I opened it, I was only half surprised. I knew it was an inside job but I never knew it was him. "I have a plan for how I want to handle this. don't act different with him."

"What about the other one? I don't like his ass anyway," Teq stressed.

"I said act normal. The shit I have planned for them will let everyone know not to fuck with us."

"What about the driver? We still don't know who it was," Meesha spoke.

"I have an idea about that. Anyone heard from Bart?"

"Naw, he went to visit his father and hasn't came back ye—" my phone rang, interrupting me. I answered without a second thought, placing it on speaker, still thumbing through the folder. "Hey wifey, how is work going?"

"It was going great until that wicked witch Anita walked into my office on some bullshit. I swear I'mma kill that bitch one of these days."

"Stop talking like that on the phone, you know you're a good girl. What did she do?"

"The bitch came in my office on some 'you're the reason Bart is gone and God will be next to leave' bullshit. I told her if she didn't get the fuck out of my face, I would slit her throat with the ENGAGEMENT ring you put on my finger."

I smirked. *Her ass was just on the fence about marrying me.* "Wifey, don't let her take you out of character, let me call her an—"

"I will cut your fucking throat, too! That's what she wants you to do. She knew I would call to snitch on her and she thinks you will call her. Don't you dare even let me catch you looking at that bitch or I'm fucking both of y'all up!" She released an exasperated sigh.

"Calm down before you upset my baby." All eyes went to me, I shrugged. "I won't call her but you need to finish up for today and go home. You've been temperamental, and I don't want the other employees picking up on it."

"You're right. I think I will walk down to Rae's office to chill with her for a minute. I'm sorry for interrupting you at work, my love. What do you want for dinner?"

"I want some curry goat!" Simon blurted out before I could answer.

"Okay big bro, I got you, rice or mac and cheese?" Vitani didn't even flinch at being on speaker.

"You know I love your mac and cheese! Let me be quiet. Your man over here giving me the death glare."

"Okay, bae is that fine by you or you want something else?"

"Are you on the menu?" I gave two fucks that everyone was listening.

"As long as you're on the menu as well. I love you Godrique," she purred and I could hear her blushing.

"I love you too, wifey." I disconnected the call with a wide grin on my face.

"She's pregnant?" Peter asked.

"I suspect as much, but I'm not sure and she keeps saying 'I'm on birth control'. Her ass looks bigger and her hips look like they're spreading, plus her attitude has been all over the place. Don't even get me started on the nausea and vomiting every other morning."

"Damn nigga your ass be stalking her every move. What her shit look like?" Simon asked trying to be funny.

"She's been constipated lat—"

"Eww nigga, nobody wanna hear that shit," Peter laughed at me and Simon.

"I'm glad you and Vitani are finally on the same page. What's up with Turk?" Teq questioned.

"He is still wrapping shit up, but it will be over soon."

Peter looked down at his phone when a message came through. "We have a problem." We all looked at his dramatic ass waiting to find out what was up. "Jack's body was found in his home two days ago, he had been dead for a week, but that's not the kicker."

"What's the kicker?" I asked.

"Your gun is the murder weapon." We all grew silent as I slipped off into my thoughts. *So, this is what that fool was planning. Whole time I been looking out, he been tryna fuck me over. To think I saw him as family and welcomed him with open arms, even convinced him to work for me instead of doing the bullshit he was on before.*

"Why is this not out yet? Vitani can't know he's dead, otherwise she'd be blaming me."

"They are building a case against you, so they are keeping everything under wraps until they're ready to charge you. So, watch your back and don't do anything crazy until we handle this," Meesha chimed.

She was the attorney of the crew. I didn't tell Vitani about her occupation the other night because she's technically not part of my crew, Peter is, and she is our little sister.

"My goddaughter said some real shit to me a few weeks back and I think it's time I remind muthafuckas who I am. I been on the straight and narrow, but these bitches about to feel me! Teq find Bart yesterday, he should've been back by now."

"Bet."

"I'mma head down to my office to get the paperwork together for when they do decide to arrest you," Meesha said as she gave all of us hugs.

"I'mma head out, too. Gotta go see what they know down at the station," Peter dapped me up.

"Thank y'all. You don't know how much y'all loyalty means to me, but I truly do appreciate it."

"Nigga, gone somewhere with that sentimental shit, Vitani rubbing off on your punk ass."

I flicked Simon off, looking back down at the face in the folder. I knew this would tear me apart, but it had to be done. "Si, I need you to set some shit up for me and it has to be perfect. This bitch thinks I'm stupid or some shit, but I got something for her."

He nodded, "Just say the word and whoever you want is dead."

"I know, but I gotta get Teq to give me the okay before I fill you in. Just be ready when I hit you up, so no leaving the country right now."

"Nigga, I ain't your bitch, don't be trying to tell me what to do," Si smiled.

"I hate that your dumb ass can't ever take shit serious."

"If I did, a lot more people would lose their lives. You coming to Ma Nichelle house for dinner Sunday?" he asked as he sat in the chair across from me and pulled a cowtail out of his pocket.

Who the fuck eats them nasty things? "Naw, I forgot to tell you that she's been acting weird as fuck with Vitani. I don't understand the shit because she loves LiLi."

"Well, there is your answer right there. And you call me the dumb ass. She fucks with LiLi so she's not liking that Vitani is trying to take her place."

"Si, LiLi never had a place to take, but I do get your point. Mommy better get over that shit because Vitani is gonna be my wife before the end of the year. Maybe by the end of the month," I said as my hand unconsciously went to my chin. I hoped my mom came around because I needed the women in my life to get along so I could stay stress free. "I still won't be there Sunday. I promised Miss Tam I'd go to church with her."

"How she got your nonreligious ass to agree to that? Never mind. Demon pussy. Aight, I'mma head out."

"Quick question. You know that coffee shop Bart used to frequent all the time, what color are their cups?"

Si smacked on his candy. "Red with white writing. Why?"

"Nothing, just wanted to be sure. You heard from him?"

"Hell no, I meant to ask about him earlier but got thrown off with that information Peter received. His pops never liked you, so maybe he convinced him to stay in Europe."

"Yea, maybe. I'll see you at the ball on Saturday, be safe out there in them streets."

"You too, bro."

Rae

"Dayyyyum sis, you're wearing the hell out of that dress! You better be glad God isn't going or you might not have made it out the bedroom," I hyped my sis up. For some reason she was nervous and I couldn't understand why. it's not like this was our first time rubbing elbows with the rich and famous. Her dress was an off-white backless diamond-studded gown with a high split that stopped mid-thigh. It was so beautiful on her.

"I am glad he had somewhere to go tonight so he didn't ask me too many questions. Thanks again for letting me get dressed here and picking out this gorgeous dress. I truly appreciate it. I appreciate you for being such a great friend to me," she hugged me tight and I hugged her back.

I leaned back saying, "Bitch, you're scaring me. Are you okay? Your ass acting like you're about to die tonight. Where is your engagement ring?"

She chuckled, "I hope I don't die tonight, but if I do, just know that I love you. I took it off, don't want Lex in my business."

I rolled my eyes at her overly dramatic ass. I hope this guy Lex was not an asshole like he was before. Vitani had told me about her first encounter with him and I hoped he wasn't on that same bullshit. *How does a federal agent blackmail someone into going out with them? How the fuck does Vitani keep meeting these crazy ass men? Damn, I need a drink.* I sauntered over to my dining table and took a shot of Hennessy, shaking my head to clear the nasty taste. I only took shots when I really wanted to get fucked up, otherwise I mixed it with hypnotic.

"Rae, that dress was made for you. I love how it gives the illusion of fire," Vitani said as she walked over to take a shot. I chose to wear an orange-black one shoulder beaded ribbon gown that also had a high split. I smiled because I picked this out with Teqwyn in mind, he said he would be there tonight. I knew how he liked to play with fire, so I was turning up the heat.

"Thanks, bestest! You know we about to shut this shit down, all them white people about to be trying to figure out who we are."

Vitani scrunched her nose. "I'll pass. Jen said she will meet us there."

"Don't make that face, your ass done started fucking the boss and think you're too good for the white folks now," I teased.

"Bart owns the company," she shrugged.

"And his ass is MIA. So, who does that leave in charge? Oh okay."

We made our way outside after Vitani received a message stating the car was outside. They had sent a blacked-out Denali to pick us up and take us to the ball that was being held at the RP Funding Center near downtown Lakeland. It didn't take much time getting there since I lived off of Kathleen, which turned into Harden Blvd. The venue was huge and it was packed to capacity. The truck pulled up to the main entrance and a guy who I presumed was Lex stood there waiting.

"Vitani, you look so beautiful. Who is your friend?"

"This is my sister Rae, she is my guest for the evening. I hope you don't mind."

"Oh, I thought we would be keeping each other company, but she is welcome to join us." Lex's smile didn't reach his eyes as he placed his hand on Vitani's back, leading her inside.

Ugh, I swear it's going to be a long ass night. I followed them into the white and gold decorated ballroom, admiring the lavish chandeliers. They approached an older white man with a young woman draped on his arm. I noticed it was the governor.

"Lexington, who is this lovely young woman escorting you tonight?"

"This is Vitani Banks, the woman that worked on the assignment you personally placed me over. She got us the information we needed."

"Vitani? That name sounds familiar. Nice meeting you, thank you for your service. Please enjoy yourself," the governor said, walking off before Vitani could respond.

I eavesdropped wondering what the hell was going on. The governor almost appeared spooked when Lex introduced my girl to him. *This shit keeps getting weirder.* I told Vitani not to get wrapped up in the bullshit, we could have worked to purchase her a building. Now, her ass doesn't even want to be a private investigator, so all of this was for nothing. Well, not entirely, since she met God from this assignment. And I met Teq. *With his sexy ass.*

Lex leaned closer to Vitani saying, "The contents of that cup were Zolpidem, Acetaminophen, and Dextromethorphan. Basically, NyQuil and Ambien. It came from a mom-and-pop coffee shop but someone ordered with one of those prepaid cards and used a fake name. Sorry I couldn't give you more."

"Thank you, that makes things a little easier for me."

"Are you sure you don't want a permanent position with the Bureau? We could use someone with your skills. Normally these operations last a few years, but you uncovered the money laundering within a few months. That's impressive."

"I am sure I don't want anything to do with you or the Bureau after tonight. You must be trying to get me killed," Vitani snapped.

"I'm trying to save you!"

"I don't need to be saved, I need you all to leave me alone!"

Lex excused himself as Jen came over, he seemed upset. She was looking gorgeous in a hunter green one shoulder gown with a high split and a mermaid train that made her dress a little longer than mine and Vitani's. Jen's hair was also green, but a lighter shade than her dress. I swore any color she wore looked good on her.

"Hey girl, look at you!" I gushed.

"Oh stop, look at y'all. Not that we all have on similar dresses without even coordinating, in this bitch looking like Destiny's Child," Jen laughed.

"We really do! I wasn't gonna say anything, but we all look fly as hell, like we looking for a soldier," Vitani added.

"You better keep your head low. From what I hear you have the commander, damn a soldier," Jen teased Vitani. My sis started blushing and we hadn't even said God's name. *What is he doing to her?* The announcement was made for everyone to have a seat for dinner to be served. We discovered Jen was sitting at our table and Lex had returned with glasses of Champagne for us. He looked good, but there was something about him that I didn't like.

"What do you think about Lex?" Vitani whispered.

I smiled because I was just thinking about the same thing, "I don't like him."

She smirked at me. "Stop comparing him to Godrique and give him a chance."

"Bitch, I wish I would. You can't even do that or you wouldn't have brought my brother up."

"Brother? Since when?"

"Since he sent me that new desk after I caught y'all fucking on mine."

Vitani's face scrunched before she laughed out loud, causing people to look our way. Jen was on the other side of Lex so she couldn't hear, but she gave us a knowing smile. "You're so materialistic, that's all it takes for you to switch sides?"

"That's all it took for you to fall in love?"

"Touché bitch. Touché. Godrique is so different from any man I've ever encountered, I couldn't help but fall in love. I feel so bad about getting involved with the Feds." Vitani bit her lip nervously.

"Did you tell him?"

"Hell no! He would probably kill me. Plus, I don't see a point when after tonight all of this will be over with."

"Wrong. After tonight you will no longer be involved, but it is far from over," I chided. *Why is Vitani being so naïve?* The food was served and I was in heaven. They gave us filet mignon and chicken marsala with mushroom, rice pilaf, and asparagus. The table grew silent as everyone started eating and enjoying the food. I noticed Vitani take two bites then push her plate to the side. She hadn't touched the champagne, either. "Are you okay?" I asked because her ass could eat if she didn't do anything else.

"Yes, just don't want to chance getting sick. Lately I have been feeling off, but I got my period a few weeks ago so I can't be pregnant," she concluded.

"Sorry to burst your bubble but that could be implantation bleeding, or it could be like what happened with my mom. She was pregnant and still got her period for six months."

"Please don't say that," she groaned. "I'll take a test when we leave here."

"Dammmn," I smiled when Teqwyn and Simon strolled into the event looking fine as shit. I licked my lips and noticed Jen did the same. Her ass could act like Simon didn't affect her all she wanted, I knew the truth. Teqwyn suddenly turned and flashed a killer smile my way, sucking the air from my lungs. Suddenly feeling famished, I picked up my glass and downed my champagne while still holding his gaze. He winked at me and I felt faint. *What the hell is he doing to me? I need to get it together.* I nudged Vitani and nodded in their direction, then watched as the color drained from her face.

"Oh shit, I have to go to the restroom," she leaned towards Lex and said. "Please excuse us for a moment."

Jen stood to "escort" us to the restroom that was on the opposite side of the venue from where Teq and Simon were. The restroom looked like a family restroom because there was a baby changing table and a diaper genie in the corner. "If Simon and Teq are here then God is coming, too!" Vitani panicked.

"That is not what that means. Wouldn't they all come together?" I reasoned as I watched her pace back and forth.

"No! Remember the first time we met them, Godrique showed up later."

"You told me he said he wasn't going to come and changed his mind at the last minute. Calm down, he more than likely won't come tonight. You can say you were here with Jen if Teqwyn or Simon tells him they saw you," I forced a smile. *Hell, I was just as nervous as she was.*

"They will tell him and I am gonna be dead. You two don't know Godrique like I do. He takes loyalty serious," she cracked the restroom door and looked out, then closed and locked it again.

"V, I got you if some shit pop off. I won't let him hurt you," Jen assured.

"And what the fuck is you doing? Pacing and opening doors and shit, you tripping, sis. God ain't gonna hurt you," I frowned at how freaked out she was.

"Shhhhhh!" She said her eyes bugged out of her head at me. "Don't use God's name in vain like that. He'll come down and smite thee for that shit."

I had to laugh because this girl had the fear of God in her, and it seemed like he'd smitten her already. I ain't know what kinda lightning bolt he had in his pants, but it had my friend over here spazzing.

"Did he beat something other than your pussy up?" I had to ask to be sure that she was just dick crazy and nothing else. "'Cause I'll kill his ass on-sight if that's the case."

"No. But do you hear yourself? You'll kill who? Matter of fact, do you two hear yourselves?! This is God we're talking about. Not to mention all of The Disciples. Y'all are mere mortals and are no match for them. I have to go! We have to get out of here before he shows up," she moved to open the door again.

"Okay, this is what we'll do," I stood in front of the door. "You go out there and give Lex a dance and while y'all are dancing, fake sick, then say you need to get home. I will go talk to Teqwyn to find out if God is coming tonight, Jen you do the same with Simon," I schemed.

"Okay, I can do that." her hands were visibly trembling.

"I can't. Why do I have to talk to Simon?!" Jen whined.

I didn't even answer her ass 'cause she knew she wanted to get close to him. We all left the restroom determined, Vitani made her way towards Lex as Jen and I made our move.

Chapter Eighteen

TEQ

Rae made her way towards me and I knew she was nervous by the way her brow furrowed. The dress she was wearing fit her curves just right and I felt like I was entranced by fire. The closer she got, the longer the split crept up her thick thigh. Simon and I came here before God to scope shit out because of the information God just received from his mother. Honestly, I knew about Vitani being hired by the Feds when she first started, but she never gave them too much, so really she was doing us a favor by keeping them at bay until we figured out how to handle Bart's ass. God had suspected him of doing shady shit behind our backs, so he sent me to get more intel. Bart's obsession with Vitani kept him distracted enough for me to not raise any suspicions with him. Him leaving was no surprise to me. It allowed me to fix the company without someone breathing down my neck.

"Rae, I didn't expect to see you here. But I'm glad I did, because you are beautiful, as usual."

"Teqwyn, I didn't expect to see you here, either. You're looking handsome, as usual," she blushed.

"I guess I'm chop suey," Simon chuckled from my side.

"You and me both," Jen added causing Simon to frown.

"Well, you might be," Simon jabbed. I elbowed him.

"I think you clean up quite well, Simon Grey."

Simon flashed a dimpled smile. "Chop suey is suddenly starting to look like a green goddess," he licked his lip as I spoke to Jen. "What brings you ladies here?" Simon quizzed.

"I am here on business, Vitani and Rae are my guests," Jen lied with ease, but Simon's eye twitched. That let me know that he didn't believe her. Simon didn't know what God and I knew about Vitani and Rae. God had just found out tonight when his mom called telling him Vitani was working for the Feds against him. How the hell she found out is what I would like to know.

"Is God coming tonight?" Rae asked casually. Simon's eye twitched again.

"Naw, he had some things to handle. Teq is here with me because of my business with the governor," Simon told a half-truth. Jen's brow raised slightly at the mention of the governor. *Wonder what that's about.*

"You have business with the governor? You must be special."

"I can show you how special I am, just give me one night, Jenisis," Simon smiled.

"I'll think about it. I hope you guys enjoy your night." Jen grabbed Rae's arm to walk away just as God walked up with John. Rae looked like she had seen a ghost, but Jen kept her composure. "God, I thought you weren't attending this event," Jen spoke looking around the room. Rae was scoping the place as well causing me to follow her line of sight. Vitani was dancing with none other than the Head of the Bureau. *Damn, son about to pop off.*

"Jen. Rae. Where is my wife?"

"Uh...uhmm...she...she's around here somewhere," Rae stuttered.

"Let me holla at you, God," I attempted to diffuse. That shit didn't work, he immediately searched the room for Vitani. His jaw tightened when his eyes landed on her. I stepped in front of him. "Don't do something that will draw attention that we don't need right now."

"Teq. Get the fuck out my face," he seethed through clenched teeth.

"Bro, just take a breather and let me escort her to you," Simon reasoned.

God didn't even respond as he moved past both of us heading in Vitani's direction. Her back was to him so she didn't even know what was coming. Jen jumped in front of God and got him to slow down a bit, but he lifted her and moved her out of the way as if she weighed nothing. Simon, John, and I were close behind, not knowing what the fuck to expect. I'd never seen him this upset before about a woman. Surprisingly, Rae didn't seem scared for her girl because she was smiling.

"You're not gonna warn your girl? Yell across the room...nothing?" I asked.

"Hell no, this needs to happen. They need to get their shit together and out in the open so they can be happy together."

"What about you? Are you going to air your shit out, too?"

She stopped walking. "I never wanted to keep things from you. I will tell you everything, I promise."

I smiled at the sincerity in her voice. We caught back up with them just as God grabbed Vitani by the back of her neck.

"Oh shit," Rae murmured.

"Hey wifey, once again you take me for a fucking joke," God spoke just before he pushed her head down and dragged her towards the exit. I could tell she wasn't hurt, he was basically guiding her like a mother would do a bad ass child. The guy she was dancing with went to reach for his gun and Simon stepped in his face shaking his head from side-to-side. Recognition shined in his eyes.

"Oh my God! I thought this was a private event. Who let the thugs in here?!" A random white woman yelled.

"Someone call the police! He's kidnapping her," another white woman yelled.

Jen ran behind them, I'm guessing to attempt to follow God, but Simon grabbed her arm and they disappeared into a hallway. John walked away as if nothing had happened.

As John walked past a woman he smiled and shook his dreads, causing her to scream, "They let the thugs in here to rob us!"

Rae touched my arm saying, "Can you give me a ride home?"

I nodded yes, but first I needed to wipe the security cameras. The Fed that Vitani was dancing with stood in the same spot with a look of hatred on his face. He was gonna be a problem. What also caught my attention was Anita standing with her phone out and a smirk on her face. Rae noticed her as well and rolled her eyes.

GOD

I drove through the city of Lakeland with murder on my mind. The women in my life had all been working my nerves. My mom thought I was stupid, I knew where she got her information from and I ain't with that messy shit. Her disdain for Vitani should not outweigh her common sense. I decided to take Vitani to my house in Plant City because I was not fucking with Grady. Vitani didn't even flinch when I touched her, almost like she knew I was coming. *If she knew I was coming, why the fuck did she try me?* She hadn't even put up a fight when I put her ass in my trunk, it lowkey turned me on because she ain't no punk. She already knew there wasn't a point in begging for her life. *If I wanted it, I'll take it...simple.* I loved my baby for being a gangsta, but I hated that it had to come to this.

Pulling up to one of my cribs in boonies, near an old winery I reached down and popped the trunk from inside the car. She had nowhere to run even if she tried. When I walked around, she was standing outside of the trunk, rubbing her shaky hands up and down her arms. I realized it was a bit nippy out tonight and pulled my suit jacket off to wrap around her. Her eyes met mine and I broke contact because all it did was further piss me off. *Why did she have to ruin our lives?*

"Walk," I snapped.

She did as instructed and paused for me to unlock the door. Then, I grabbed her arm and led her to the room at the back of the house. This house was built like a cabin and I loved the privacy it provided for moments like this. I made the chicks that came out here sign NDAs because I wanted to keep it confidential. They had never been to the back room, though. I was saving it for my wife. *Hell, I might as well use it to kill her trifling ass since there will never be anyone else who makes me feel the way she does.*

"Take your clothes off." I purposely left the light off so she wouldn't try to run before I could tie her up.

I sent a quick text to The Disciples, then Teq, letting them know to meet me here in 30 minutes. Their lives were put on the line by Vitani's actions too, so they could decide her fate.

"Are you completely undressed?"

"Yes."

I walked over to her and rubbed my hands along every part of her body. I pinched a nipple and massaged her soft ass. She moaned and that snapped me back to reality.

"I had to make sure your trifling ass ain't got no wire."

I walked out of the room to pull myself together and grab a t-shirt for her to put on. When I returned, I put the t-shirt over her head, backed her up, and lifted her up to wrap her legs around my waist. I raised her arms above her head, secured them, and then did the same with her legs. I unbuttoned my white shirt, placed my Alpha and Omega mask over my face, and turned on the red lights.

"I trusted you, Vitani. I love you and our daughter, but you betrayed my brothers and me."

"Godriq—"

"Don't use my name, you can call me God like every other trifling bitch in my life." I winced when tears cascaded down her face. "Fuck is you crying for? I'm the one that got played," I snapped.

"I never meant to hurt you or our brothers," Vitani cried.

"They are no longer your brothers. You made sure of that, rat. I see why your name translates to demon of war, you're a fucking Trojan horse. Did the feds teach you how to suck dick like that?" She flinched at my words but didn't respond.

I heard movement and knew my brothers were here. What I didn't expect was for Rae to walk in with Teq. "What the fuck, Teq?" I snapped.

"Chill bro, she was already in the car with me."

"Damnn Vitani, you look real comfortable up there on that cross," Rae turned to look at Teq, "Teqwyn do you have one, too?" She smiled before licking her lips.

These women are out of control. Simon walked in the room with a Styrofoam plate full of food, smacking. "Bro, what the fuck? Where you even get that from?"

"Violet fixed it for me, since your dumb ass ain't give me time to eat before you pulled that dumb shit." He looked up at Vitani on the St. Andrew's cross and said, "I knew your ass was into that kinky shit...but why the fuck are we here? Oh, hey sis, sorry he's on some weird shit today."

I shook my head in frustration just as John, Peter, and Meesha walked in. "Si, who the fuck is Violet?"

"Granny," he shrugged as if I should know that. This dumb ass went by Vitani's mother house before coming over here, knowing damn well what I planned to do. Then Teq's stupid ass brought a witness. *These niggas get on my nerves.*

"Vitani, when you started working for the Feds did you know God was a part of the company?" Meesha asked.

"No, I swear I did it because they offered me money and a job to take care of my daughter."

"Our daughter," I corrected. *I could see why the Feds would send her in to investigate, since Bart's slow ass was laundering money through the company. But that doesn't justify her keeping secrets from me after we made things official. I even gave her a ring!*

"Did you actively pursue God knowing who he was?" Meesha continued.

"No, I didn't know he was involved in the company when I... we uh... when we met."

"You did find out before I told you the other night at the restaurant. So why did you play stupid instead of being honest?" I asked.

"Then what? What would happen if I was honest? I would be in the same place I'm in now. Hell at least there were witnesses tonight if I come up missing."

I slowly walked up to her and wrapped my hands around her neck. "The only thing a witness can do is end up six feet under with you," I warned, then released her neck as she gasped for air and cried harder.

"I didn't mean to hurt you...any of you. I was thinking about my daughter and once I found out about the investigation into all of y'all, I told them to count me out. The only reason I was there tonight is because Lex basically blackmailed me into going with him."

Blackmailed? So, he decided to fuck with my wife instead of coming for me himself. That's some pussy shit and he will pay for that. "Why didn't you tell me you were going to the ball tonight?"

"Would you have let me go? I'd probably be tied up at home screaming mercy. I know you, Godrique."

"I don't fucking know you! That's the problem," I boomed. *Calm down nigga, you're showing your emotions. She needs to know you're serious.*

"On that note, I will catch you all later. As your lawyer I advise you not to kill her. As your sister, I advise you two to talk it out like adults. I think she's telling the truth," Meesha patted my shoulder and walked out.

"Yea bruh bruh, she seems like she's telling the truth. I don't want any parts in this. Lil' sis, stay up, this nigga all bark and no bite when it comes to you," John flashed his golds and left.

"I hope you know what you're doing, bro, you're already in the hot seat," Peter walked out shaking his head. *The fuck this nigga say that for? He acting like the police...oh he is.*

"I could've stayed with Violet for this shit. Got my sister up there half naked and shit, nobody wanna see that," Simon walked out, still stuffing his face.

"Yo' don't do anything I wouldn't do. You know how to reach me, I gotta get Rae home," Teq headed out.

"Vitani your ass better call me in the morning to let me know how this turned out. I'm jealous, bitch! Remember how we used to fantasize about getting kidnapped? Now your ass out here playing with God, you know he's a jealous God!" Rae laughed as she followed Teq out the door.

I had a damn headache fucking around with them, but I'm glad they came because it gave Vitani a chance to explain herself before I put a bullet in her head. To know that she wanted out a while ago but they wouldn't let her live, fucked my head up. *They put my baby life in danger over some bullshit.* I was about to pull my mask off, but I remembered what Rae said. *She wanted to be kidnapped, huh?* I was gonna give her exactly what she thought she wanted plus more. By the end of the night, she would know not to play with GOD.

Chapter Nineteen

VITANI

I looked around at my surroundings. I quickly took everything in and the room I was in was one I had never seen before. He dimmed the lights before he made his way back over toward me. I sucked in a breath as God wasted no time ripping his shirt off my body. His dick was hard as fuck, but I could feel the waves of anger coming off of him. He was going to be petty, and I knew it. I was fully naked from head-to-toe, my arms and legs stretched outward. He moved out of my line of sight, making me wonder what he was up to. He was way too quiet and that was never good when it came to him. *Now that Rae ran her mouth, I have no idea what was about to happen.*

I thought me and Godrique were okay after he had me questioned in front of everyone. He had to know that I didn't intentionally keep it from him because I got out once I found out what they wanted from me. Now, he knew the entire truth about everything. *So why—*

I caught a movement out of the corner of my eye, and I realized it was Godrique. He made long strides until he was standing in front of me. I swallowed my nervousness as he towered over me, his eyes expressionless as he watched me.

God's face was unreadable and cold. He was still in his expensive, tailored suit, but missing the jacket. His dress shirt was unbuttoned, giving me a view of smooth dark brown skin I wanted to touch. I secretly loved admiring him in a suit, but now wasn't the time. I had to make sure I was paying attention because the look in his eyes told me I was about to feel God's wrath. *I can't wait.*

He stepped closer and dread along with pleasure filled me as his eyes roamed over me. His sensual and soft mouth, which had given me multiple orgasm before, was now set into a hard line. I could feel the cold rage rolling off him even after he got the truth. Both of us refused to break eye contact, and since he wouldn't speak, I decided to fill in the silence.

"Now what?" I asked, my voice sounding croaky and hoarse. "What are you—"

"You're not the one that gets to ask questions today."

I flinched at his harsh tone and how cold he looked. I'd never really seen him like this when he was with me. It dawned on me that the man in front of me was no longer my Godrique but the most feared man in the city. *GOD.* It didn't matter what the others had to say about this situation. He wasn't going to forgive me until he was ready.

"You know," he drawled out softly. "I knew there was a little snitch inside my circle. I didn't want to believe you of all people were one of them," he sardonically murmured, shaking his head. "I guess I was just too blind to see it."

"I—"

"You should have told me, Vitani. Don't you think so?"

I nodded. "Yes." However, he knows that already. *Doesn't he?*

It dawned on me what was happening, and my core clenched painfully in knowing what he would give me. Maybe Rae running her mouth might work in my favor. The smell of Hennessy hit me, and I couldn't fight the frown on my face as I assessed his features. After he finished off his drink, I watched as he poured another before he pulled his mask back down. I still wasn't sure if he forgave me or if he really was going to kill me.

His eyes were shimmering, telling me to trust him and to give in to whatever he wanted to do at that moment. Either he was going to believe me or naw. *What he WILL DO is let me off this damn cross!* I knew he could make every one of my fantasies come true if I just let him ride this thing out.

"Jack's dead."

"What? What did you just say?" I asked. I snapped my head up to glare at him, only to be caught in a gaze cold as ice. I was done playing with him because this was not funny anymore. "Godrique!"

"Why you mad? I thought you didn't give a fuck about him?" *He is crazy as hell.*

"I don't, but he is still my daughter's father! Get me off this thing," I gritted.

"You funny."

"You said that you wouldn't–"

"You think I killed him?"

"I–I didn't say that you killed him, but what am I supposed to think right now? I need–"

"I don't know why you acting like that nigga ain't a sperm donor. Ice is my daughter and right now you seem more worried about what that dumbass nigga got himself into instead of your own shit," he grunted.

He took a step toward the table and picked up his glass. He raised his mask again never taking his eyes from mine and took a drink. I swallowed my reply because he wanted me to argue with him and I refused. God put the empty glass back on the table and pulled his mask back down.

I was not afraid of God, but his *retribution* was a different story.

"Is Rae right, Vitani?"

"N-no," I whispered breathlessly. My mind was all over the place. The news about Jack and the position God had me in was all too much. He trailed his finger over my body, making me shiver. *What the hell is wrong with me?*

"Oh, so you still lying? I know your ass is lying by how wet you are right now. You like this shit," he answered, his voice dangerously low. He twisted my nipple hard before pinching it at my answer.

"Ahh, shit," I hissed. He was right though, because I was wet as hell. It was something about the way that he watched me. I was becoming hyper-aware of his every touch, more addicted to this high. I fought hard on the restraints, but it was useless. He reached over to the end of the table next to the St. Andrew's cross, and I felt cold from the loss of his touch.

I craved it, even though I shouldn't. Then, my eyes widened when I saw he had taken out a nipple clamp with the chains connecting the two. I fought on the restraints, and I could only cry out as he fastened them on my nipples. It was a mix between pleasure and pure pain at how hard I was.

"What the hell are you doing?"

He didn't wait before tugging on the chain connecting the two clamps, sending electricity into the tip of my puckered nipples. The movement was firm and fast, making my already heavy breasts turn even more swollen. He continued to toy with my nipples through the clamps as he resumed his interrogation, which I would willingly give.

"God...Godrique," I choked out weakly. "P-please..."

"I can feel just how wet you are, even smell your arousal," he snarled darkly. After what seemed like forever, I felt him pushing a middle finger against the opening of my pussy. He doesn't penetrate me but ran the tip of his finger up and down my slit.

Against my shaved skin, I was much more aware of his touch. I can feel the moisture slicken the outer walls of my opening with my own arousal. He was using my own body against me, and I knew how much easier it would have been if I had just caved. The need to cum was so powerful, it was smothering me.

"Hurry up," I whimper.

He chuckled. "Is there something you want, love?"

"You," I gasped, spreading my legs wider still. "You, please."

I gasped when he pulled hard on both my nipple clamps as satisfaction bled through his expression. He was happy I had this reaction, that he had this huge effect on me. "What's the matter, Vitani? Are you turned on by shit like this? You fantasize about shit like this? You want to cum, don't you?"

All I could do was nod feverishly. I was dripping so much, his hand was covered in my wetness. He pressed the pad of his thumb on my clit, but not hard enough for me to cum. No, he massaged it in a slow circular motion and then smacked my breasts hard. It bounced, and a gush of liquid heat spilled from my body and coated his fingers even further.

"So fucking sensitive, wifey," he praised, his eyes widening as his pupil dilated. "You like that. You like that edge of pain and pleasure. Do you know why? Because I *trained* your body to enjoy it."

My lips parted, yet no sound tumbled from my mouth. My pleasure gives him power and he gets drunk off of it. Much like his dominating nature. He finally entered his fingers into my tight entrance and curled it to hit my sweet spot, but it wasn't hard enough where I could get off.

"Ah," I cried out, arching my back off the St. Andrew's cross to the best of my abilities as he continued to finger me. "Please."

He didn't say anything as he curled his finger inside me and mercilessly pressed at my g-spot. His thumb continued to tease at my throbbing and twitching clit. He hit my breasts, making me moan as I became more sensitive to the clamp on my nipples.

It was too much...yet also not enough.

Suddenly, I felt him withdrawing his hand that was on my breast and swipe at my wetness. I whimpered, closing my eyes as I shamelessly ground onto his hand to the best of my abilities before I felt his one finger probing at my puckered opening. I stilled suddenly, my whole body frozen.

"Relax," he hissed, "or I'll accidentally put it in your ass."

I wasn't sure why, but I felt my inner walls tighten up around his two fingers even more at his words, and he let out a string of curses. "Fuck, you tightened like you *want* it, but your sexy ass ain't ready for no anal," he chuckled.

He was most definitely right, but the thought still turned me on.

"I want to cum," I cried out softly.

I soon realized this wasn't about reward but *submission,* of pleasured pain, of denial for what I had done.

He lowered his mouth to add another element to his torture. As he got down on his knees, he sucked on my clit, which was swollen and hot. He continued his torment of interrogation, always bringing me near the edge before stopping and starting again. I was beginning to grow delirious myself from his rough treatment. My release seemed like it was never going to happen at this point as I took what he was giving me.

He alternated skillfully between spanking down onto my pussy and making me count. My head was pounding with need and driving me wilder. I don't even know if I counted right as he continued playing with my body like a puppet. I tried to fight the sensual pain and pleasure and the rising need to cum each time. I was sure I was soaking the floor with my juices as he penetrated me with his fingers. My arms and legs felt like gelatin as I stopped struggling against the restraints.

"Please," I whimpered. "Please, *God.*"

He chuckled darkly before he withdrew his hand from my heat. He shifted till I could see his face clear as he brought his drenched hand to my face. It was shimmering, coated in so much wetness as he carried it to my parted lips.

"Open wider," he demanded. "Stick out your tongue."

I did as I was told and he placed his fingers on my tongue. The burst of my own essence filled my mouth as I stared at him.

"Suck your juices off my fingers," he growled, and I quickly began to clean my arousal off his fingers. It was so dirty, lapsing up my own juices, and yet I couldn't stop. Not when he was praising me for it. "Such a good wifey. You better clean it thoroughly. Tell me, do you like how you taste?"

I could only nod as I continued my task at hand. We stared at one another, and I could see the furious look in his eyes. Even when Godrique was mad, he was sexy as hell. And despite everything, I still wanted him. I had fallen for him along the way, and nothing would change it. His scent was everywhere, clean and inviting, with a hint of Hennessy.

"Did you know they wanted to investigate me, too? Is that why you fucked me that night?" he questioned darkly once I finished lapsing my own essence up from his fingers. Quickly, I shook my head from side-to-side, because he knew the truth. Still, I couldn't help but answer.

"No, never. I was doing what was asked of me from the beginning and that was to look into the laundering. As soon as they asked anything about you or my brothers, I told them nothing. I told them that I was out and I didn't want anything to do with any of that."

He stared at me, his hand still wrapped around my throat. He looked unconvinced and still angry as he gave me a dark smile. He thrust two fingers into me unexpectedly and curled at my g-spot. He continued thrusting hard and fast as he murmured, "Then why were you dancing with him? Answer honestly, and maybe I'll let you cum."

"I told you! He blackmailed me to go to the stupid ball. While there, I told him that I wanted nothing to do with whatever he had going on," I whimpered, trying to meet his thrust as I raised my body off the cross I was tied to. "I would not betray you."

"That's right, you know better."

I meekly nodded. "Yes."

He let go of my neck to slap two fingers onto my clit. Then, I became undone like a rocket. The orgasm hit me so hard that I was sure I almost blacked out from how powerful it was.

I was still cumming, trying to catch my breath, when I watched whatever control he had slip from his face. He got up, and I could barely open my eyes as I heard him unbuckling his belt and the zipper opening. I was so turned on and I felt like I needed to cum with him to be satisfied.

I watched him quickly strip off his clothes, his dick so hard that it curled upwards to his stomach. It was swollen and the veins popped out, making my mouth water. His dark chocolate brown skin was already glistening with sweat. Pre-cum dripped from the head and I knew that he would make sure I wasn't able to even stand tomorrow.

I watched him stalk back towards me, aligning the head of his dick with my tight entrance once he lowered the cross low enough. He licked my neck, his tongue snaking out, making a trail to my earlobe before biting it. Even though I anticipated the penetration, he grabbed me by the thighs and pushed himself fully into me, making me moan.

"Oh God," I groaned.

No amount of wetness or preparation was enough for me to take his girth and length so quickly. It burned in a good way as he pulled all the way out of me and speared into me again, making my back arch. A forced choked cry escaped my throat. All I could do was whimper at how full I felt when suddenly he bit down onto my neck. I knew I had climaxed again, and the smirk on his face told me he knew, too.

"That's right, fuck me, wifey," he hissed before lapsing into the crook of my neck again.

"Please...please, God...."

I tried to struggle around the ropes tying me down to the large cross, while another part of me felt nothing but pure ecstasy of being held down, at his every mercy, to do whatever he wanted. He didn't wait for me to adjust as he thrust into me hard, deep, and fast, relentlessly. His powerful and muscled body was glistening with sweat as he moved, his eyes piercing into my soul.

"Vitani," he seethed. One of his hands again found its way around my throat.

He thrust into me like he was trying to remind me who I belonged to. Yet, I didn't need the reminder. He owned my body, mind, and heart without even trying, especially by the way he was pounding into me. Paired with the clamps on my nipples, I was so close. One more thrust, and I'd become undone again. I just needed—

Suddenly, he stopped thrusting, and my eyes enlarged in horror as he pulled out of me. I felt so empty that it hurt.

"No, please," I moaned. "Don't stop."

"It's called edging. You push me to the damn edge, so it's your turn. And we're going to do this all fucking night if we have to and what did I tell you about that stop shit?" He growled out, pushing back into me, but it wasn't like before. It was so slow, I was in pain. He pulled at the chains of the nipple clamps and my back arched in response to him. "I'll break you. I'll ruin you so your body won't even cum for anyone else, but me. Now, who owns you again?"

"God, oh... *Godrique*."

I was rewarded with two spanks on my clit as he rammed all the way in me. I was so full, so painfully stretched to take him as he cursed. "You always loved being taken by a God like me. Look at you, panting for this dick like you need it."

"Please," I choked out as he made teasing small circular motions on my clit. "Please, just let me cum!"

He started to lick my throat almost hungrily, sucking gently as he finally started to thrust madly back into me. "You keeping anything else from me?"

I shook my head quickly. "No." I moaned. My mind was everywhere, but I couldn't concentrate on anything but cumming.

"You're not lying to me, are you?" he hissed, his eyes finding mine. "Don't ever keep shit from me again, Vitani."

"No, I won't. Just, please, God!" I cried out, eagerly meeting his thrust with my own.

"Good, because if you do, I will kill everybody involved. My wife doesn't keep shit from me," he groaned out. I knew I should be fearful, especially since he said he was willing to murder me and everybody else, yet I grew even wetter. "Say it. Say you belong to me."

"Yours," I gasped out. "Yours. I belong to God."

"You're mine to touch, mine to fuck, and don't you forget it."

He was crazy as shit, but something inside me loved it, and I didn't want him to stop saying it. *Am I just as crazy as God?*

"Yes," I nodded enthusiastically. It wasn't a lie either, and I gulped when I saw his eyes were now darkened. He wrapped his hands around my throat and squeezed tightly, making me dizzy momentarily as he stared into my eyes.

I whimpered, closing my eyes as the pleasure took over me, but was lightly slapped on my face. I could barely open my eyes, but I pried them open enough to stare into his near-black ones.

"Look at me."

I forced my eyes to open wider and stared into his eyes, a window to his soul, momentarily before he pulled me in for a kiss. Unlike before, I felt my body tense, slowly dissolving at his loving nature. I wished I wasn't bound so I could run my fingers over his body, because he belonged to me as well.

At the sound of his name slipping out of my mouth, he started to madly pound into me with such force that the cross creaked under us. The light fixture shook from the way he used my body to bring us both over the edge. I whimpered against his hold, thrashing my head to the best of my abilities as his pelvic bone rubbed onto my clit with his every hard thrust. His slick, wet chest rubbed onto me, causing the friction to build deliciously fast, and I needed to cum more than anything else.

"Dear God," I gasped loudly. "Please!"

"Cum now," he demanded and gripped harder onto my throat, cutting off my breathing altogether. It was the push I needed to cum, it had me gripping him like a vice.

"Fuck, Vitani. Fuck," he growled, releasing so much into me that it ran down my thighs, our cum mixing together.

I could feel his dick still pulsating inside me, his cum filling me to the brim. I never felt so connected to him than in that moment. I felt lightheaded and sated. I barely noticed my arms and legs being untied. I felt myself being lifted and carried, but I could barely keep my eyes open. The next thing I knew, I felt cool sheets and warmth as God pulled me tighter to him and covered us with the comforter. I blinked as he rolled me onto my back, waking me up slightly. I was sore everywhere and had a little pain where I was tied down, but I was not about to complain.

He held himself up by his arms as we lay next to one another, catching our breath. For the first time, I didn't feel guilty. I felt peaceful being next to him after confessing everything to him. God rubbed my wrists until the pain resided. He picked me up and settled me on his chest. His arms wrapped around me so I couldn't go anywhere. I wasn't even about to try at this point. I looked up at him and we stared at each other before he smirked.

"When we get up, you will put my ring back on your finger and never take it off again."

I knew at that moment that we'd be okay.

Chapter Twenty

GOD

I woke up to an insistent ringing that was about to piss me the fuck off. After the night I had with my wife, I just wanted to relax today. Maybe go to the park or some shit and have a family day. But whoever was calling would not give up. I looked at my phone to see that it was Black. He and Turk went to what was supposed to have been the final meeting last night to wrap shit up. "What's up?" I spoke groggily.

"God! I have been trying to call you since three in the damn morning. Turk got shot—"

My heart dropped to my stomach. *I can't have heard him right.*

"Don't fucking play with me lil' nigga, I don't do that prank shit," I barked into the phone, causing Vitani to jump from her place beside me.

"NIGGA, ain't nobody playing on your phone. My mans got hit last night and we're at Lakeland Regional. He's still in surgery."

I looked down at my phone as if it were a foreign object and saw that it was now seven in the morning. Vitani and I had woke back up and fucked some more before dozing off again around five, so I knew my wifey was tired. Yet, she was up putting on some of my baggy clothes.

"Godrique, why are you sitting there? Let's go!" Vitani yelled.

I was stuck as a world of emotions crashed into me like a derailed train. My brother, my friend, had been shot while I was more worried about Vitani's betrayal. *If only I had stayed my ass home. This shit just can't be real.* I looked at Vitani but no words came from my mouth as my heart pounded loudly in my ears and my chest caved in. My mouth opened, but nothing would come out. Vitani ran over to me and straddled me pulling me into a warm hug. I let my forehead rest on hers as tears leaked from my eyes like a burst pipe. My wife pried my phone from my hand and told Black we would be there and to call if there were any updates.

"Godrique, my love, you are allowed to cry. You are allowed to feel pain. But you are not allowed to blame yourself for something you can't control. I can see the guilt written all over your face. I am here for you, but you need to be there for our goddaughter."

She kissed my forehead further making me feel like a lil' bitch. *She's right though, I need to focus on my goddaughter for now.*

"Thank you, wifey."

I tried to smile but it didn't work. My wife climbed off of me, went to the restroom, and then brought back a warm rag to wipe my face and a toothbrush with a small cup to spit in. *Damn, I love this woman.* She picked out some sweats and a t-shirt for me to throw on, then we headed out, not having time to shower. I popped my trunk and grabbed her purse, which was still back from last night, then got in the passenger seat since she had walked to the driver's side.

We made it to the hospital in less than twenty minutes, taking frontage to HWY 92 E, and I almost laughed at Vitani gagging as we walked into the hospital. We went to the desk but Black waved for us to follow him up to the Neurology floor. *Neuro? Did my brother get shot in the head?*

When we made it to the empty waiting area I asked, "What the fuck happened?"

"Goddy!"

I turned around to see Alianna standing there with Teq, Simon, and John. I held out my arms for my goddaughter to run into them as a piercing scream filled the room. She was now shaking as tears lined her face. I hugged her tighter, not knowing what to say that would make her feel better. I knew this was a possibility with the line of work he was into, but that doesn't mean I was prepared. I was his medical proxy until Alianna turned eighteen and I was afraid of the decision I might have to make. Turk always said he doesn't want to be hooked up to any machines, but standing here hugging my goddaughter, I knew I couldn't make that kind of decision in my current state of mind.

"I knew something was wrong Goddy, I felt it. People think I'm crazy when I get strong vibes or weird feelings out of nowhere. I knew it, Goddy! I begged him to take me to the movies instead."

"I'm sorry, baby girl, but you and I both know once your father makes his mind up, it's hard to change it," I spoke softly. Vitani walked over and hugged both of us, then Alianna removed her arms from around me and wrapped them around Vitani as they both cried. I took that moment to step outside of the waiting area for a minute. Seeing my goddaughter like that ripped at my soul. The guys followed me out.

"How did y'all know what happened?" I asked curiously

"Nigga, you texted us to pick Ali up and meet you here," John said with raised brows.

My wife must've texted them in the groupchat on my phone. I was glad she did because I need them now more than ever.

"Teq, I know you don't know me like that but Turk told me about your skills. I managed to snatch the video from the convenience store where shit went down," Black spoke, pulling some sort of memory device out of his jacket pocket.

"Wait? Y'all never made it to the meeting," I questioned.

"No. We stopped by the store because Turk had to take a leak. I decided to go in and try to piss too since we would be at a location that was not ours. As I was taking a leak, I heard three gunshots and hurried up to run out and see my mans on the ground bleeding from his hands, chest, and feet. When I got closer, I noticed he was also bleeding from his head. The ambulance came and I rode with him, leaving the car and the work in it. Oh shit!" he said if it had just dawned on him that he could get in serious trouble for drug trafficking.

"Calm down. Give me the name of the store and the street name, I'll handle the rest," Teq chimed. Black did as he was told and handed Teq the memory drive just before Teq headed to the parking garage to work in his car. Hopefully he had brought his van with all of his things, it reminded me of the vans the CIA be using in movies and shit.

"God, he was shot in all the places Jesus was nailed in on the cross," Black solemnly spoke.

This meant it had nothing to do with Turk and everything to do with me. My brother was shot because someone was gunning for me. I nodded and turned to walk back into the waiting area when I heard a male voice. *This shit just keeps getting worse.*

"Family of Tevin Matthews?"

"Yes, how is my dad?" Alianna asked.

"Your father is a fighter. He sustained five gunshot wounds that proved to be non-threatening in both arms and feet. The fifth was in his chest, but that went through and through with hardly any dama—"

"Oh my gosh! Thank goodness! Can we go see him?" Alianna cut the doctor off.

"Well, the gunshot wounds were not fatal. However, when he was shot, he fell and hit the ground hard causing his brain to bleed and swell from the trauma. I am sorry, but your father is in a coma and I do not know if he will ever wake up. If he does wake from the coma, he may never be the same."

Alianna's head snapped around to look at Black with a death glare just before she ran up on him swinging. "This is all your fault! You should have been there to catch him!"

Surprisingly, he didn't react how most young dudes his age would have. He let her hit his chest a few times before grabbing her arms and whispering something nobody else could hear. I cocked my head to the side because I knew damn well he wasn't trying to smooth talk my goddaughter.

"Sorry, I was acting out of anger." She snatched away from him then turned to the doctor saying, "May I please see my dad?"

"Yes, but only one visitor at a time, per recovery room protocol."

As soon as Alianna followed the doctor out of the waiting area I strolled over to sit next to Vitani, who stood and sat on my lap.

"I'm glad to see you're still alive, sis," Simon smirked.

Vitani smiled at him but didn't respond. She started rubbing my head and my eyes felt crossed like a knot by how good it felt. I felt more relaxed despite the present situation. My eyes felt heavy so I moved my head away before I dozed off.

"God, I came to check on you. The whole hood has been talking about what happened with Turk. Are you oka—" LiLi paused, looking at Vitani saying, "You can leave now. I got my baby's father. He needs a ride or die that be on the same shit he be on. You ain't it, ditzy bitch."

Vitani stood up. "Move around LiLi, today is not the day."

"No, bitch, you move the fuck around. This is my nigga and he will always be mine. You might be fucking him now, but trust he will be crawling back to me," LiLi walked closer to Vitani. I noticed her stomach didn't look as big. *Is she taking care of herself? My baby?*

"Aye, LiLi chill with the bullshit. You already know what it is, so go back to work," I tried to defuse because I really didn't have time for this petty beef shit.

"Naw, I let this bitch slide too many times. She talks big shit when it's a crowd, but when I walked in that hospital room her ass was mute with that ugly ass lil' girl hanging onto my man looking like a damn monkey."

I didn't know my wife could move so fast. Before I could blink, she had LiLi by the hair decking her in her shit. "You just don't listen. I told your hoe ass I was gonna beat your ass before it was all over!" Vitani yelled as she kept hitting LiLi.

LiLi got a hit off on Vitani's jaw and that pissed my wife off more. She stood to her full height, lifted her knee up, and brought LiLi's face down on it, causing her nose to sputter blood. That got me to snap out of my shock and as I went to grab Vitani. Simon grabbed LiLi.

"Let me go, that hoe had the nerve to call my baby ugly but her dense ass is a Miss Piggy doppelganger! I will fucking kill you! I swear to God you better count your fucking days because every time I see you in public I'mma beat your ass like the circus pig you are," Vitani continued to yell and fight against my hold.

"I want to press charges! I'm pregnant!" LiLi yelled as the cops arrived on the scene.

My head snapped in her direction, "You want to do what?"

Her head dropped low, "Never mind. I don't want to press charges, just please escort that bitch from my place of employment."

Vitani's phone rang and she ran to grab her purse to answer it. I walked over to LiLi and the cops. "She doesn't want to claim trespassing, she's just upset. You all can leave now—"

A hard crash snatched my attention as I turned to see Vitani passed out on the floor.

"What the fuck?!" I ran over and picked her up yelling, "Someone help my wife! She's pregnant."

I didn't know if she was truly pregnant, but I would say and do anything if it would get her help faster. As I walked past LiLi she wore a stupid looking smile on her face that caused a chill to creep down my spine. I don't believe in omens but I had a feeling before it was all said and done, I would have to make her grimy ass disappear.

Chapter Twenty-One

VITANI

I woke up to my head feeling as if it was about to explode. My eyes felt sewn shut as I tried to open them. I tried to remember where I was and how I got there. Suddenly, it all came crashing into me like a wave. My daughter was taken by CPS and my grandfather was being rushed to the hospital. That's the last thing I remembered my mom saying to me on the phone before everything went dark. I groaned at the pain in my jaw, that bitch LiLi got me good but I dawged her ass as best I could without touching her stomach.

"Vitani, are you awake?" Godrique caressed my hand with his as I peeked through one eye. Simon was standing in the corner with his arms crossed and John was sitting in the recliner, all of them were staring at me.

I cleared my throat, "Yes. What happened?"

"You tell me. You took a phone call then the next thing I know your ass is out on the floor like a preacher laid hands on you. Who was on the phone?" Godrique asked. I tried to sit up, because I had to check on my grandfather and see about my baby. Godrique pushed down on my chest and I looked at him like he had lost his mind. "Wait until the doctor clears you."

"I have to get to my baby." My throat tightened as I felt tears swell in my eyes. "I have to check on my grandfather." I felt so drained.

God's brows creased as he stared at me for a moment before saying, "Tell me what's going on, wifey." He kissed my tears and I cried harder.

I was just consoling him this morning and despite the shit he had been through, he was still here by my side. I couldn't ask for anyone better to be my husband. "They took my baby. They said I am unfit to be a mother."

"Who?" God stood and began pacing, giving me the opening I needed to stand up. I snatched all the stickers off my chest and went to snatch the IV out before he stalled my movements.

"I don't know. More than likely that bitch Susan."

"I got it," Simon walked over to remove the IV with such precision you'd think he was a medical professional. He smiled down at me saying, "I was a Corpsman." *Well damn.*

A doctor walked in as soon as he placed the band-aid over my wound, "Ma'am you need lay back down. All of the tests haven't come back yet."

"I don't care, I have to leave."

"But ma'am, you're pregnant and—"

"I'm what?!" I choked out. A smile graced God's face and I wanted to smack it off. "But I'm on birth control."

"Yes, I pulled your records from your doctor since they partner with us and see that you are very consistent with your DEPO shot. However, you are of the rare 1% that does everything right and still get pregnant. Congratulations."

God hugged me from behind and whispered, "I told you that you are special."

I pushed him off of me, scoffing. Ugh! I had to get out of here.

"Trauma 1. Black female around 20 years of age, full cardiac arrest." Blared over the intercom. I realized I had been taken downstairs to the ER. I dashed out of the room in the hospital gown and all to find my grandfather. I looked in the rooms around me then went to trauma.

"Vitani!" Granny yelled my name from the end of the hall.

"What's going on? Where's grandad?"

"He's in there," Granny pointed to the hospital room with granddad.

What...what happened?" I asked, not sure that I wanted the answer. He was talking to Ma so he seemed like he was alright. But I was still headed in there to fuss at his ass for doing too much as soon as I found out the details.

"We were at your house to pick up Ice and your grandfather was playing with Ice. She was showing him some apps she'd downloaded on that iPad that Goddy got her, before we got ready to leave. There was a knock on the door and when your mom answered it, this white social worker woman came in with paperwork tryna take Ice. She said something about you being unfit and you know that ain't sit right with him at all. He was ready to take her on and the cops she brought with her. They were tryna take Ice and the mess they were talkin about you and putting her in a dangerous situation. Said they had video of you in a violent altercation," Granny continued.

I was ready to kill that bitch Susan and everybody else that came to my mom's house on that shit. I knew they were talkin' 'bout God, but I also knew that he'd take a bullet for Ice and would never put her in danger.

"That was one of the reasons I loved his old ass. He was gone protect y'all if he ain't do shit else," Granny said, pulling me back to the present and shaking her head, having a fond moment about Grandad. "Ice was holding onto him for dear life and he tried to keep them from taking her but..." she said, frowning and her eyes turning black like she was ready for war. "They pulled a gun on him and threatened to tase him and send him to jail if he didn't comply. He laughed at 'em, Vitani. Told us they were coming to get Ice for you putting her in a dangerous situation, but what do you call what they did? Traumatized my baby. Your mom had to step in and calm the situation down. She promised Ice we'd be to get her and she and I ran to get dressed while she was on the phone with an attorney. Came back and he was on the floor. All we did was turn our backs for a second," she said, tears rolling down her cheeks. Her and Grandad had their issues but there was still love there.

"Granny, we're gonna get to the bottom of this and Grandad is gone be just fi—"

Just then I heard machines going crazy and saw doctors and nurses begin rushing in our direction. I sent positive energy to whoever was coding and hoped they could bring them back. That was, until they turned right at the door that led to the room that Grandad was in. It was then that I realized I had just been sending positive vibes to myself. They all crowded his bed in the room and my mom came out with tears threatening to tumble from her lids.

"That social worker lady came to the house and took Ice, that's the reason for this. They took my grandbaby, please God don't let them take my father, too" my mom broke down. I hugged her and my granny joined in. Why is this the worst day of my life? So much had happened within the last twenty-four hours. It was too much.

"Why you out in this hall with an open gown showing all God's favor?" Granny scrunched her face. Leave it to her to make light of a serious situation like she ain't just tell me some heavy shit.

"I would like to know the same thing," God spoke from behind me. I rolled my eyes.

"Hey grandson, you are letting her do what she wants out here. Better tame her fast ass," Granny laughed.

I didn't find shit funny as I looked on into the room with my grandfather. The doctor that was doing compressions stopped saying, "I'm calling it. Time of death—"

"You better do everything you can to bring him back or your ass will be lying next to him! Lazy ass doctors, it hasn't even been five minutes," I snapped, running into the room, pushing the doctor. God came and stood in front of the doctor that looked petrified and I pushed his ass, too. Going to the bed I looked down at my grandfather's lifeless body and I couldn't even cry, I wanted revenge. I wanted blood. I kissed his forehead and walked out of the room and my granny grabbed my arm to stop me.

"I know how you are once you make your mind up, but you have two kids to worry about now." I nodded but still said nothing. I went back into the room that had my things, got dressed in God's baggy clothes I came in, then headed to the garage.

"Wifey, let me help you how you helped me. Please," God grabbed me from behind and hugged me. It momentarily gave me a sense of peace.

Momentarily.

I hopped in his car and he jumped in the passenger's side as John and Simon got in the back. I drove to the police station which was around the corner from the hospital in downtown Lakeland. I barged in and tried to rush the officers when I seen my daughter crying for me. "Give me my baby!" I yelled. My heart was breaking into a million pieces.

"Ma'am, if you keep this up we will have to tase you," an officer removed his taser from its holster.

"Put the taser up. She is just emotional right now," Simon flashed a badge that I couldn't see. "Where is your supervisor?" The officer went to get a woman who smiled at Simon. That pissed me off more because this bitch up here thinking about dick while my child is being kept from me. "Sgt. Moore, what does Miss Banks need to do to get her daughter?"

"We're on strict orders that she cannot be anywhere near her daughter. Apparently, Miss Banks was seen in a violent situation and is considered a threat to her child. The next of kin can get custody if they can prove they have a stable income."

"I'm a threat to my daughter?! Bitch, I'm a threat to you, not my daughter," I seethed through gritted teeth.

"See, that is a threat to an officer of the law and I should lock you up, but I have kids so I understand your frustration."

"I will ki—" I was cut off by my mother walking in my line of sight.

"Vitani Seline Banks! I did not raise you this way, so you better start acting like you have some sense," she then turned to the Sergeant saying, "I will take my granddaughter home with me. Prepare the paperwork."

All I could do was stand there in shock with no tears left to cry. My mom was able to go over to console Ice, calming her down. I walked out of the precinct, bumping into Rae. I looked at her and broke down again as she hugged me. Damn, I thought I had no more tears. I cried for what felt like forever. "How did you know what was going on?" I asked.

"Teqwyn called to tell me everything, he thought you would need your bestest at a time like this."

"I'm glad he was thinking. I'm spiraling, sis. I want whoever is behind this's blood."

"Welllllll... I was doing some digging into the person Anita was chatting with and found out that it is someone by the name of Susan West. You know her?"

"Those bitches! I'm going to kill them!!"

"Fill me in sis," Rae prodded.

"Susan is the social worker that took my baby, but Anita must be behind it. She is still mad about Godrique and I being involved."

"Oh well, they are cousins."

"What?! I knew she looked familiar, just couldn't put my finger on it."

"When do you want to handle that?"

"Handle what?" God asked as him, Simon, John, and Teq walked up.

"Nothing," Rae and I said in unison.

"Godrique, where is Alianna? Is she at the hospital alone?" I asked.

"No, Black is up there with her. I need you and Rae to go back to the house in Plant City and stay there. Ma Tam has Ice, so you know she's safe. Don't stress anything. I have some things to handle. Since Ali is with Black, I'm sending her security detail with you and Rae. Invite Jen over and y'all can have a girls night," God instructed.

"I don't have any clothes there. I don't need security!"

"You will do as I say. I'll see you soon," he spoke with finality as a chill raced down my spine to my pussy, making me remember all the filthy things he had done to me last night. He kissed my lips then whispered, "That kitty knows how to respond to its master. I love you, wifey."

I stood in a daze, watching him and The Disciples walk away. "Bitch, what did he do to you last night? Ooh MASTER!" Rae teased, causing me to laugh.

"You don't even want to know. Let's go by the house so I can get some clothes. We have shit to do, too," I smiled deviously.

"He said what he said. I have your bag in the car. Teq thought it would be smart to bring you some clothes...on second thought, maybe God orchestrated that, too."

"Yea, I'm pretty sure he had something to do with it. If he thinks I'm about to sit in the house and be a good girl, he has me all the way fucked up. Mom having Ice is the best thing that could happen since now I can fuck some shit up with the peace of mind that my daughter is safe. Once all my enemies are dead, I'll get my baby back. My grandad didn't deserve to die like that. Susan will be last, I want her to know I'm on her ass."

"Your crazy ass is a demon of war. Let's go get that bitch!" Rae giggled. She was just as crazy as me. "Wait, should we call Jen?"

"Naw, I don't know if I can trust her...well, I don't know if I can trust the agency she works for. Therefore, I can't trust her by default."

"You're right, she can't be trusted."

Chapter Twenty-Two

GOD

You would think people would know not to fuck with me by now. Nope, they insisted on getting me out of character. Teq found out that Devun and Chez had been working together laundering money through IntelliCorp with Bart. No wonder his pussy ass skipped town. Teq stayed back at his spot where all his gear was while The Disciples and I rolled out to go find Chez. Devun was out of the country, him and that social worker bitch. But Chez still didn't know I was onto his scheme to have me locked away. LiLi and Chez were cousins, so I was sure her trifling ass was in on it too. I didn't put two and two together until now that the nigga I saw at her house that made me stop fucking with her seriously was the same nigga that was about to run his mouth before Chez shot him. I still didn't have concrete proof of that though.

The coordinates to where Chez was holed up in Davenport were etched in my brain as I speed down I-4 East with my brothers behind me. Teq jammed all street cams and police speed traps. We were all on our motorcycles except John who insisted on driving a big slow ass semi-truck with a trailer attached. About thirty minutes later, we pulled up to what appeared to be an abandoned warehouse with about ten cars parked outside. *Does he know we're coming?* He couldn't know, unless…I checked my texts and realized Vitani had texted in the group chat with Bart in it about Turk being shot. We were a good distance away so not to alert anyone of our presence. This further let me know that Chez, Bart, and Devun were all working together. Good thing Rae cut him off, or she would probably be collateral damage.

"He knows we're coming. No need in sneaking around, Peter got here a minute ago and is set up on that water tower ready when we are. There are no cameras inside so they will be as blind as us. Did you all look over the blueprint?"

"Bruh chill and let's go get this nigga. I have a dinner date with Violet to console her since her baby daddy just died," Simon shrugged. "What's you plan?"

"I say we go in, guns blazing. I haven't had a shootout in a good minute," John smirked.

"I'm game. Let's go fuck some shit up," I checked all my surroundings and saw the red dot on the ground near my feet, letting me know Peter was growing impatient with us sitting around talking.

These niggas were sloppy 'cause I really didn't see anyone looking out. I didn't see anyone in the back, and I damn sure didn't see anybody looking out on the roof. Maybe they didn't know when we were coming, but Chez should know I wasn't about to let this shit ride.

He tried to kill Turk! He tried to take my brother, and that shit was not about to go unanswered.

I looked up in the direction where I knew Peter was set up. The red dot flashed on my feet impatiently, and I shook my head. Peter was ready to go, and I felt him on that, but I wasn't about to rush in and miss some shit. I wanted to make sure no one got away from here alive. Before the end of the night, they would all be repenting for their sins. But they wouldn't find any mercy. I waved to my left at Simon and then to the right so John could head in that direction. We were going to hit this shit right and hit it hard.

We approached each side of the building, checking each vehicle a few times to ensure we didn't miss anything. No one was inside, just like no one was looking out. I hoped this wasn't a sign this nigga thought I wouldn't come for his ass. If he knew me, he would know that I always had a plan to handle my business. I got to the front doors and realized that Chez might have put a little thought into his hideout, because both of these doors were brand new and were made of steel. It also had a fingerprint security lock on it to get inside. I leaned away from the doors and looked up to see a camera. Luckily, we brought the jammer with us to make sure no technology besides our own would be working. I looked left and right, catching John and Simon's eyes and bringing up a finger. We all moved as one, meeting behind the cars.

"The front is locked tight with steel doors and a fingerprint lock," I said.

"Yeah, same on my side," Simon grunted. I looked at John, and he nodded as well. I shook my head because it was always something trying to stand in the way of my plan, but not tonight.

"Fuck it. I wanted it quiet, but we can hold off some calls for a little bit, right?"

"Everything phone, camera, or whatever will be down once I make the call. Also, if anyone sees anything or tries to call it in, Teq has a program to misdirect any responders to a different location," John said quietly. I nodded once and held up four fingers. Peter already knew what that meant, and so did the others.

"Yeah, this the shit I like," Simon grinned.

We're all crazy as fuck.

We got lower as we waited for Peter to hit that bitch with the RPG. That nigga was fully loaded for this shit. We were about to hit these niggas hard as fuck, leaving nothing but scorched earth. Peter was going to blow the doors right the fuck off, and we were going to walk up in there and drag this nigga out screaming. We were taking everybody out and leaving no witnesses. *Fuck it.* They were all gonna feel the wrath of God.

Two flashes hit our feet, and I knew Peter was in place.

"Get in position," I said as I got down on one knee to ensure I didn't get hit with any debris.

As soon as I heard the explosion, John hit send to make the call. I knew that would give us some time to get this shit done but not a lot, so we had to move.

"That's why we always take the truck with us," John said showing off his golds. I looked at him and could see the killer was coming out full force tonight.

"You two make sure nobody that isn't us leaves this building," I said, pulling out my steel from my shoulder holster. I started moving before them niggas, but I knew they were always watching my back as they moved silently behind me.

I was first through the door when I heard screaming and shit. I couldn't help the laugh that escaped my lips. These pussy ass niggas didn't understand how much they'd fucked up.

"Don't let them motherfuckers get through the doors!" Someone yelled.

I moved through the smoke the explosion caused and dodged to the left, lifting my gun. I squeezed the trigger letting off two shots, hitting two dudes coming from around a corner screaming they were being attacked. I used the smoke to my advantage because they couldn't see me coming.

"Double-tap these bitches. I don't want nobody walking out of this shit!" I shouted as I gave the one nigga I had shot in the gut a headshot as I walked past. I looked over to Simon, and this nigga was coming upon them with blades cutting throats while smiling. I turned around and saw Chez running up a set of stairs leading to a catwalk.

"Chez, you bitch! Don't fucking run now," I said, putting my back to a wall. I peeked out and looked up the catwalk, where I saw Chez's hoe ass moving as he pushed his own niggas out the way and tossed some over the side.

"Fuck you and your fucking disciples! Let it loose!" Chez screamed as I heard a door open on the opposite end. Loud shots started to let off like a fucking belt-fed machine gun.

"Shit!" John roared as he dodged behind a pallet and pushed some nigga right in the line of fire. I heard rapid fire again, but it was coming from where I saw Chez running. I peeked out again and saw that his dumbass fools were shooting. I leaned back and waited for the break. They stopped, and I leaned out and shot back at the men on the catwalk. I took aim and shot, hitting the nigga in the shoulder, making him spin out, dropping his gun as he fell a few feet to the floor. I did the same with the next one, not wasting any time between shots. I could still hear the rapid-fire going, but I knew Simon would handle that. I saw Chez peek out of a door, and I took the shot aiming for his fucking head. He ducked back inside just in time, the bullet missing him by seconds.

"You fucking bitch!" Chez growled. He stuck his arm out and shot twice and then two more times before pulling his arm back inside. I started to move at that moment, making sure I stayed behind the stacks of boxes on the floor. Another nigga came out holding his gun where I was last, so I knew he didn't see me. I aimed to hit him once in the thigh, then in the head, and watched him slump to the ground in the doorway, leaving it open for me.

"Chez," I sang while moving to where I last saw his bitch ass. I heard the rapid gunfire stop, and I knew Simon had gotten to whatever nigga was thinking he was doing some shit. All he was doing was making noise for no reason 'cause his ass wasn't hitting anything.

"Jit, go handle that shit while we clean up down here," John said as he dragged an unconscious body behind him. I looked back, ensuring they would be straight before going for the door.

"Bet."

I ran for the stairs. I climbed up and gave each person I passed a headshot just in case. I knew Simon and John would make sure we had the right amount to make our statement clear to the streets. *You fuck with me, my disciples, or my family, and you better prepare yourself for judgment.* I stepped through the door and saw another door on the other side left open. I walked over to it and cracked it open, then stepped back. I looked inside and saw another set of stairs leading down. I checked my clip and reloaded it before going back to where John and Simon were, letting them know I was going down to take care of Chez.

"I'm going for him! It's another door with steps going down. Clear out this fucking shit and get ready to burn this bitch down!" I said as I checked my clip one last time. I made my way to the door to get this nigga Chez so we could get out of here before any police started showing up.

I moved down the stairs, hearing yelling and Chez telling somebody to handle that shit. *Little did they know, shit was already done in this bitch, and they are last on the list.* The door opened, and I lifted my gun, aiming for whoever was first to show their face. I took my shot when I saw a head poke out. I hit my target and watched as he started to fall backwards. I kicked the door open and saw a woman going for a gun on the floor and another nigga with his mouth open looking at ole boy who got the first headshot. Then I saw this nigga Chez, holding another gun. I moved fast, seeing the woman jump sideways to get out of the way of the bullet. I ran up on the dude, looking like a fucking dumbass, and put my heat to the back of his head.

"Got you, bitch." I whispered as I pulled the trigger. The chick screamed as the body hit the floor, snapping Chez out of whatever paralysis he was in at seeing me. He moved as he lunged for the girl pulling her up by her hair.

"Let me go! Fuck you, Chez! Let me go," she shouted while fighting his grip on her.

"Shut the fuck up!" Chez snapped. He put the gun to her temple as I cocked my head to the side as my brows drew together.

"Chez, please let me go. I don't want no parts of this shit," she cried. Her eyes found mine, and they pleaded for me to help.

"Yeah, Chez, be a man about this shit. You acting like a little bitch hiding behind a female," I laughed. I felt someone behind me, and I knew it was Simon. Only he could move that silent.

"Naw. Naw, fuck you! You think y'all can get away with all this shit!" Chez spat. His eyes grew wide, and I now knew for sure it was Simon behind me.

"Wrap this shit. We ready to get the fuck out of here," Simon said as he looked around.

"Yeah, it's about that time to end this shit so I can get home to my wifey," I said.

"Please, I had nothing to do with any of thi—" Chez shook the girl as he jammed the gun harder into her temple. "Shut the fuck up!" Chez gritted. "You might be a killer, but you ain't killing no innocent," Chez said as he moved, keeping the girl in front of him.

"I know this nigga don't think he is getting out of here, does he?"

"I think he does," Simon laughed. "I find it funny that he thinks this stunt will work as long as he has been around us. Let's get this shit over with, so I can meet up with Violet," Simon grunted as if he was getting bored.

"The chick?"

"That's the bitch he been fucking for a minute now. She ain't innocent, and even if she was, who gives a fuck?"

"Yeah, you're right," I said and shot her in the stomach. Chez let her go as she sank to the floor in a pool of blood. Chez didn't even realize that I took another shoot hitting him on the shoulder, until his gun dropped to the floor.

"Oh shi—" he exclaimed as he stumbled backward. I took another shot in the other shoulder and then blew out both his knees. His screams filled the room as he crashed to the ground. Simon moved from behind me and kicked the guns away from both of them. He stood over the girl who was choking on blood and shot her in the forehead.

"We got everything already set up. We just waiting on your slow ass so we can light this bitch up," Simon said as I joined him. We stood over a screaming Chez and the thought of his ass looking at Vitani flashed through my mind. I sucked my teeth before bending down and pistol-whipping the shit out of his face. Blood splattered all over the walls and floor. I felt a hand on my shoulder and knew I had to stop. It wasn't time for this bastard to die just yet. A statement had to be made, and he was crucial for making that shit happen. I wanted everyone to know I was coming for them. I wanted this shit to make every headline in Polk County, so niggas knew if you fucked with me, this was what they could look forward to.

"My fault. I was thinking back to the cookout for a minute," I said, taking a deep breath.

"Yeah, sis, got your head all the way fucked up off that demon pussy. I don't think this nigga even had a chance to fuck with her," Simon chuckled. He grabbed a moaning Chez by his pants leg and then looked at me. I laughed and grabbed the other side, and we dragged his bitch ass out of the room and up the stairs to where John and Peter were waiting.

By the time we made it through the warehouse, I was sick of hearing this nigga moaning and crying. I was ready to get this done and get my ass back to my wife.

"You know we need to finish that other shit before you go home to little sis," Simon said as he dropped Chez's leg to the ground.

"Ahh! Oh, God! Please! Ahhh!" I looked at Simon and noticed John moving fast in our direction. I stepped to the side while still eyeing Simon, trying to figure out how this nigga knew my thoughts.

"Who?"

"That bitch Anita," he said, watching John and Peter drag Chez's body to the other side of the lot where three large crosses stood tall.

"I didn't forget about that bitch. We will handle her and get home, so we all got an alibi for the night," I said as I took the cloth he handed me. I cleaned off my gun and hands before putting it back in my holster.

"Will y'all come on! We don't have all fucking night," John said, flashing his golds as he gritted his teeth. Peter and John were hoisting Chez up on the third cross next to two other niggas.

"John, I can't believe you had these crosses just chilling and waiting," I said, standing in front of Chez.

"Shid, I knew we would need them sooner or later," John smirked. Peter and John held Chez up to the cross, and because I shot out his kneecaps, he couldn't stand on the little pole. So I climbed up the other ladder and held out my hand. Simon placed three large, spiked nails in my hand along with a mallet.

"Well, you were right, as usual," I stated while hammering a spike into Chez's wrists, nailing him to the cross. After I finished nailing his feet, I stared up at this nigga, watching him cry like a bitch. Peter and Simon had gone back inside the warehouse to make sure we weren't leaving any evidence behind while John loaded the truck back up. I took a step back so I could see all three of these clown ass niggas and reached for my heat. I pulled it out of its holster, aimed at the dude on the right, and gave him a headshot. I did the same for the other one, saving Chez's punk ass for last. I closed my eyes as flashes of Turk lying in a coma played through my mind, and the agony on my goddaughter's face fueled my rage. I opened my eyes and stared at a bloody face with pleading eyes.

"God, pleas–"

I cut him off because I didn't want to hear shit he had to say. "At least you will be good for something. Your bitch ass will be the sign for every nigga on the streets to remember that I am the Alpha and Omega."

I raised my gun, aimed for his head, and pulled the trigger. I wanted the fear of death and pain to last longer, but I knew we had to go. This was just the beginning because I knew more enemies would need to meet the same judgment. I did one more look around to make sure we left nothing tying any of this back to us.

"So, we lighting this thing up or what?" Peter asked, holding the gas cans. I looked back to the crosses, then to the still smoking warehouse, and came to a decision.

"Naw, leave it. I want them to see the bodies, and I want niggas to know we are not playing any fucking games. Let's go deal with that bitch Anita and get back to the spot," I said, heading for the vehicles.

John had already rolled out with the truck, and that was a good thing because I could hear sirens in the distance. We wasted no time getting out of there to head to our next target on the list.

Chapter Twenty-Three

VITANI

"You ready?" I asked Rae as we stood near the top of the stairs about to put my plan in motion.

"Yes, but do you really have to do them like that?"

"Yes, their big ass would take us down in no time. What do people call it? Necessary roughness."

"If you say so. God gonna beat your ass and I'mma blame everything on you," Rae giggled lightly.

I moved to descend down the steps when one of the big burly security detail guys turned to glare at me. I smiled.

"We are going to get some wine and chill in the den, if that's okay." *Good thing he doesn't know I'm pregnant.* He nodded and turned back around just as the other guard walked over facing us with a menacing look on his face. He probably knew we were up to no good since both of us wore all black from head-to-toe. Once we got to the bottom Rae tased the guy that wasn't facing us in his thick neck as I pulled my stun gun from behind my back and shot the other one, continuing to press the trigger until he was out cold.

"You're fucked up for this. I'm sure we could've said we're going to the store or something," Rae frowned.

"Shut up, they were given strict orders and we don't have time for shoulda coulda wouldas. Hurry up and let's tie them up before they wake up and shoot us."

"Us? They better shoot your ass! I am just the accessory, but you on first degree. Better repent now before we walk out of God's house," Rae joked.

"Girl, make sure your knot is secure so we can go."

I watched as Rae double-checked her knot then we both ran out the door. I had to take God's car since mine was still at the other house. Honestly, I didn't know this house existed until last night, so I guess I wasn't the only person keeping secrets. Rae made sure to use her paper roadmap for directions to Anita's home. Everyone is scared of God and what they think he'll do, but he isn't the only one that has a mighty wrath. I know I shouldn't indulge in crime now that I know for sure that I'm pregnant, but I couldn't have that bitch thinking I was weak. LiLi's ass was next as soon as she had that baby. I know I shouldn't kill God's baby mother, but he killed my baby's father, so we'll be even.

We blasted a local artist by the name of Toddrick's song "Know the Meaning" as we cruised down Galloway to take the back way to the south-side where Anita lived in a nice-sized mansion. Such a shame it would be back on the market after tonight. Not really, the shit was painted an ugly ass blue color that was fit for a nursing home. With all that money she brags about having, you'd think she'd have some sort of designer on her payroll.

I stopped on the corner of her street and Rae pulled out her laptop to jam her cameras. I couldn't believe she only had one camera and that was on her doorbell which was easy to hack for someone like Rae. For the life of me, I still couldn't figure out why Anita didn't like me, it's not like her and God had anything going on. It was all so confusing, but her life was now about to be cut short for getting my daughter involved. I backed into Anita's long driveway when Rae gave me a thumbs up, signaling that she was in the camera system. She put her computer away and we both got out of the car. I grabbed a brown paper bag marked with a restaurant logo. It was around 9p.m. and the street was pitch black with nobody in sight. If we were in the hood the block would be on swole at this time of night.

I knocked on the door and stood off to the side so she couldn't see out of the window or the peep hole. I held up the bag and her stupid ass opened the door without even asking who it was.

"What th—"

I pushed her inside and Rae closed the door behind us. Anita stood in some kinda Tae Bo stance and I almost laughed. She looked like the white woman off *Bringing Down the House* that got her ass whooped by Queen Latifah. She lifted her leg like she was about to kick me but threw a left hook instead, and I lifted my arm to block that weak shit.

"Tsk. Tsk. Tsk. don't you know us hoodrats like to throw hands?" I headbutted her and she screamed at the top of her lungs for help as blood leaked down her forehead.

"You're going to jail, you bum bitch. Wait until my cousin hears about this. You will never get your daugh—"

Whap!

I decked her in her mouth. "So you were the one that decided to play with my child's safety." I grabbed her hair, slamming her face into the wall. "Not gonna fight back? Thought you were about to give me a challenge," I taunted, yanking her head back to see the damage I had done. I dragged her into her dining area that was just past her foyer.

"You and that fat bitch that's over there laughing will be in jail by morning. I refuse to engage hostiles," Anita snapped as she spit her blood in my face.

I smiled wickedly. "There's the desperate bitch I remember. You know what happened to me last night? Doesn't matter, I'll tell you. I spent all night sucking and fucking on my fiancé, you know him right? Godrique.

You missed out on some fantastic sex. It was so good I almost forgave you for all the shit you did to me in the past few months."

I slung her to the ground and she landed in front of Rae. She immediately put her foot on Anita's chest.

Walking over to the kitchen area I rinsed the blood off of my face, then lifted my shirt to dry it. I looked down at my gloves to be sure they hadn't ripped, then walked back over to Anita, kicking her hard in the stomach.

"Ahhh," she groaned.

"You see, the little stunt you pulled with your cousin Susan signed both of y'all death sentence," I smirked when her eyes bulged at the mention of Susan's name. "Not only was my daughter taken away from me today, but I lost my grandfather as well."

I leaned over and grabbed her hair dragging her over to the sink, she started yelling for help again. Rae pulled out her .22 and pointed it at her head, effectively muting her theatrics. I kneed her, making her do a backwards arch as I turned the water on to run down her face.

"Ever heard of waterboarding? You don't have to answer, I know it's kinda hard in this new position," I pressed down on the knob giving her a break as she gagged and choked to catch her breath. "Do you know how it is to feel like you're drowning from all of the trauma you've endured?" I turned the faucet back on over her face.

"Did you hear something?" Rae asked.

I turned the water off and listened closely. I couldn't hear anything from Anita gagging and shit all loud. I covered her mouth with my free hand and shrugged since I still didn't hear anything. I turned the water back on and laughed as Anita's slow ass tried to swim in the air. Then she tried to claw at my face, but I dodged her blind attack. "You know I'mma kill you, right?" I taunted further, shutting off the faucet.

Cough. "Please—" *Gag.* "Don't kill—" *Cough.* "Me." Anita pleading for her life was like music to my ears. It's always the slimy muthafuckas who want to beg for their lives after they have done people dirty their whole life.

"I was wondering how long it would take for you to beg for your life. I am sorry to inform you that your request has been denied by the counsel of YOU GOT ME FUCKED UP," I lifted the faucet and my pussy started pulsating. Death was inescapable, kinda like an orgasm. You could try to run all you want, but it would still take you the fuck out when the time came. I turned the water off again and reached over to grab one of her kitchen knives. I chose the ridged one to make a jagged cut that would be pretty, like a little design.

"Pleas—"

"Wifey!"

I froze in place, afraid to turn around. Rae had heard something, but I didn't expect him. Anger consumed me as I turned to face him, The Disciples, and Teq. "What are you doing here? You been fucking this bitch on the low?!"

He chuckled. "You could at least lock the door if you're gonna be on some rah-rah shit."

I turned the water back on before saying, "You'll watch her die before I kill you, too."

Godrique lifted his mask as he stalked toward me and I felt my core clench. He couldn't have come to fuck her because he wore his Alpha and Omega mask. He wrapped his hand around my neck and licked my lips before prying them open with his tongue to greet mine in a twisted affair. I moaned, then pushed him back so I could turn the water back off. I didn't want her to drown. Naw. *I have to be the one to take her life.*

"How did you know I was here?" I asked.

"I didn't. We were tying up loose ends. She's the one that tipped the social worker off. Imagine my surprise when I pulled up and seen my car outside. Wait, where is Danny and Doug?"

"Uh, well they are kinda tied up at the moment." His brow arched. "They're alive," I confirmed.

"Uh huh, and how did you find out about this one?" he asked, pointing to Anita.

"I can't disclose my sources. You're not the only person with a techie," I winked, and in one swift motion I cut Anita's throat and watched her choke on her own blood while staring into her eyes.

"Jit ain't even blink. She a real hitta!" John said.

"Ooh, my sis has heart. She looked that bitch in the eyes like 'yea, I just took your life'. Bro, you better not get caught slipping," Simon praised. "Oh shit, she has twinkies!" He reached for a cake and started eating it.

"Si, what the fuck are you doing?" God asked.

"Eating. Your ass wanna keep a nigga out all day and not feed me and shit. That's why I be ignoring you when I'm with Violet. She feeds me."

"Man, you shot the fuck out," Peter laughed.

"It's y'all thinking this is our first rodeo for me," Rae laughed.

Teq squinted. "You're her techie!"

Rae smiled. "In the flesh. For the record, I told her ass to stop playing with God a long time ago, but I think she likes trying him."

"I should waterboard your snitching ass next! You talk way too much." I frowned and noticed Peter wiping shit off. "We're not dumb ya know."

He looked up and smiled, "I am just putting some other DNA in here to throw the cops off."

"Who's DNA?" I asked curiously.

"Chez."

I gasped, "Wha— what happened to Chez?"

"You'll see. Let's get home wifey, so we can all have an alibi," Godrique gripped my ass.

I stabbed the knife into Anita's chest where her heart was located. Everyone looked at me like I had lost my mind as I sauntered over to the key bowl I'd seen near her garage door. Looking at the many keychains, I picked a purple sea turtle that I thought would go great with my collection and put it in my pocket.

"Oh shit, she's a sociopath!" Peter surmised.

I turned to look at them. "I ain't no killer, but don't push me."

Epilogue

BART

"WKJA, News For You. Florida man or shall I say Florida men found nailed to crosses down in Davenport, Florida. A homeless man near the scene said it reminded him of a hood crucifixion. Sources say they do not have any suspects as of yet, but they have their top investigators on the scene. The County Sherriff made a statement and I quote 'I don't know who was foolish enough to come to Polk County and commit a crucifixion, but I will gladly turn their wine into water when I put them in the County Jail.' Also in Polk County, a South Lakeland woman found beaten and slaughtered in her home by a scorned lover. We received word that the two crimes may be connected but we are waiting for confirmation. After the break, Larry will let us know whether to wear beach clothes or a poncho. Back to you, Sarah."

I sipped on my glass of gin and turned the news off. I was in D.C. with my dad for a business meeting, but I was still in Europe on record. My father forced me to stay there after discovering that I was double-crossing God. He said he never liked them, but he wouldn't suggest getting on their bad side. *Fuck God. I will go back for my woman as soon as I get this business settled with my father.*

"Son, you worry too much. I will protect you at all costs. You're my heir. Let that black guy you were working with handle them, we have bigger things to worry about."

"Father, I can't just forget about it. God stole my woman!"

My father scoffed, "She is not good enough for you."

"Yes, she is. You don't know her, she's perfect. I will get her back."

"If I help you get her, will you stay home at the villa for good?"

I smiled. "Yes Father, I will accept my place by your side with my *African Queen.*"

"Consider it done. Let this be the last I hear of this."

LiLi

God texted to check on me and the baby but I didn't respond as I sat in the federal office across from Mr. Sharpe. He wanted God, but I was only willing to give him Vitani. *That bitch has to go. I know if she is out of the picture God won't even care about me not being pregnant. Hell, I could probably trick him into sleeping with me to get pregnant again.*

"LiQuesha, we have a common interest. Help me help you," Mr. Sharpe smiled.

"I want immunity," I demanded. I wasn't a fool. That way if I were to kill Vitani, ain't shit they can do to me.

"I can get you that, but will you go into protective custody?"

"Yes, I need your best agents as my security, because those guys are dangerous."

"I will have my best agent with you. Her name is Jenesis Carter. She will protect you with her life. You will meet her by the end of the day when she escorts you to our safe house in the Bahamas. Pack light," Mr. Sharpe instructed.

"Yessir, I will be ready."

To Be Continued

Before you go, check out a sneak peek of
Cold As Ice
Taken By A Yeti
By
Author Penz & Blossom

Sneak Peek

CHAPTER ONE

RAHEEL "RAH" SILVERMOON

We never get the chance ever to hit up Club *PHANTASY,* but since we had to allow for the wedding, there wasn't a reason not to see who wanted to be tied down tonight. Neither Saheel nor I liked being stuck in a tux, but it was for a good cause and friend.

"Raheel, what room are you going into tonight? I want to hit the bar first. Izumi assured me they had Frosted Whiskey and Cool Blizzard on tap. Not to mention she said the pixies run in packs on the dance floor." Saheel smirked. I was in the mood to play, and a few pixies would fit my agenda. I could do a little rope play with one while the other watches restrained, and I could make use of the spreader bar. A drink didn't sound bad, and if the pixies weren't down, I knew there were others upstairs.

"Let's get that drink first," I said as we walked up to the door. No one was in front of it, but I knew something was around. A tall brown-skinned man wearing all black seemed to step out of the shadows as we approached. We didn't say a word as he opened the black door for us to enter. There wasn't a line or anyone else waiting to get inside. The street seemed to be dead quiet. If I didn't know Izumi Nivia as I did, I would have thought this was an ambush.

"Any friend of the Tigress is a friend to this club. As long as you follow its rules."

There was no need to answer because once we stepped through the door, I could feel the magic of the spell that filled every inch of this building. I smiled as it settled over us and could feel Izumi as if she was right next to us.

"I guess she sent us to the special entrance," Saheel joked. The hallway was wide and dark. The walls were black leather, but the scents that filled my nose told me many species were here tonight. "She told us to behave and not fuck anything up. I told her we were always perfect gentlemen," Saheel smiled.

"No wonder we had to pass through that door. She knew your ass was lying like shit. Anytime we enter the building, it's nothing but fights to be our Subs for the night. She dampened our presence," I laughed. The Siberian Tigress did nothing to our power but placed a spell on us to seem less than what we were. It was hard for any being not to be attracted to our animal magnetism.

"Oh, that is dirty," Saheel said, shaking his head. His liquid silver eyes looked around, missing nothing. The shadows along the walls moved, but nothing was there, but I knew something was watching. The light ahead began to get brighter as the heavy bass of hip-hop had me nodding my head.

"Naw baby brother, that's not dirty. She is busy with her cousin's wedding, so she is making sure we don't fuck shit up here," I stated. We stepped out of the shadows above the bar and looked down into the crowded club.

"I get it. I'm not mad about it either. Makes the chase, and when they submit even better," Saheel grunted. He was right about that because I hated when it was easy. I liked to work for what I wanted. I liked the chase and the satisfaction when they began to beg for what I had to give them.

"Well, let's get that drink cause the pixies are already on the dance floor."

"Bet," Saheel said. We both moved to the stairs and made our way to the bottom floor. I could tell whatever Izumi did was working to a certain extent. I loosened my blue silk tie and unbuttoned the top button on my dress shirt. We were not dressed for the club scene, but it wouldn't make a difference. I caught the eyes of two pixies who floated a few feet off the ground. The one pixie's wings were almost the exact shade of my eyes. They went the Persian blue like mine but maybe slightly lighter. I stared into her large brown eyes, then let my gaze roam her light brown skin with shimmers of blue that dusted over her like a powder. I knew what it was, though. I knew why all the human men clustered around her and why her friend leaned on her shoulder. She licked her tongue across her lips, tasting the pixie dust. I caught the scent of her orgasm as we made it to the bar. I turned away, deeming them both too easy, and started to search for someone else.

"Your kind doesn't make it here much. We have a few selections for you," The demon said, grinning. Saheel took his gaze from the Vampire watching him and looked at the bartender.

"Izumi said you have Cool Blizzard on tap," he said.

"That's right. I didn't know why, but I get whatever she tells me to get with no questions. No one wants to feel her claws."

"Good, then you should have the frosted Whiskey as well. We will take one of each."

"Gotcha, it will be right up." The demon moved down the bar to make the drinks. That's when I noticed the Vampire and a Witch was making their way over to us. I breathed in their scents and knew this one was Pure Blood. I didn't know exactly who she was and why she was here and not at the wedding reception.

"I haven't tasted Yeti blood in three hundred years," she smiled. Her gunmetal gray eyes only stared at Saheel as she spoke. I looked at the Witch, who seemed to study me before looking down.

"If you are who I believe you are, my safe word is..."

I turned and grabbed the Frosted Whiskey from the demon and threw the shot back. I sat the glass down and grabbed the other before looking back at the Water Witch.

"Your safe word is what?" I growled. I could see that she was nervous as she pushed her thick curls from her face.

"Wh...Whiskey. It's Whiskey," she stumbled. I think I was going to like this one. Playing with a Witch was always fun for me.

"I think that will work just fine," I grunted.

Saheel

I knew exactly who this Vampire was all in my face like I would ever let someone from that family get a drop of my blood. Still, I couldn't help but admire her height and thick figure.

"Nadia Vanderlee, do you speak this way to everyone? I thought someone of your high blood would be more...more discreet about asking for someone's blood," I smiled slowly. I took the drink from the demon and took a swallow while staring into her light brown eyes. Her French accent did get me hard as fuck, and the way she licked her pouty lips told me she was a pro with sucking. Point intended.

"When we are in a place such as this, why should I play at niceties? You're here to fuck, just like I am here to do the same. Your blood calls to me, and since your kind once served us, I feel as though you should..."

"See, that is the problem with you, Pure Bloods. You think you can say what you want to who you want, and nothing will happen," I chuckled. I sat my glass down on the bar and stepped close to her, smelling her berries and champagne scent. She had to be about five feet ten inches. I was six feet and three inches, so she still had to look up. "I serve no one. The only person who would be serving anything would be you on your knees in front of me until I said otherwise. But no need to worry because you and your bitch sisters can crawl back in your coffins and die,"

"You should choose your words wisely, Yeti. If you know my name, then you know my family and how powerful..."

"Excuse me. Saheel and Raheel, please follow me," a voice from my left said. I flicked my eyes to the tall man. I had no clue where the fuck he came from or when he appeared. He wasn't in a black tux like the rest, but he wore a black long-sleeved tee-shirt and black jeans.

"What's this about, Tiger? My brother was minding his business when the Vamp started talking..."

"Honestly, she is of no consequence. This is urgent, so please follow me," he said. He waved a hand in a circle, moving his fingers in a motion I couldn't form. Something close to a portal opened, but that wasn't what it was. It was more like a tear, and I figured that was right when I saw a single claw elongate.

"A tear in space?" I said. Before dropping a couple of bills on the bar, I took another drink and stepped forward.

"Yes. As I said, this is urgent," he said and stepped through the opening. I looked at Raheel, but he was already moving. The relaxed state he was in was now gone, and so was our night.

"I will catch you next time, Nadia," I said, following after my brother.

The rip in time shut behind me, but we were already stepping out into a room. It looked like a meeting board room. The colossal steel table sat in the middle with chairs around it, and a flat-screen T.V. sat on one wall. I thought we had left the club, but I knew we hadn't by the view of the city below us.

"What's this about?" Raheel said agitatedly. I turned to the two and saw the man pull out a cell phone. He dialed a number and waited.

"The name is Saber. The Tigress informed me that she needs to speak with you, I don't know what the hell is happening, but whatever it is, it's happening at the wrong damn time," Saber said. The line picked up on the fourth ring, and all we heard was screaming.

"I'm not messing with none of you, Bigfoots! I am here because my cousin is dumb enough to marry into this damn family!"

"Hello, hold on," Izumi snapped.

"Izumi? What's good? Are our cousins giving you a hard time again? You need us too…" Raheel started. He looked at me like I knew what the hell to do. I didn't understand why she called because of something like this.

"No, no, some people can't keep their big hands to themselves! This is about something else. I received a call a few minutes ago, and I think you both need to head home with this little info. Something is up with the letter agencies. One of my Streaks just informed me about some government team digging up something in Alaska and an upcoming trip. Something about a found treasure or something buried deep. I don't know all that you do there, but she couldn't hear all of the conversations about whatever they are looking for under the ice. Whatever they found, she felt they shouldn't be messing around with it. She didn't like the scent of them, which means they up to some fuck shit."

I looked up at Raheel, and his eyes hardened into ice as he stared out the windows. I could hear the metal of the phone starting to break in his grip. I took the phone from him before it could happen. I felt my beast howl at the intrusion into our land and what we had sworn to protect.

"We got it. Thanks for the heads up," I said.

"If I figure out more, I will let you know," she growled.

"Aight, bet. Handle your business and know we got this shit handled. Tell my cousins to chill the fuck out," I said.

"Yeah, it's no problem, but if you see a confirmed sighting of a Big Foot on the news, you know what happened!"

"Just...just make sure you don't hurt any of them too bad," I said.

"Yeah, not making any promises. Just...just leave as soon as you can. I don't like this shit," Izumi said before ending the call. I looked up at Raheel, who hadn't said a word. He slowly turned toward me, and I could see the beast in his eyes.

"We can't let them get close to that tomb," he growled.

"Let's move," I said as I felt for the elemental beneath this building. I could feel the prominent earth being, and it helped me rip open a tear in time. I wasn't touching the ground, but it wasn't needed. I roared as I punched out, creating an icy portal for us to go home.

CHAPTER TWO

ZANIAH "ZYA" ARCTIC

"Hello?" I mumbled into the phone. "I know you're playing with me! Wake up. We have to be at the airport in an hour," my best friend Amari yelled in my ear. I pulled the phone away to look at the screen and groaned when I saw it was 3:30 am. This girl was always trying to be early, but she had me fucked all the way up if she thought I was supposed to be at the airport three hours early. I put my phone on speaker and closed my eyes as I laid my head back down on my memory foam pillow.

"The plane doesn't leave until seven. Go back to bed."

"I'm too excited to go back to sleep. You know how I get, plus our kind doesn't really sleep at night," Amari sucked her teeth.

She was right about us not usually sleeping at night, but I had been up for the last forty-eight hours getting things prepared for the month-long assignment we had landed with an undisclosed government agency. They had tasked us with locating a hidden ancient tomb in Barrows, AK, because we are local archeologists based out of Fairbanks. The agency offered us ten million a piece, and there was no way in hell we would pass up the opportunity.

I sighed, "I had things to do."

"You should've packed weeks ago. I know you waited until the last minute to rush and handle things. I hope you don't forget anything. There are not many stores where we're going," Amari chuckled.

I hung up because she was right on point. I could never pack in advance. My brain didn't function like that. The real reason I was so tired is that I had fucked this alpha wolf a few hours ago, and he wore my ass out. I liked my men to be dominant so that I could dominate them. If people knew a bunny was making these alpha males cry, their reputations would be ruined. I'm not a small woman by any means, but I ain't big either, so it's fun when I make these men my bitches. When I say to bend the knee, that's what the fuck I mean. I chuckled to myself as I stood to get my hygiene together.

Once that was done, I finished packing and grabbed my keys off the rack. Amari could be a pain in my ass, but she kept me on my toes. Our parents are from the same Snowshoe Tribe-based Alaska. We have been best friends since leverets lying side by side waiting for our parents to bring us food. The funny thing is, our mothers hated each other but never attempted to keep us apart. I loaded my things and picked up Amari from her apartment near the airport. Once we parked and got inside, I was glad I listened to Amari. The airport was thicker than my fur.

"I told you," Amari rubbed it in. We had on matching jogging suits with sneakers, but hers was soft pink, and mine was red. Amari's small frame fooled a lot of people. Her little ass packed a powerful punch. She was a little beneath average height for a female and was skinny with big titties and a big booty. Her deep mocha complexion and light green eyes gave her an exotic look that made people constantly question her ethnicity.

"I hate airports. Why couldn't we be flying squirrels or some shit," I whispered. Amari burst out laughing and hit my arm. "Ouch," I rubbed my arm and joined her laughing. As we headed to check our bags in, I smelled something that favored honey with a pinch of chocolate. My nose wiggled as the scent tickled my nostrils, causing me to lift my head and take a deep breath. *Damn, that smells delicious.* I licked my lips.

"I think I'll pass on the flying squirrel. Do you smell something smoky? Almost like sweet mesquite?" Amari questioned as she, too, sniffed the air.

"Not quite smoky, but definitely sweet." The scent was strong at first, but then it faded into a subtle linger as we checked our bags and went through the TSA checkpoint. When we boarded the plane, my mind was still focused on that delectable scent that had me trapped. Amari and I stayed on to get off last when the plane landed. We finally walked down the corridor that was now empty, and the scent of honey and a hint of chocolate were so intense it nearly knocked me on my ass. I immediately searched for the source needing to get a taste.

"Why your slow ass can't ever get the shit right? You've had more than enough time to master it?!" I heard someone growl as they exited the male restroom. When I looked into the crisp blue eyes of the finest man I'd ever seen, my legs moved of their own accord towards the strength he possessed and the scent that held me captive since entering the airport back home in Fairbanks.

"Fuck you, bro, you try doing that shit after having one of the strongest drinks in all of the realms," The other man chided as he walked beside him. Both men were fine as fuck, but the one with the blue eyes and snow-white dreadlocks had me in a trance. My pussy throbbed between my legs harder and harder the closer I got. I felt drunk off the smell of him. There has never been a human man that could capture my attention so swiftly and precise. I had to get a taste of him.

Amari

I smelled the man with the piercing silver eyes and skin the color of the milkiest chocolate before I saw him, but when I laid eyes on him, I couldn't take them off. He smelled of the juiciest grilled carrots, and I was lost in the sight of him. My feet moved toward him, and I didn't want to stop them. When I stood in front of him and the other guy, they both looked agitated. I wondered if they were on their way to a wedding because both of them wore suits, and dang, if they didn't look good.

"Are you lost or just rude?" Silver eyes asked me. His deep smooth voice effectively snapped Zya and me out of whatever trance we were in, and I looked over to her for help. She was more vocal of us regarding our natural sexual urges. "Are you mute?" Silver edged.

I raised my hand to slap him across his smug face before I could stop myself, but he caught it before it could connect. I snatched my hand back with a gasp, "I'm sorry. I don't know what came over me. Please forgive me!" I was so embarrassed. Hell, if I must admit, I'm a little scared. His tall, muscular frame towered me like a rottweiler to a kitten.

"Feisty and rude, I see your little ass wants to be punished," Silver eyes chuckled and licked his lips. My eyes followed the motion of his tongue, and I thought of what it would feel like. It left his lips moist, and I was now leaking between my legs.

"I would apologize for my brother's actions, but both of y'all is wrong, so we can just keep it moving. Come on, Sah, we have shit to do," blue eyes said from beside Silver.

"He owes my sis an apology. How the fuck is he gonna call her rude then proceed to insult her more? Both of y'all are assholes," Zya spat as she stepped closer to blue eyes. Zya stands around five-nine and is considered full-figured, but believe me, she's agile. Her skin is a fair tortilla shade, and her eyes the color of toasted ginger. I watched as he smiled before looking to Silver and nodding as if they were having an inside conversation.

"I apologize, little lady. Let me make it up to you by taking you to dinner." Silver touched my hand, and I shivered. His touch was different. I couldn't tell whether it was hot or so cold that it felt hot. I closed my eyes as a feeling I had never felt before coursed down my spine. I needed to feel this man deep inside of me, but I am not like Zya. I can't just boldly declare that I want something. I bit my lower lip as I opened my eyes and noticed all eyes were on me. "My name is Saheel Silvermoon, and this is my older brother Raheel Silvermoon. Take my card and send me the location at around seven. We'll pick y'all up at eight."

The command in his voice almost caused me to shift and hop away. It was funny because a part of me felt like hopping away, but the other part wanted to hop on his face. I allowed my eyes to travel down to his large hands that held the card out and stood frozen. Zya laughed and took the card on my behalf, then said, "we'll catch you guys later. My name is Zya, and this is Amari." She then pulled me towards the elevators to go to the baggage claim area. "You gotta work on how to talk to men if you ever want some good dick," Zya mused. I hated not being able to speak my mind like Zya, my mother was very strict, and I had to bite my tongue a lot, so it caused me to have social issues according to humans.

"I know. I will try tonight. My panties are soaked, and I want to taste him. He smells so yummy."

We got our bags and went to our room, a two-bedroom suite, at a local bed and breakfast to set up a zoom meeting with the lead investigator of the agency that hired us. I was excited about the money and the job that needed to be done, but Zya thought there was something more behind the scenes. Barrows is not very populated, and the site for the tomb is ten miles outside of town. Zya wants to go check it out before the humans arrive to ensure it's safe. We loaded up the zoom call.

"Zaniah and Amari, how are you?" The agent asked.

"Good, is everything still on schedule as planned?" Zya questioned.

"Yes, everything is in place. We have a team of six accompanying you two at all times when you are on-site. There are two agents outside of the Bed and Breakfast you will be taking up residence at as we speak to ensure your protection. Do you ladies have any questions?"

"Why do we need protection?" Zya asked with raised brows.

The agent's face turned red, "we just want to keep our assets safe."

We talked a little longer before disconnecting. I was starting to understand why Zya was untrusting when it came to the government. "Do you believe him?" I frowned.

"Hell no! There is something fishy going on, and I need to find out what it is before one of us gets hurt. Don't go anywhere without me, not even to the front desk," Zya chastised.

"Yes, ma'am," I laughed.

"Hand me your phone." I handed Zya my phone and watched as she pulled the black card from her pocket and sent a text. I suddenly grew nervous. I hope he wasn't as impatient as he came off because he would have to chase me for my cotton candy, but the way my body responded to his touch had me questioning everything I thought I knew about myself. "Amari calms down. That man will fuck your brains out tonight and tomorrow. You will never see him again," Zya smiled at me, and I joined in.

We did that a lot, love them and leave them. It is in our nature to be sexually active with multiple partners. I liked to think of it as getting men back for how they do other women. "It's all fun," I started.

"Until the rabbit has the gun," Zya finished.

Author's Note

Thank you for reading and for your support! I hope you have enjoyed reading this story as much as I loved writing it. Please leave a review if you can and stay tuned for more!